URBAN SHOTS
CROSSROADS

Ahmed Faiyaz grew up in Bangalore and now lives in Dubai. He's a book and film addict, and apart from reading books and watching cinema of all genres, he is a passionate writer. He is the bestselling author of *Love, Life & all that Jazz*, *Another Chance* and *Scammed*, and the editor of *Urban Shots: Crossroads* and *Down the Road*. He has written and directed six short films and two feature films, including *Graveyard Shift*, based on his novella by the same name.

URBAN SHOTS
CROSSROADS

Edited by
Ahmed Faiyaz

RUPA

*To all the young writers out there
who aspire to tell beautiful stories.*

Published by
Rupa Publications India Pvt. Ltd 2014
7/16, Ansari Road, Daryaganj
New Delhi 110002

Sales centres:
Allahabad Bengaluru Chennai
Hyderabad Jaipur Kathmandu
Kolkata Mumbai

Copyright © Ahmed Faiyaz 2014

All rights reserved.
No part of this publication may be reproduced, transmitted,
or stored in a retrieval system, in any form or by any means,
electronic, mechanical, photocopying, recording or otherwise,
without the prior permission of the publisher.

ISBN: 978-81-291-3086-0

First impression 2014

10 9 8 7 6 5 4 3 2 1

The moral right of the author has been asserted.

Printed by Parksons Graphics Pvt. Ltd, Mumbai

This book is sold subject to the condition that it shall not, by way
of trade or otherwise, be lent, resold, hired out, or otherwise circulated,
without the publisher's prior consent, in any form of binding or cover
other than that in which it is published.

Contents

Foreword ... ix
Rohini Kejriwal

Everyone Has a Story ... 1
Gayatri Hingorani

Hako ... 10
Chandrima Pal

Priorities ... 20
For Deepalaya

Getting off a Virar Fast at Borivali ... 30
Vinod George Joseph

The Crows' Feast ... 40
Sanchari Sur

Song of the Summer Bird ... 46
Anita Satyajit

The Power Cut ... 54
Maryann Taylor

Mervin *Ahmed Faiyaz*	59
She Got off Easy *Sanchari Sur*	72
The Gap *Saritha Rao*	77
Pity *Paritosh Uttam*	86
Pasta Lane *Siddhartha Bhaskar*	91
Mindgames *Manisha Dhingra*	99
Look How Far We've Come *Shreya Maheshwari*	105
Paradise *Anitha Murthy*	114
Crossroads *Ahmed Faiyaz*	118
Virtual Reality *Vrinda Baliga*	125
Footsteps in the Dark *Mini Menon*	135
Gautam Gargoyle *Shailaditya Chakraborty*	144
Baba Premanand's Yoga Class *Paritosh Uttam*	153

Wrong Strokes *For Deepalaya*	164
The Last Week *Venkataraghavan Srinivasan*	172
The Pink Slip *Malcolm Carvalho*	182
Plummet *Avnee Rajesh & Pranav Mukul*	187
Tainted Love *Rohan Swamy*	191
Hunch *Karthik K*	204
Rajasthan Summer *Ayesha Heble*	212
Childish Love *Reeti Gadekar*	220
Jump, Didi *Sharath Komarraju*	233
Categories *Rohini Kejriwal*	241
Contributors	246

Foreword

ROHINI KEJRIWAL

In each of our lives, at some point or another comes a crossroad where time stops to savour the moment and all is still. Be it the day you turn twenty-one and you share your first legal drink with your father or the day you are told that you have only six months left to live, it is a turning point in your life and more often than not, there's no going back.

Two roads diverged somewhere in my life and I took the one less travelled only so that I could have an experience unlike any other before. Or maybe I did that to take on an adventure I had never even fathomed possible until the moment I made the choice to travel by it...

Crossroads is a wonderful collection of short stories by Indian authors about such experiences that change lives, in small and big ways; Sometimes, without even knowing it. The reeking smell of Old Monk on the lip that makes you smile, a small gesture of unselfish love you received, or even realizing the loss of the memory of an experience is an experience. And as we all know, the core of humanity lies in holding onto experiences. Each story shared in this book takes you through the vividness of the subject's feelings and paints a clear picture in your head as they express their thoughts in words.

It might be the 'Song of the Summer Bird' that fills your heart with childhood reminiscences or a feeling of 'Tainted Love' after a moving conversation unveils the realities of being a prostitute; it could even be a walk down 'Pasta Lane' remembering the first time you put a cigarette to your now blackened lips. In the end, the only thing one must accept to hold on to their sanity is that a memory is a memory is a memory.

Rohini Kejriwal, 20, is a writer, journalist, blogger and co-editor of Down the Road, *a collection of campus tales from Grey Oak Westland.*

Everyone Has a Story

GAYATRI HINGORANI

Meena Tukaram Tirade, more commonly known as Minu bai, cracked the betel nut in her palm and swiftly installed it in the farthest corner of her crimson mouth. She loosened the small lump of sari formed near her navel and stuffed the extra length behind, till she could feel the cloth sting her deep inside the sensitive crack of her derrière. As a final move, she slightly squatted, only as much as her fifty-eight year old knees would permit, to let it all fall into place. She was among the few bais of this generation to wear a navari sari to work every day—possibly the only one in the locality she operated in. For years she had looked down on salwar suits, believing that the navari sari was functional, uniform-like and made kaamwali bais look professional, like they meant business. Salwar suits, on the other hand, were prone to fashion trends, such as plunging necklines, knotted backs, shorter hemlines and so on, and gave the wrong impression about her sorority to the sahibs. The latest trend of jeans and kurtis among bais was almost blasphemous for her, and at the faintest cue from her memsahibs, she derided those 'heroines' who came to work to conduct 'other' business.

Before ringing the doorbell, she examined her hair in the small mirror she carried with her everywhere. It was always tied in a neat bun and she ensured that no loose strand escaped the discipline she had enforced on it with bob-pins. Earlier, she used to even check if the big red bindi was right in the centre of her forehead, but that was before Tukaram left her for those heroine-types. The day he kicked her out of their one-room tenement in a fit of drunkenness was the day he left for his heavenly abode—figuratively, of course. It was much later, after producing two children with that heroine that he succumbed to alcoholism. She had not felt a tinge of sorrow the day he died. In fact she was joyous, in a triumphant sort of way, for many days after that. Tukaram had always been a source of misery for her. She would never forgive him for letting that poisonous liquid seep its way into her son's childhood and leave its abhorrent smell lingering all through his adolescent years. Poor Babloo had to take up odd jobs to supplement his mother's meagre income until they had enough to rent out a small house by the highway. Tukaram had not felt the pain in his heart when Babloo came home with his face smeared with boot-polish, or the salt in his mouth when Babloo's fingers were bruised with nips and cuts at the electrician's shop. He had detached himself soon after impregnating her and bestowing upon her life's best gift, almost like the snapping of the umbilical cord.

That seemed like a distant dream now. Years had passed, problems had come and gone, but not before bringing new ones along. Babloo was now married and had a two year old daughter from a vile woman whose tongue was sharp as a house-knife at the beginning of the day and sharper than a dagger by night. After twenty-five years of toiling and scraping, the least she had hoped for was a relaxed and lazy old age. But that was not to be.

She rang the bell to the Parekh house, her first and most laborious stop of the three houses where she cleaned vessels and clothes and swept floors. There were seven members in the family, and a huge pile awaited her at the sink and the bathroom every day. There were three memsahibs across three generations so the khit-pit was additional. But they paid well and gave her generous gifts during Diwali (two saris, old utensils, one mithai box and a one month bonus). They sometimes also gave her leftover breakfast, because they didn't like stale food even if there was a big fridge to store it in. It was a busy household with people scurrying around, phones ringing and the TV on at the maximum volume in the background. Only during the fourteen days of mourning, when the patriarch of the family had passed away, had one felt silence in the house. He had left behind an aged wife who mostly stayed cooped up inside her room and shouted if she needed anything. Things got back to normal shortly afterwards, including the kitchen politics that seemed like it was being played out of the saas-bahu serials currently on TV.

Everyone seemed to want control—the old memsahib, her older daughter-in-law and her newly wedded daughter-in-law. While the old memsahib was nice and had treated Minu bai well through the years, Minu had taken an immediate liking to the younger daughter-in-law, Komal-ben. If she had a choice, she would have wanted a girl just like Komal for Babloo. She always treated Minu bai with respect and made small talk with her every day. On one occasion, she had listened to Minu's life story patiently and sympathized with her deeply. It was also easier to talk to her because she understood Marathi well—her mother was Maharashtrian. Minu tried to help her as much as she could in the kitchen—Tuesdays and Thursdays were the days allotted to Komal to make lunch for everyone. Wednesdays and Fridays were days Minu would delay as much as possible to pique Komal's sister-in-law and adversary.

In the short time span of one hour and fifteen minutes that she spent in the Parekh household, Minu got a good grip of the family dynamics and understood who was on the winning side that day. Over the years, she had learnt that Komal had entered into the family by way of a love marriage, while her sister-in-law, five years older and well-entrenched in the system, had come in through the traditional route. She had won over her in-laws by the time Komal came in, and for Komal to replicate her success story was difficult, since her sister-in-law put several spokes in her wheels. The mother-in-law, the old memsahib, tried to stay neutral as much as possible, which aggravated the situation and made it far more sensitive than conclusive—taking sides would have settled the matter once and for all.

That was not the end of trouble for poor Komal-ben. She had always wanted to be a Chartered Accountant but, after marriage, her education was stalled because she had to be trained in 'other areas of life' as her mother-in-law had advised. That frustrated her no end. And maybe it was this frustration, combined with the insipid poha she had made for breakfast (that her sister-in-law had expectedly taunted her on in front of everyone) that made her suddenly start wailing in the middle of the chaotic morning in the Parekh kitchen. The sobs got louder and louder and made the entire household come out from their cubby-holes in the expansive apartment and make their way to the rasoi.

The mother-in-law came in first and saw the grey-haired pesky Minu bai patting her volatile daughter-in-law. She immediately tore her away and took her vulnerable daughter-in-law in her arms. Even the men folk, who usually steered clear of the domestic affairs ministry, stood agape as Komal cried her heart out. For those few minutes everything came to a grinding halt in the Parekh house, as it had when the head of the family passed away. While Minu dried up the vessels with a rag, a family drama unravelled. Though it would have amused her to stand around and watch, she realized it would be wiser to get going. By the time she had reached the front door, regular life had resumed—the TV was on again at full volume, the phone had started ringing as if on cue, and the old widowed grandmother was shouting from her room.

'Yes?' he enquired cheekily. A good-looking man in his mid-thirties, dressed only in boxers, had answered the door of Priya madam's house. If Minu bai had not been a mature woman with experience in dealing with unusual situations, which she prided herself upon, she would have started cursing aloud and possibly even driven the suave man from the house. If he had been unrelenting, she would have screamed 'Chor! Chor!' and alerted the watchman in the gallery. But she decided to play the situation by ear. She declared, 'Mina bai,' as if it were not her name but a judgment. She suddenly saw a blush cover the man's face, then his neck, moving downward to his bare shaven chest. Before her roving eyes could go any further, he opened the door fully and let her in.

Minu had been working for Priya madam for eight months now. Before Priya, she had worked for another single woman who had rented the same apartment, but had moved back to Haryana after an unsuccessful bid to make it big in the city of dreams. But Priya madam was smarter, more ambitious and better endowed for her job as an air-hostess. Even though Minu would never admit it publicly, working for Priya madam had been thoroughly enjoyable.

Every other week, she discovered something in her fairly empty yet modern apartment that would make her suffer a culture shock. She would spin a story around her sightings and relate it with a sour face and screwed up nose to her other bai friends in the area. But her stomach was full of butterflies during these narrations, just like the time Tukaram had first touched her in the cinema hall.

She recalled how she had come across a fuchsia pink brassiere and matching skimpy underwear from below the sheets within the first week that Priya moved in. After that, there had been many colours and designs of lingerie, which she would describe with a stick in the muddy patch outside her house, ensuring that she was always encircled by women and none of the teenage boys were mischievously prying. The other milestone in her voyeuristic journey was a savagely torn pack of condoms found under the bed, with just one ignored condom left inside. For some reason, she had kept the pack with her and felt foolish afterwards. Not so much because of what it was, but she had in the process broken her first rule of work ethics—that of not lifting anything from her memsahibs' houses. Then one Sunday, she had found a man sleeping in Priya madam's bedroom. Priya had stepped out of the bathroom to attend to Minu's doorbell and hurried back in. But before she could close the bedroom door behind her, Minu had spotted him splayed out on the bed in deep slumber, obviously satiated and at peace. When Priya later instructed her to not sweep the bedroom and not even hang the washed clothes on the balcony line, Minu smiled knowingly. She saw the man several times after that and had almost accepted him as the sahib, when Priya surprised her another Sunday morning by having a new man in the same bed. Minu bai hoped against hope that he was just madam's brother, or possibly the sahib's brother, but of course her old-fashioned self had not seen much of the world just yet.

Two other men came and went from Priya's life just as seasons changed, but none of them had been defiant enough to open the door of the house and look her in the eye like the one she had just encountered. When inside the house, she went about her usual business. With her deftness, it didn't take her more than half an hour to complete all the work. The cheeky man had disappeared inside the house and she was not motivated to bump into him again when she went to dry the clothes, but her second rule of work ethics was to always complete the job to her best satisfaction. She trudged along to the bedroom and further down to the balcony when she saw the sacrilegious spectacle—the man who had opened the door was sprawled on the bed alongside another man! Minu didn't know where to look. Ethics were important but not when the work atmosphere was as polluted as this. She dropped the bucket in the balcony and rushed to the front door, put on her slippers and closed the door behind her slowly as if she meant to not awaken a sleeping baby.

Mr and Mrs Soneji were the perfect couple with the perfect house. Mrs Soneji kept everything ready and in order for Minu, so she could do her job systematically and with ease. It was always a pleasure working for them, even though they paid less than the market rate. She never cribbed about it, as she did in the Parekh household, because it would be thoughtless to demand more from Mr Soneji's hard-earned savings that were meant to last them their limited lifetime. Mr Soneji had retired from his well-paying bank job about three years ago, when their only son Pankaj was set to migrate to Australia. Minu knew that Mr Soneji had invested a large share of his collected wealth from over twenty-five years of service on his son's future in foreign lands. Mrs Soneji, on the other hand, had sacrificed time and aspirations in raising him to be a first-class student who topped almost every exam he sat for.

Minu empathized with the elderly devoted parents and admired the way they had pledged their life for their son. If she had a choice, she too would have left no stone unturned in securing a bright future for Babloo. Minu could feel the heaviness in their hearts the day Pankaj was to leave. Since then, the heaviness had transformed itself into a dark cloud that loomed in every room of the Soneji house that Minu cleaned. No amount of jhadu-poncha or dusting could help get rid of it, nor the cobweb removal and wet washing that Mrs Soneji made her do as part of the Diwali cleaning.

Only recently had sunshine made its way amongst the omnipresent dark clouds in the form of a computer, a device with which they could see, hear and speak to their beloved son for half an hour every day. They had made a special place for it in the living room adjacent to the showcase that was adorned with Pankaj's pictures and medals. It was not only their primary medium for communication with Pankaj (speaking on the telephone regularly was unaffordable even for them), it was a gift that their son had bought for them after completing a year of his part-time job in the university. Their joy knew no bounds. Life now revolved around getting to know the machine better and switching it on with great expectation every morning at 11.00 am, only to switch it off an hour later with much dejection.

In the last five days, however, this little piece of sunshine had also been robbed from them. Mrs Soneji told Minu that Pankaj had gone for a picnic with his friends and was to return to campus after a week, when Minu enquired why the computer was not yet on when she came in. Suddenly, during this short period of Pankaj's absence from the computer, news flashed across all television channels about the merciless killings of Indians in Australia. The Sonejis were shaken up and couldn't sleep the night the reports trickled in. The next day, they had tried calling the numbers they had for Pankaj's friends and teachers, but no one knew of his whereabouts. Every morning Minu came in and checked with Mrs Soneji if they had heard from Pankaj, though she didn't need to because the dark circles under her eyes and the wrinkles all over her face were an eloquent negative.

It took longer than usual for Mrs Soneji to open the door that day—long enough for Minu to start worrying about the well-being of the old couple. When the door finally clicked open, Minu let out a small sigh of relief and started to reproach Mrs Soneji. But then she saw her face and knew. Just a few steps inside and she was engulfed by distant voices, happy cries and exchanges of many words back and forth via the privileged computer. The dialogue was uncoordinated, with many pauses and breaks, but obviously not meant to convey or elicit anything specific. It was just an outburst to liberate them all from the anxiety trapped within.

Minu bai speedily completed her forty-five minute job in the Soneji house. She felt like an outsider, a potential predator on their happiness, and wanted the old couple to savour their joy in peace and solitude.

As she shut the door and made her way down to the road back home, Minu considered the events of her long day at work. In a short time, she would have her own life to deal with—that of poverty, insecurity and failing health. Her problems were no different from many others in her neighbourhood. Yet, hers was a different story. Everyone had a story of their own, even her memsahibs. And to have a role in this maze of stories, however small, made life worth it.

Hako

CHANDRIMA PAL

Hako lived in a house which was a shout and a lamp post away from ours.

It was the oldest and only house in our neighbourhood that still had a garden of its own—with a mango, chiku and guava tree and hibiscus bushes that exploded in scarlet blooms every other day.

All the other houses had long ripped off the hedges and sawed off the trees to make room for cars and bikes and extra rooms.

Even then, our neighbourhood was usually quiet. Apart from the piercing cry of the old maulvi from the green minarets of the mosque twice a day, the occasional auto rickshaws and our school buses which unfailingly picked us up from our stops and released us in the afternoon to our mothers, nannies or grannies.

But all that was set to change, our parents said, as they went through the morning papers and dissected the headlines. The neighbourhood is not what it used to be, they said, shaking their heads and squinting at the march of the cloud-bursting towers from the south.

Every house braced itself for the big change. Walls were made taller, thicker and more evil, with spikes, barbed wires and shards of glass. Menacing iron gates were given teeth and spears and people did not leave their bikes out on the road at night anymore. Some even brought home puppies and stuck 'Beware of Dog' boards on their gates. There were whispers of how strange men were talking to some of the old house owners, telling them stories of how much more their homes could fetch them, and showing them pictures of tall buildings with glass doors.

But Hako's home remained untouched.

The powder blue slanting roofs, the red tiled path that started at the creaky gates and went right up to their door, the walls which were perhaps once painted a bright red, but had now faded to a sad nameless shade—everything remained the way it had always been.

Every afternoon, after school, we gathered outside the rusty gate and yelled, 'Haakkoo!' The door always opened with what sounded curiously like an old man yawning, and Hako strutted out, grinning widely, dressed in his blue shorts and chequered red and blue shirt, dragging his bright orange Toby cycle with him. The door would close behind him again, keeping its secrets to itself, shutting out the world and a bunch of pesky kids.

We never went inside. We were often tempted to stone the bright green guavas and sweet and sour pairi mangoes into submission, but instinct and rumours made us give Hako's house a wide berth.

Perhaps it had something to do with the fact that Hako seemed to be the only cheerful thing to emerge from the house. Everyone noticed how his parents seldom spoke or smiled at us and mostly kept to themselves. Even Hako's birthday was never celebrated—he would mysteriously disappear on that day, only to show us the gifts he had received from his parents a day later or so.

Dwarfed by houses that had been repainted, scrubbed, cleaned and spruced up, Hako's house looked terribly uninviting. And on some winter evenings, almost scary. The aggressive trees kept daylight away, moss grew thick on the walls and the smell of all things old and dying stuck to it like cotton candy on a stick.

And then there were the rumours. No one was sure what Hako's father did for a living, but everyone said he had the temper of the devil and a tongue like sand paper. And that was enough to keep us away from Hako's house.

But Hako? He was different. He was a quiet boy who had the funniest laugh you would have ever heard. He was also the fastest runner and best seeker among us. But what made Hako, despite his forbidding house and mysterious family, such a hit with all the neighbourhood kids were his stories.

Hako was the best story-teller among us all.

There were days when the road that ran right down the middle of the neighbourhood got too busy. And we would gather behind Almeida's bakery shop and corner Hako into telling us stories.

'Hako, yaar, we're not going to play with you unless you tell us a story!'

'Ya, tell us a ghost story!'

'Hey, you never finished that one in which Terminator meets King Kong!'

Hako obliged all of us. Well, almost—because he had no way of knowing what I really, really, wanted.

When all the kids hung around him as he spun his yarns, I would be there too. But my eyes would be on his bright orange Toby cycle.

As far as bikes went, Hako's was a masterpiece. His father had tweaked parts of it to make it stand out from everyone else's. Each of the three wheels, for instance, was of a different colour—red, blue and yellow. At the heart of the wheels were little gleaming metal hearts on which Hako had pasted rhinestone stickers. The seat was a bright shade of green, the handles like dog ears, with candy-coloured tassels hanging from them. And attached to one of the handles was an old-fashioned truck horn that startled everyone who came in his way. Nothing in the world was quite as beautiful. Not even my mother's hand-knitted lace that covered our dressing table mirror.

Hako's signature orange Toby cycle was stuff that kept you awake and appeared to you in your dreams. And it was completely out of bounds.

Hako, who was otherwise generous with his chocolates and comic books, never let anyone touch his wheels. And from the day the orange wonder rolled into our neighbourhood, all I could do was look at it lovingly and pray every night that the next morning I'd wake up older, wiser, and the proud owner of my own custom-made Toby cycle.

But that was not meant to happen soon. And every afternoon, I watched sadly as Hako pulled his Toby out of the dark house and joined us as we went pedalling around the neighbourhood's quiet back alleys.

I tried to ride as close to Hako as possible. But he was always faster.

'At least I am riding next to the Toby,' I'd tell myself and push my pedals harder, happy that the orange blur of Hako's Toby was close to me.

That day, however, I had no bike to ride. My rusty blue Avon, which once belonged to my brother who had long graduated to a sports bike with a gear and other fancy stuff, had finally given way.

'You'll get a new cycle on your birthday, sweetie!' My mom patted my cheeks, kissed my forehead and packed me off. 'Now run along and play some new games with your friends, okay?'

It was far from okay. I was the only one without wheels in a gang that was insanely obsessed with riding, and Hako's Toby was in full form that afternoon.

'Dad just greased the wheels, see?' Hako declared before turning into a blur down the lane. My heart sank.

And as the boys and girls whizzed past me over and over again, I curled up behind Almeida's bakery shop and stared at my feet. I did not want anyone to see me cry.

I was gulping my sorrow hard when, suddenly, an orange apparition screeched to a halt before me. It was Hako.

'What happened?' he asked softly. I sniffed hard.

'Why are you crying?' Hako sounded more scared than concerned, quickly turning back to see if anyone was watching.

I just couldn't say anything.

'Oh, come on,' Hako pleaded. 'Don't cry now please!'

The sight of Hako standing so close with the Toby did funny things to my eyes. I broke into a wail.

That did it. Hako quickly got off his cycle and moved close to me. 'If you stop crying now, I promise I will let you ride my cycle tomorrow—how about that?'

I could not believe what I had just heard. 'Really?' I had suddenly run out of tears.

'Promise!' Hako smiled and straightened up, with one arm still cradling the Toby protectively.

'Let's go Hako, one last round!' the boys yelled at him from a distance. Hako suddenly turned crimson, jumped back on his Toby and shot away.

'Promise, tomorrow?' I shouted after him.

'Yeah,' Hako yelled back, blasting away at the truck horn.

Next day, at the end of what seemed to be a painfully long and slow school day, I was outside Hako's gate with the others.

'Haakkoo!'

My heart was thumping really loud. It was my big day after all.

'Haakkoo!'

I wanted to be the loudest. I wanted Hako to know I was there, waiting for my turn.

'Haakkoo!'

Something was not right. The others started getting fidgety. Hako's door remained shut.

Two more shouts and everyone decided to carry on.

But I could not move.

As soon as I was sure the others had left, I called for Hako again.

'Haakkoo! Won't you come?' I was choking on my hurt and I hated it.

Hako did not step out that day, nor for many days after that. No one saw him get out, no one saw him go to school either.

And then, one day, one of the boys came back with the news that Hako's father had done something really bad and the police were looking for him.

'Why? What has he done?' I summoned the courage to ask.

'They say he ran over some people in his car and killed them.'

Cold dread clamped our mouths shut.

The calls for Hako had stopped completely. No one waited outside his gates anymore in the afternoons. Not even me. My birthday was still a few weeks away and I was stuck with the other group of girls who hosted tea parties for their dolls and played with cups and saucers. It was no fun.

I missed Hako terribly, but I was not allowed to go looking for him. Every time I passed by his house, I'd steal a quick glance, hoping to see him walk out with his Toby. But it did not happen.

And then, one Sunday afternoon, just when I had been dragged into a silly game of Statue, where I was supposed to remain still until someone managed to make me smile, I heard that familiar sound—Hako's horn.

Everyone—the girls playing Statue, the older kids riding their bikes—had stopped what they were doing to watch Hako as he emerged from his house, the Toby next to him.

'What?' he asked incredulously, as no one budged from their place, staring at him as though they were seeing him for the first time.

'Hako!' I called out happily. Hako looked at me and smiled.

'Come, don't you want to ride this?'

All eyes were now trained on me. It was scary.

'Well… I…' I didn't know what to say.

Hako looked at me and smiled bravely.

'Come, I will take you to a new place,' he said, now sitting on his Toby.

I must have taken a step towards him when someone shouted, 'Don't! We will tell your mother!'

Hako stopped smiling.

'Come, don't listen to them!'

I looked at the Toby and at the angry eyes piercing me.

'You know what will happen if you go *anywhere* near him!' It was my brother, in his coldest, angriest voice ever.

I looked at the Toby again and at Hako who was on the bike, hands on the dog-ear handles, the tassels fluttering in the breeze, and the seat, shining, inviting.

And the next thing I knew, I had squeezed myself onto the Toby, right behind Hako, my feet grazing the concrete footpath, my arms around Hako's sweaty belly as he broke away from the circle of annoying kids and hit the pedals hard.

I was on the Toby at last.

'Don't stop! Don't stop!' I cheered, as Hako rode faster and faster.

I quickly turned around to check if we were being followed. It would have been such a thrill to be hotly pursued, as the Toby whizzed way ahead of the others.

I looked again. There was no one. It just did not feel right. A funny feeling rising from my stomach, I turned back again.

'I will ride faster,' Hako grunted, when suddenly I realised we were on a road I was totally unfamiliar with.

'Where are we Hako?' I gulped, holding him tighter. There were cars, buses and way too many people. This was not our familiar neighbourhood.

'New road. Like it?'

I did not, especially when I saw a black car speeding right at us. I wanted to get off, go back.

'Stop!' I screamed. 'Stop!'

'Why so scared? Trust me!' Hako was saying, swaying dangerously from side to side, the Toby groaning under our combined weights and the momentum.

I was suddenly annoyed at how clumsy he was.

'Hako!' My fingers dug into his flesh. 'You will kill us! Like your dad!'

The Toby screeched to a halt, as if it had run into a wall. I opened my eyes and saw my brother.

There were some other people too and, in a flash, I found myself being dragged away from Hako, who just stood there surrounded by some very angry adults who were all trying to tell him something, all at the same time.

I looked at Hako. He was looking at his feet, but I knew he was crying.

That was the last time we saw Hako. We heard his father had been taken away by the cops, and one day we heard he was gone too. With his mother, who had sold the house to one of the strangers who had been seen walking in and out of several other houses on the street.

'It is only a matter of time before…' Adults had this weird habit of never finishing what they started.

My birthday arrived but I had forfeited my right to a bike and was asked to be happy with a set of new board games instead, which included a jigsaw puzzle and Battleship.

Cycling around the neighbourhood had been banned, all thanks to me. And we were quickly running out of innovative games to play every afternoon.

It was on one such day, when our fingers were aching after striking the carrom discs for too long, that someone suggested, 'Let's go to Hako's house!'

'Why?' I asked nervously. 'There is no one there.'

'Exactly! Now we can stone as many guavas as we want!' the kid said, and suddenly it seemed to be the best idea to have emerged that afternoon. And even if I did not want to be party to this misadventure, I was in no mood to be left out again.

We marched towards Hako's house—some eight or nine of us—and pushed open the rickety gate. This was the first time we were stepping into the place we used to visit every day. The hibiscus bushes were withering away, untended grass and other nameless plants and shrubs were running riot in the garden.

The kids got busy at the guava tree, chucking stones at the bright green fruit. I walked on. The house looked as if it was held together by some miracle—the doors and windows were cracked and mossy.

Had it really been that long? I wondered. I went around the house and behind it. And there I was greeted with the most spectacular sight I had ever seen.

Next to a large bird bath, a tattered lamp and some other junk, was Hako's custom-made Toby cycle.

And as I looked carefully, I saw my name scratched on one side of the bright green seat.

Our neighbourhood is a different place now. There are several tall towers where our homes used to be. Hako's was the first house here to be taken apart, brick by mossy brick.

Priorities

FOR DEEPALAYA

Sameer got back from college and dragged himself up the stairs. His head was splitting and his joints ached as they never had in years. He gave a feeble knock at the door while leaning against it. The usual walk up two floors seemed like a chore. Mohan and he shared the room on the roof of Messrs. Vineet and Kunal Bhandari's home off B.V. Road, a short walk from their college. Both of them were in their final year of the Masters in Media and Mass Communications in St. Xavier's College, Nashik.

A sleepy Mohan, wearing a pair of old shorts and a singlet, opened the door. 'Arey dude, it's you,' he yawned. 'How was college today? Did you manage to give me proxies?'

'It was okay. Man, I have a splitting headache. I did manage to get you attendance for a couple of lectures. Your friend Vibhod Shukla was looking for you in class as usual.'

'Thanks for the proxies yaar. Thank God I bunked that chutiya's lecture! I better get dressed. It's good you woke me up. Mudassir, Pranav and I are going for a trek to Singhda Valley. The weather is good and it should be fun. Why don't you come with us?' He stood in front of the mirror to admire his non-existent biceps.

'No dude, I'm tired. You have a good time,' Sameer said, getting up and taking a Crocin tablet with a sip of water. He was devoid of energy and felt an irritation in his throat.

'I'll do that. Do you need me to head out and get you some medicine?'

Sameer shook his head to decline the offer.

'Are you sure?'

'Yup, just a fucking headache, and I'm a bit tired with all the late night dinners and partying. You enjoy,' he grumbled with a sniff.

Mohan took his backpack and walked out the door while Sameer lay down with a throbbing headache.

༺ⴰ༻

Sameer woke up in a daze when he heard someone knock furiously at the door. He managed to sit up and looked at the time on his watch. It was past 5.30 pm and he had slept for over three hours. He slowly got out of bed and opened the door. His long hair was all over the place and his eyes were bloodshot. It was Sakku Bai at the door.

'Arey kya baba? Itna time se I'm waiting.' she grumbled, walking in huffily. Sameer felt irritated. Sakku Bai was difficult to deal with. She could understand little of what he said and vice versa. They often communicated through Mohan.

'Morning mein, your friend didn't open the door. You babalog stay awake in the night and sleep during the day. Hope my son doesn't become like this. I will give him two raps if he tries!'

༺ⴰ༻

Her son was the one person she idolized. Every day Mohan and Sameer learnt about her son's shenanigans. The ten-year-old boy was the sole ray of light in Sakku Bai's miserable life. Her abusive husband worked in a factory on the outskirts of Nashik. He spent his time drinking and playing cards when he wasn't beating her or his son. She often came to work with a swollen eye or a swollen lip.

Sakku Bai picked up her broom and began sweeping the place. 'That Mohan throws biscuit packets and crumbs on the floor. Can't he see the dustbin over there?'

'Arey baba, what happened? Oh my God! Get up baba!' While she made her usual complaints, Sameer had collapsed to the floor and had fainted.

An hour later, Sameer woke up to see Sakku Bai changing strips of Eau de Cologne and water on his forehead. His temperature had come down a little and he began to sweat.

'Why don't you look after yourself baba? All you boys these days are like this only. My son also gets a headache and tells me after three days. Aaila, your body was so warm! Give me fifty rupees and write the tablets you want and I'll go and bring them.'

'Sakku Bai, thanks. Why don't you go home? It's almost seven. It seems like there is a drizzle outside.'

'No, no, I cannot leave you like this. Where is that fellow Mohan? He's normally sleeping here at this time.'

'He's gone away for the weekend.' Sameer shut his eyes, he felt drained out.

'Lie down baba. I will get you something to eat.' Sakku Bai left before Sameer could say anything.

She came back a short while later with misal pav, sabudana and hot vegetable soup. 'Memsahib on the first floor let me use her kitchen to prepare something for you to eat. She's a good lady, God bless her. Here take this, baba, and this packet of medicines too.'

'I will go and get a cup of hot tea for you,' she added, and walked out before Sameer could say no. He attacked the food on the plate as if he hadn't eaten for days. He felt really weak and his temperature seemed to be rising again. Sakku Bai came back in a short while to play nurse. It was a side of her Sameer had never seen. Mohan and he were often irritated with her for the amount of noise she made, the number of times she showed up late or decided not to show up because of her domestic problems.

She grinned at him with a look of satisfaction while he took large sips of tea. 'I've put cinnamon and ginger in it,' she said proudly. She took the empty cup from him and made him lie down.

'Sakku Bai, go home,' Sameer mumbled, lying down.

'Sssshhhh… Lie down quietly baba, you are like my son. How can I leave you in this condition? Look at that Mr Vineet Bhandari downstairs. He doesn't care about anything apart from filling his belly! The amount of money he takes from Mohan and you, he should look after you, right? He tells me to lock the tap in the morning and give you only two buckets of water every day.' If it was up to her, she would evict the miserly Mr Bhandari from his house. He used to charge Sameer ₹50 a month for the newspaper he borrowed every evening.

'Don't talk about him like this, Bai. The window is open and your voice carries. The next thing I know, he'll be writing to my mother telling her how badly behaved I am. Go home. Your son must be waiting.'

Mr Bhandari had written a letter to Mohan's parents after he caught Mohan kissing his girlfriend Priya behind the overhead tank. He had come up to inspect his dish antenna, which was giving him a poor signal. After Mohan was caught in the act and screamed at, no girls were allowed to come up to the room on the roof.

His letter to Mohan's Dad went like this: 'It gives me great displeasure to inform you that your son is a very bad influence on my own son and the other children in the neighbourhood. Out of respect for you, I cannot describe his behaviour with young girls on my terrace. Your son has to realise that mine is a culture and value driven family and we've lived here upholding our principles for…'

Predictably, Mohan received a tongue-lashing on the phone from Lucknow and went without pocket money for two months. This also led to Priya leaving him as she got tired of paying for his cups of tea at the canteen and sitting at home on Saturday nights. His credit amongst friends had dried up too and nobody wished to lend him any money.

Sameer remembered what Mohan had told him soon after the incident. 'What a pompous and self-righteous prick! His son comes up here to surf porn on my computer and read trashy magazines… Double standards, yaar! I should write a letter to him.'

Mr Bhandari also failed to mention in the letter his preference for erotic fiction, which Sameer and Mohan had noticed when they went down to pick up the newspaper. They wondered how his docile wife had put up with him all these years.

Sakku Bai applied Vicks on his forehead and nose and made sure he had his medicine before leaving.

She was back early the next morning and was sitting on the floor next to Sameer's bed when he woke up groaning. He was a lot better, but he still had a slight fever and body ache.

Sakku Bai started applying some oil on his feet. 'What are you doing Bai? Why don't you go down and finish your work? Mr Bhandari will find a reason to cut your pay for a day.'

'Arey, you lie down baba… That fat miser has gone to the

market with his old bag. He'll go and ruin some poor vegetable vendor's day. Panauti, that fellow is!'

'Haha! Yes, some poor guy will sell vegetables at a loss today. What oil is that? It's making me feel warm.'

'It's from the Nilgiri Hills. My Aai has used this for years. It's very effective.'

She was back at lunch and again at dinner, fussing over Sameer and treating him like a spoilt child. Sameer was overwhelmed with emotion for the lady who had treated him like one of her own. He gave her ₹50 for her son, which she tucked into the sleeve of a small pocket attached to her sari before leaving in the evening.

Sameer was getting dressed to leave for college. It had been a week since he had recovered from his raging fever. He rushed down the stairs as his girlfriend Nidhi was waiting to be picked up from her apartment which she shared with a couple of others down the street.

On his way down, he saw Sakku Bai come out of the younger Bhandari's house on the first floor. He hadn't seen her for the past three days. She had failed to show up for work and he felt she was having problems again.

'Baba!' she said, with tears running down her cheek. She quickly wiped them with the pallu of her sari.

'Is your husband troubling you again? We should go and finally complain against him.'

'No baba, that poor man, even he is very worried. My son is not well, he has a headache and he can barely walk. He keeps holding his head, crying in pain. I don't know what is wrong! We took him to different doctors every day and they gave him medicines but he hasn't improved…' She looked at Sameer with agony and helplessness.

'Here, take this,' he said, putting a five-hundred-rupee note in her hand. 'Bribe the guys at the Government Hospital and get a scan done. He has to see a neurologist, Bai. Take the tests and go to him, okay? Let me know what happens. He'll be okay. You've been going to quacks. Maybe he just needs glasses. Get his eyes tested too.'

'Thanks a lot baba.'

Sameer ran down the stairs and rushed out on his bike.

Sakku Bai did not show up for work for the next four days. Mohan and Sameer had been washing their own undergarments as they had no other option. Mohan heard Mr Bhandari complaining and shouting at his wife for keeping a servant who was playing truant. One morning, Sameer heard a knock on the door while he was combing his hair. It was Sakku Bai who walked in and collapsed on the floor crying uncontrollably with her hands on her head.

'What happened Bai?' Mohan asked, while Sameer looked at her with apprehension in his gaze. Something is drastically wrong, he thought.

'My Sachin has brain cancer! We got the tests done and took them to two doctors. They said they cannot do anything. He will live for six months they say! They tell me that I cannot afford the medicine and his treatment. What can I do baba?' she said, gazing in Sameer's direction with agony in her voice. 'Mr Bhandari has not given me my pagaar for the last ten days. He appointed a new maid this morning. Where am I to go?'

Mohan and Sameer looked at each other. They had no answer.

Sameer felt crushed and could not get his gaze to meet hers. Sakku Bai was shattered and broken. Her Sachin was her pillar of strength and her hope for a better future. He remembered her saying many times, 'I will make Sachin study like you, baba. You must promise to help him get a job. You will become a big shot one day.'

They gave her the ₹350 they had on them. 'We are very sorry Bai. Please go home and don't worry about your job with us. Do come back when Sachin is a little better. I will talk to Mr Bhandari and we'll see what we can do. Let me speak to my family too,' said Sameer, trying to reassure her.

She wept inconsolably for a while, crying for her sick son who would never recover, who would never be the same again. 'He holds his head and screams at night, baba,' she said before leaving. She looked tormented and seemed like she had been to hell and back in the past few days.

Sameer and Mohan went down to Kunal Bhandari's home on the first floor.

'Oh, how can I help you?' he said, uninspired by their presence.

'Sir, we wanted to talk to you about Sakku Bai. Her son is suffering from…'

'Yes, she had come here crying and wailing about her plight. Very sad, but too much trouble, you know. These servants have a lot of problems! We have our own priorities. Kunti is studying to do her entrance for medicine. Rajiv is trying to get into IIT again. This is his third attempt.'

'Maybe there is some small way you can help her, sir? We could pool in to buy some medicines that might give him some relief.'

'No, you see she doesn't work here anymore. My brother downstairs didn't even pay her for the days she's missed work. I gave her salary till the end of the month before we relieved her. What can I do?'

'Actually...'

'I have a lot of work. Why don't you boys run along now?' he said sternly and stood up. He turned his gaze to Sameer and patted his back. 'Please talk to Rajiv this weekend. He wants to take my money and open a restaurant instead of studying for his IIT entrance. Why can't he study? He should become an engineer! Please convince him.'

Sameer and Mohan walked out looking exasperated. 'I'm not coming to the big brother's house. I don't want to hear that chutiya go on about tradition and cultural values. He'll start a discourse in moral behaviour while his son hides porn magazines under the water tank on the roof. See you in college,' he said and left before Mr Vineet Bhandari saw him.

Mr Bhandari opened the door beaming with a broad smile to see Sameer standing before him. 'Sameer! Since when did you start paying your rent in advance?' He looked at Sameer with a wry grin.

'Actually, I'm here to discuss Sakku Bai's problem with you.'

'You too! My wife has been eating my head since this morning. If she doesn't come for work, I'm going to cut her pay. Why has she sent you to negotiate for her?'

'Sir, I'm not here to negotiate. Let's do something for her son. The poor lady is in a bad shape.'

'Look son, it's the government's job to take care of healthcare for the poor. I paid my taxes for so many years till I retired, after thirty years with Suraj Auto,' he said stoutly.

'Sir, government hospitals are...'

'Look here son, please don't spoil my mood. My daughter Richa is coming from America this weekend with my grandson. My son-in-law is coming too. We are going away to Goa for a holiday. You should come and say hello to my son-in-law. He is a vice-president of something at Pittsburgh Mutual Bank. Come down for a coffee on Sunday before we leave for the airport. Don't worry about these servant problems.'

'That is very nice, sir. I'm sure you are very excited about them coming. We can maybe buy some medicines…'

'Here, see? This is a picture of little Saurav. He's two years old.' He stood there, showing off the picture with a flash of pride.

'He's very cute, sir, and I look forward to meeting them when they are here. But before you leave, maybe we can…'

'Ok, I have to go now. We have a lot of work you see. I have to get Richa's old room painted and buy new mattresses. I also need to go and buy some toys and clothes for Saurav. Do you want to come?'

'I have to leave for college, sir.'

'Okay then. Good day, son. I have to run along.'

Sameer heard the door slam behind him. He went to college with a heavy heart feeling miserable about not being able to do anything for Sakku Bai. Seeing him walk into class, Nidhi greeted him cheerfully.

'I got Anuj to book two tickets for *Humko Hua Pyaar* at C-square tonight. I so look forward to the movie,' she gushed.

'Sorry, I'm not in the mood. Please go with someone else,' Sameer said despondently before walking away.

A Grey Oak Foundation initiative. For those loving and good-natured human beings who toil and strive everyday doing physical labour and cleaning up our homes and neighbourhoods, while putting up with filth and squalor in their ghettos/tenements with the hope for a better tomorrow.

Getting off a Virar Fast at Borivali

VINOD GEORGE JOSEPH

I think it was the Old Monk that dulled my senses and made me board a Virar Fast that evening.

'Let me show you the real Bombay,' Javed said to me earlier as we walked out of the Nariman Point skyscraper where we worked. We went to a Mangalorean restaurant near Fountain where Javed ordered Old Monk and Prawns Koliwada for both of us. I would rather have gone home directly and caught the second half of the World Cup cricket match between the West Indies and South Africa.

'Bombay's changed,' Javed said wistfully as we got through a couple of rounds of Old Monk each. 'We don't even drink Old Monk these days. Everyone is into single malts or some fancy vodka.'

"Bangalore has changed a lot as well.'

'Have you started missing it already? It's been just a week since…'

I shrugged my shoulders and Javed moved on to another topic. It was nine when Javed dropped me off at Churchgate and drove off to his lonely flat in Marine Lines. I rushed inside the station and saw a Borivali Slow filling with passengers. The second class compartments were already crammed, but the first class for men still had a few vacant seats. I hesitated, hoping that a Borivali Fast would be announced. The Borivali Slow would take seventy minutes to reach Borivali, whilst a Borivali Fast would do it in an hour. Were my eyes deceiving me or was that a half-empty compartment? No, it was not the ladies first class, which was also only half-full—it was the compartment for the disabled and cancer patients, half the size of a normal one. Since I didn't have a doctor's certificate stating that I had cancer, I prepared to board the men's first class. At that moment, a Virar Fast entered the station.

Conventional wisdom dictated that passengers for Borivali should never board a Virar Fast, though the Virar Fast would get them to Borivali in fifty minutes. The Virar bunch was known to harass passengers who wished to get off at or before Borivali. 'There are many trains, which terminate at Borivali. Take them if you are not travelling beyond Borivali,' they were reputed to admonish those who tried to alight at Borivali or any station before that. At times, they even physically prevented passengers from getting off, forcing them to travel till Dahisar or even Mira Road and then reversing their journey. But surely that couldn't happen so late in the night, could it? It would be almost ten by the time the Virar Fast reached Borivali.

I joined the mob that poured into the first class compartment of the Virar Fast, even before all passengers had alighted. With luck, I would catch the final moments of the South Africa—West Indies match. I took out a paperback from my expensive leather briefcase, plonked the briefcase in the overhead rack and took a window seat. Within seconds, all seats were taken and passengers filled up the aisle.

I turned around when I heard a devotional song, sung full-throatedly in chorus by a group of middle-aged men, most of them standing, a few seated. Some of them held sheets of paper that they referred to as they sang. I looked at my watch. It was now ten past nine and there were at least fifteen men standing. I wondered why the train did not start. As if in response to my question, the platform started to move backwards.

'Ganapati Bappa Moriya,' the men in the second class compartments shouted. A few of my fellow commuters in the first class took up the chant, but their enthusiasm and decibel levels were nowhere close to what emanated from the second class. The train picked up speed and I tried to immerse myself in my book. From time to time, the notes of the devotional song drifted up to me, over the din made by my fellow commuters.

At each stop a larger number of passengers got on. None got off. Since the compartment was filled to bursting with men standing between seats, in the aisle and in the section between the two exit doors, getting in at Mumbai Central meant gaining a foothold, then a handhold and then sliding and squeezing as much of one's body into the compartment as possible and hanging the rest of it outside. At Dadar, an important station where the Central and Western Lines meet, getting in meant throwing oneself into the passengers standing by the door and allowing the weight of those behind to push oneself into the compartment to whatever extent possible. At Bandra, fewer people got on than at Dadar. Many were left behind on the platform and by then I could feel the compartment was packed as tightly as a tin of sardines.

As soon as the train left Bandra, a pretty voice started to repeatedly announce in Marathi, Hindi and English, 'The next stop is Andheri.'

I could still hear the devotional song being sung. On the Virar

Fast, Borivali came immediately after Andheri. If a substantial number didn't get off at Andheri, I knew I would have some difficulty in alighting at Borivali.

'The next stop is Borivali,' the pretty voice announced just after the train pulled out of Andheri. As far as I could tell, no one had got off at Andheri. Five minutes later, I got up from my seat, took out my briefcase from the overhead rack and slowly eased myself into the crush of men who stood in the aisle. I would somehow have to get close to the door before the train reached Borivali in another ten minutes. The question was which door should it be— the one to the left or the one to the right? Only regular commuters would know.

'The next stop is Borivali!' The announcement was repeated over and over again. I wished they would announce how many minutes away Borivali was. Every cubic inch of space in the aisle was occupied.

'I have to get off at Borivali,' I politely told the two men blocking my immediate progress.

'Borivali?' The man facing me was incredulous.

'Try to do so,' the other man told me, facing me sideways, his body hunched forward as a result of a very tall man who was leaning into him.

'Can you let me through?' I asked the man facing me who gave a good-natured chuckle, but nevertheless wiggled his body around so that the two of us slowly moved in a circular motion. I could smell an expensive perfume, which overpowered all other smells nearby. I wondered if I reeked of Old Monk.

'The next stop is Borivali.' One of the men we pushed against gave an exasperated gasp, which made us pause for a moment, before we resumed our circular movement. I started to sweat, despite the overhead fans. Soon, I was one ahead and the man who had faced me was now behind me.

'I have to get off at Borivali,' I repeated to the people surrounding me. I had to get past three passengers before I could reach the area between the two doors.

They let me through. One by one, each of the men in front of me swapped places with me and after three sets of the circular movements described earlier, I was finally at the end of the aisle, beyond which was the space between the two doors, an area approximately twelve feet long and six feet wide. I still clutched my leather briefcase in one sweaty hand.

'Which side will the platform be at Borivali?' I asked the young man to my side as the pretty recorded voice chirped yet again, 'The next stop is Borivali.'

After a moment's hesitation, the young man jutted his head to the right.

'That side?' I asked him, wanting to be doubly sure. There was another nod. I was lucky. I had come through the right side of the narrow aisle. I now had to turn sideways and get to the door—a distance of about five feet.

'Bhai sahib, I have to get off at Borivali,' I politely told the man to my right, only to receive an exasperated look.

'Go on, let him go,' someone said and the cry was taken up by a few of the men standing near me. The man to my right, a lanky man in his twenties, a few inches taller than me, took a deep breath and said, 'Go on.'

The lanky man smelt of a very cheap deodorant, one advertised widely. I didn't need a second prompting. I pressed myself into the non-existent space between him and the back of the seat at the end of aisle. Once I was fully squeezed in between the lanky man and the back of the seat, we started to carry out the circular manoeuvre that was by now second nature to me. My breath was coming out in gasps since I was really being squeezed, but in a few moments, I was through. I drew my breath and started to request the man in front to let me get ahead. But I made no such request for, behind me, I could hear a hissing sound. I had expected the lanky man I had just bypassed to slip back into the space behind the seat I had occupied a few moments earlier. The hissing sound indicated that such a retreat hadn't taken place yet. Most probably, someone else had slipped into that space, forcing the lanky man to stay where he was. I did my best to press myself forward, so that I did not force out all the air from those lanky lungs, to no avail. I realised that I had to keep moving forward so that someone else could heartlessly squeeze the lanky man instead of me.

A man behind me had his back to me, which meant that our backs were pressed against each other. A vibration reverberated through my body. I was puzzled for a second till I realised that the man behind was wheezing. You've got to focus, I told myself. Focus on getting out.

'Bhai sahib, please excuse me,' I told the men around me and waited for my abject apology to take effect before saying, 'I must get off at Borivali.'

I wanted to look at my watch, but couldn't lift my hand. It was going to take me at least another five minutes to get to the door. I wondered how much time I had.

'The next stop is Borivali,' the useless announcements continued. They let me through once more though, by this time, I could feel the train slowing down as it approached Borivali station. I desperately tried to force the pace.

'Sahib, I have to get off at Borivali,' I shouted out loud. 'Please let me through,' I added.

The men in front of me weren't uncooperative. They didn't even smell of any deodorant. In fact, I remember one man stinking of sweat like a workman. Did I smell of sweat or of Old Monk? Were people retching or throwing up as I passed by? One by one, the men in front made way for me and my briefcase, which I was determined not to lose. My house keys were in it, as was my mobile phone. I knew that I ought to have pocketed them both before commencing my precarious journey down the aisle, but it was too late to worry about it. Maybe I ought to take it easy and wait till Dahisar to get off. It was not such a big deal. I could always take a not-so-crowded train back to Borivali. Heck no, I was going to make it. There were just a couple of men ahead of me and the train was yet to reach Borivali.

By now, I was sweating in rivulets. I was squeezed against a stout man with a huge paunch who was roughly my height and had headphones on. His eyes were closed, so that he could listen to the music better. I was sure that I was causing him annoyance and even pain, but he wouldn't open his eyes. I would have felt better if only he would open his eyes and convey his annoyance to me. Suddenly we were at Borivali. I could see the crowds all around, but something was not right. I looked for the platform rushing forward to meet the train and realised that I'd been had. My knees buckled beneath me.

'The platform is on the other side,' one of the men said with a smirk. There was a snigger behind me. A few men hanging by the edge of the door on the other side got off and their places were taken by a few who got on. I think more people got off than got on. If only I had moved towards the correct door, I would have been standing on the platform by then!

'He needs to get off here,' someone announced with a chuckle. Failure and defeat gnawed at my innards. I knew that the situation was hopeless. The train wouldn't stop for more than a minute at Borivali and I needed to cross almost ten feet and about a dozen men before I could get to the other side.

'Try karo,' someone said. I ignored him. I had to find out which side I had to be to get off at Dahisar, before I moved. I had to ask someone. I stood there, waiting for the train to move. I wanted to turn around and see if the chubby man had his eyes open. If so, I could ask him—he seemed to be a trustworthy chap. Anyone who could listen to music in such a crowded space had to be reliable.

'Try to reach the door,' the man to my left said, with iron in his voice. I noticed that he had a two-day stubble and his teeth were stained with paan. 'Chalo, make an effort,' the man repeated and actually managed to create a small gap in front of me. I felt obliged to move into that gap. The train ought to have started to move by then, but it hadn't. Maybe there was a delay. I waited for a second. Yes, of course there was a delay for some unknown reason. The train should have been moving by now.

'Try karo, try karo,' three or four voices said in rapid succession. 'Try karo, try karo,' the men around me chanted. It was as if the crowd was collectively carrying out a science experiment to find out if a human being could get out of such a confined space within a set period of time. 'Try karo, try karo,' the voices rose to a crescendo.

Now it seemed as if all the men around me wanted me out of that compartment. Men pushed themselves, and those behind them, back to create a gap for me to move forward. I was no longer relying on the circular dance motion I had used earlier. Instead, I was being pushed forward into a vacuum constantly being created in front of me. Men squeezed their bodies into a volume that was half their normal size so that I could move forward and get out.

Finally, I could see through the two men standing ahead of me and there was only one more human layer ahead of them. The door was so close. It was unbelievable. Then the train hooted. It was getting ready to move!

'Bhai sahib, I have to get off here.' My cry was a wail of despair. The train hooted again. I could feel it starting to move. No, not yet, it hadn't moved yet, but it would any moment.

'Go,' the man to my side said as I forced myself through to the last layer. Now the train was starting to move.

'Bhai sahib, I have to get off here.' A huge burly man standing by the door had his arm looped around the vertical bar that was in the middle of the exit. There was no space for me to get past him. He looked me in the eye with disgust as I pressed myself into him. Unless he got off the train, I just wouldn't be able to get out. I politely pressed forward a little bit more at the risk of being clobbered on the head.

'Please bhai sahib, I must get off here,' I said, looking him in the eye. As if in reply, he wrinkled his nose. Was he angry with me? Then, all of a sudden, he turned around and jumped out of the compartment. I had the presence of mind to move forward and quickly jump out after him.

When I gathered my wits, I found myself standing on the platform, totally disoriented, the burly man next to me. Sweet, fresh air wrapped me in its soothing embrace. I noticed that the second class compartments were much more densely packed than the one I had got out of, with a dozen men hanging out of each of them. Behind us, the train was now rolling forward, slowly picking up speed.

'Thank you very much,' I fervently told the burly man who mumbled something in reply and jumped back into the compartment. What was that smell? My belt's buckle had been pushed to one side and my shoes had many footprints on them. I was sweating so profusely that my briefcase's handle was slippery in my grip. I quickly opened the briefcase to check if the keys and mobile phone were still there. Yes, thank god! The air smelt of cooking oil and sweat. As I happily started to walk out of the station, I thought of the odour that had hit me for a few seconds as the burly man mumbled his reply. It took me a moment to figure out what it had been. It was the smell of Old Monk rum.

The Crows' Feast

SANCHARI SUR

I knew Maharajji was visiting us today. I knew it from Baba's eagerness to visit the bazaar as soon as it opened; from Ma's rush to wake us up so that she could clean the house; from the moving of the only charpoy in the house, which Baba normally occupied, into the smaller room and from the throng of gurubhais who had already arrived at our doorstep, waiting in anticipation for Maharajji.

I did not know his real name, nor did Baba, who had heard about him from another gurubhai, and had been a disciple for many years, even before my birth. He was known as Maharaj, or 'king', with the 'ji' attached as a mark of respect. His disciples, like Baba, were known as gurubhais, or guru-brothers. Baba looked up to him and believed that, with Maharajji's prayers and grace, our family would find peace and salvation. Ma said that if Maharajji did not visit us so often, then we would finally have some peace. But she never said this in front of Baba and only mentioned it when her sister, Mala Mashi, visited us.

I knew for a few days now that Maharajji would call on us soon. I had seen the off-white postcard that arrived in the mail the previous week. The postcards always had the same look to them—dusty and urgent with quick, scant, scribbled Hindi words, followed by a date. They arrived unfailingly every year to announce his arrival.

Maharajji usually stayed for a few days when he was here. He spent his days moving from one place to another, always staying at a gurubhai's residence. Whenever he visited Calcutta, he stayed at our place first. When he was with us, Baba would be extremely busy and even take a few days off from work to spend time meditating and praying with Maharajji. At that time, our house would be filled with gurubhais who would come to pray with him. Everyone saw Maharajji as a powerful and learned man as he was capable of going into coma-like trances. I recall seeing him meditate for as long as one and a half to two hours straight.

I didn't like it when Maharajji visited. For one, I had to be on my best behaviour. I couldn't play ball or yell at the crows that came to rest on our window ledges. Even Ma was too busy cooking all day to bother with me. His arrival also changed our sleeping arrangements. We lived in two rented rooms on the first floor of a fifty year old building on Bowbazar Street, not far from Sealdah station. The bigger room had an attached kitchen. One side looked into an alley and the other side gave us a view of a neighbouring building. The smaller room, which also looked out to the same building, was usually occupied by my three older brothers—Tarun, Varun and Subroto—who were almost grown men. Baba, Ma and I used the bigger room. Our rooms were separated by a small but private bathroom in the common yard, which was shared by the other tenants on our floor. But when Maharajji visited, the smaller room was vacated for his used. All of us then squeezed in on the floor in the bigger room. I had trouble falling asleep on those nights because Tarun's snoring kept me up.

Apart from prayers and meditation, Maharajji loved to eat. Ma said that he ate as much as ten men. Normally, we bought our fruit and vegetables from a grocer's down the street. But when Maharajji was here, Baba visited the bazaar to buy the freshest stock available, even if it took him longer to get there and the food cost a little more. Ma then spent all day in the kitchen, cooking ten different dishes. No one in the house was allowed to eat what was cooked for Maharajji, not even Baba. Ma cooked dal and rice for us separately. I only cared for hot rotis smeared with ghee, which was a delicacy in our house. Sometimes, I stared at Maharajji eating and waited for him to say, 'I cannot eat any more.' But this had never happened and I kept on hoping that it would happen the next time he sat down to eat.

Today too, as at every other time, Ma was busy in the kitchen. Baba was in the smaller room talking to the gurubhais. My brothers had left for school. And I was hanging around the kitchen, hoping that Ma would offer me something to eat.

'Don't stand here staring at me. You know this is only for him.'

'I know, Ma. Can't I have just one roti and maybe... a little bit of that potato and pumpkin curry?'

'No, you know you can't. Baba will get angry if he finds out. Maybe if there is something left over later...'

'But there *never* is anything left over, ever!' I whined. Sometimes, Ma gave in if I pouted and pretended to throw a tantrum. But today was not one of those days.

'Go and see if your Baba needs something,' she said in an attempt to get rid of me.

I dragged my feet as I approached the doorway when I heard, 'Maharajji is here! We are blessed! Maharajji ki jai! All hail Maharajji!'

I ran quickly to catch a glimpse. He looked just as I remembered him—tall and lanky, with a long, inky beard. His face was unlined, even though he was much older than Baba. Baba had once said that Maharajji was from U.P. and that's why he spoke in the peculiar Hindi of that region. At that time, I didn't know what people from U.P. looked like, but he was certainly much taller than most Bengalis. Dressed in a stark, white dhoti that exposed his legs, and a long white kurta, Maharajji looked like any other holy man in Calcutta, only taller.

He raised a hand to quiet the crowd and turned towards Baba, 'How are you, my brother?'

'With your blessings, we are doing quite well,' Baba responded with folded hands.

This was not true. In fact, I had overheard an argument between Ma and Baba only a few days ago, the day the postcard had arrived.

'You know we cannot afford to keep him. Think of your sons.' This was Ma.

'Do you know what a privilege it is that he is coming to spend a few days here? Not everyone gets this privilege! We should feel blessed!' Baba had retorted.

'But we do not have enough for rent this month, and I also have to pay the grocer…'

'I will ask for an extension from Dhuri babu. After all, he is a gurubhai too.'

Dhuri babu was our landlord.

'But…'

'You know Maharajji's prayers are important for our family! I do not want to hear about this matter again!'

Baba and Ma had not spoken to each other since then. Even this morning, she took the bag of fruits and vegetables from him without a word.

By this time, Maharajji had entered the smaller room and

was holding an audience with all the gurubhais. He was telling them something about life and the emptiness of desire. 'Desire is poisonous. Desire is Maya, illusion. Overcoming desire should be life's ultimate goal.'

I was bored and hungry. The smell of cooking all morning had made me ravenous. But I had to wait till Maharajji had his lunch. I knew he was hungry too. It was almost one in the afternoon and, like clockwork, Maharajji called to stop his preaching. 'My brothers, I must rest after my long journey. And then, I must meditate. I will see you all later this evening.'

After all the gurubhais had dispersed, Baba and Maharajji approached the bigger room, where Ma had already set down our best copper cutlery with different kinds of vegetable curries and a stack of hot steaming rotis smeared with ghee. The smell of the ghee was heady and even now, when I think back to those days, I can remember the smell throbbing in the air around me, swollen with my single-minded desire for a single ghee-smeared roti.

'Come, Maharajji. I hope Sumati has prepared them to your taste.'

Maharajji took the tumbler of water and washed his hands outside, then sat down to eat the feast laid out for him.

Watching him eat was mesmerizing. He tore a roti slowly and dipped it into one of the curries. As he brought the piece glistening with the curry to his mouth, his eyes closed in reverence. He seemed to savour the taste as he munched on his first bite. Every other bite that followed was in quick succession.

I held my breath as I watched him go deftly through the rotis one by one. Finally, he started to tear into the last roti. After one bite, he stopped. He placed his hands on his belly and said, 'Sister, you have outdone yourself. I cannot eat anymore.'

'No, Maharajji, what are you saying? Have some more,' Baba urged.

Maharajji smiled and shook his head. 'No, brother. I am full.'

Then he turned towards my watchful eyes, rolled up the partially eaten roti and beckoned to me. 'Come, my son. Take this roti.'

I took the roti and glanced at Baba. Maharajji continued, 'Go and feed the crows on the roof. Those winged creatures are intelligent, just like humans. They reflect us in many ways. Just as you must feed the poor, you must also feed the crows. This will bring peace to your inner being. Go, my child.'

Baba nodded impatiently at me and I turned to run up the stairs to the roof.

The rooftop was vacant at that time of the day, and I panted in the stillness. The afternoon was grey and the clouds seemed to threaten rain. I threw the roti on the floor and retreated to the doorway leading to the stairs. A ruckus of cawing filled the air as about twenty to thirty crows mobbed the roti, pushing at the others with their wings. In a matter of seconds, the roti had disappeared. I turned around to head back downstairs.

Song of the Summer Bird

ANITA SATYAJIT

I ran out of the door, as soon as Padma turned her back on me. Before she could catch me, I was jumping down the stairs, two at a time. I slowed down after I crossed the gate to look behind me. Padma was not on my trail. She would surely be calling Mummy to tell her I ran off without permission. But she was a maid—why did I need her permission?

I set off towards the library. Sudha and Ramya were hiding behind a car in the parking lot. 'Diya! Come hide. Lakshya is searching for us.'

'No. I am not in the mood. I am going to go to the library to see my dad.' Ramya made a face. I stuck out my tongue in response. They were so silly. Hide and seek was their idea of fun. But I didn't want to play today. I wanted to read. Waving goodbye to Sudha, I walked on. Ashoka, gulmohar, peepal, neem and other trees whose names I didn't know spread their arms, preventing light from brightening the black tar streets. I hopped on the spots where sunlight managed to penetrate the canopy of leaves and kiss the ground. I loved living here. It had been a month since we moved to this new home in Mumbai University. I had soon discovered which trees were easy to climb and which bricks were loose enough to use as hiding places for various things. At night, the rising and falling crescendo of buzzing insects lulled me to sleep. In the morning, the cawing of the crow unfailingly perched on the tree outside woke up me. It was a far cry from the jarring shrieks of vehicles that woke me up each morning at our previous residence.

Soon, I was near the library building and immediately walked erect to feel taller than my four feet. This was the first time I was heading there alone. As I neared the entrance, I noticed a very old man sitting by the door. His eyes, framed on the top by thick white eyebrows and on the bottom by dark half-moons, were sunk far into his bony face. The skin on his neck hung loose in layers and, in his brown pants and shirt, he looked... dusty.

Daddy had mentioned a watchman who was away on vacation. Was this the man? I remembered the cranky old man in the story Mummy often told me—the man who took children away if they were too naughty. With my head bent low, I scurried past him. But the voice that emanated from him was firm. 'Where do you think you are going, baby?' he asked in Hindi.

I whirled around. Baby! 'I am not a baby. I am eight years old.'

He bent down with a quizzical expression on his face.

It took me a moment to realise that he didn't understand English. And so I repeated in Hindi that I was eight years old and was on my way to meet my father who was in charge of the library.

'You are Maheshji's daughter? Does he know you came here alone?' he enquired.

'He'll know when I go inside,' I replied cheekily and rushed inside before he could respond.

That night, I scowled at the blank television at home. After stating that he had no problem with me coming alone to the library every day, Daddy had decided to punish me nevertheless for coming without permission this time. Actually, he was not angry. But when Mummy returned home from work, Padma had narrated a tale so exaggerated that Mummy was mortified at my behaviour. And so Mummy had convinced Daddy to ban my television viewing for the day.

Daddy was seated on his woven bamboo chair and Mummy was on her small stool, cutting vegetables for the night. They were discussing what they had read earlier that day in the newspaper. When I couldn't bear the boredom anymore, I dropped the doll I was playing with. 'Daddy, what is inflation?'

'Read up about it in the library tomorrow,' he teased and beckoned me to come closer. Optimistic at his response, I asked him if I was forgiven and could watch TV. Mummy's stern gaze was the reply. Pouting, I walked back to play with my doll.

If there was one thing that made me forget the world around me, it was books. I could spend hours without food, water, TV or play if I had a book in my hands. Both Mummy and Daddy encouraged this habit. Since Daddy started working as the librarian at the university, my appetite for books was suitably sated by the number of books he brought back home. But after I started going to the library by myself, I felt as if I had been granted access to a magical world. Every afternoon, I spent hours on the floor between bookshelves, poring over words that exhilarated me or which I didn't understand. After I was done, all I had to do was put the books back on Daddy's desk. One exceptionally hot summer afternoon, about ten days after my first interaction with Bhau, the watchman, he smiled at me as I approached the building.

'Does your father know you spend such long hours inside?' Bhau asked. I looked back at him defiantly. 'Of course he knows. He encourages my habit.'

Bhau laughed as if he didn't believe me. I caught sight of the bushy white hair that grew on his earlobe. As he turned his head to look for something in his pocket, the hair jiggled in the breeze. I covered my mouth with my hands, but couldn't stop the sound of laughter from escaping. Bhau shot me a look. Without waiting to explain myself, I ran inside the library laughing. That day, on my way back, I felt myself warm up to him and smiled at him as I left. He reminded me of Santa Claus—after he had wiggled down a sooty chimney.

I established a ritual of talking to Bhau before I stepped into the library. As I grumbled about vacation homework or how mother scolded me for sticking a paper tail on our maidservant, Bhau would patiently nod. Whenever I encouraged him to talk, Bhau would regale me with stories in which animated trees and wildlife would prominently figure. His descriptions were vivid. He moved his arms to describe a bird's flight or a rat's scuffle. And each time he mentioned a bird or tree that I didn't know, he would take the time after the story to point out that bird, if it nested in the trees nearby. It was this search for birds that started us on the habit of going for evening walks after he finished his shift at five. Bhau's sharp ears would seek the whistles of the birds and, in minutes, he would point them out. He knew so much about nature that I began to be increasingly fascinated by it myself. I even decided I would spend my adult life studying animals and birds. When I told Bhau this, he smiled indulgently, which immediately made me angry. Then he took me for a walk and soon I was lost in his stories. I asked Bhau if the people at the university had forgotten to retire him, at which he just smiled.

'I just have a week before school begins, Bhau. I am…' I saw that Bhau wasn't paying attention and was instead searching in the bushes for something. 'What did you see, Bhau?' I ran behind him. Bhau pushed aside the bushes and scurried ahead.

'A snake, little one—stay behind me. I'll catch it for you if it's not poisonous.' I was scared and exhilarated at the same time. A snake! I had never seen one before. Bhau jogged hurriedly on a small path that I had never seen before. It seemed to wiggle between trees. Soon we reached open ground. Fresh translucent grass was sprayed over most of it. Bushes had sprung up in a haphazard manner. Tall trees stood at the periphery of this patch. Wandering about, touching each tree, I noticed one tree whose trunk caved in. It was a lovely place to sit. With a whoop of joy I immediately seated myself there. Bhau scooted over to sit beside me.

'Bhau, why haven't we come here before?'

'It is a little out of our way,' he explained. 'But isn't it beautiful?' The snake forgotten, I jumped up and down from the tree trunk while Bhau became nostalgic about his favourite hiding spot by the river in his village. He spoke about his childhood, his family, their struggle for money and eventually became silent. I only caught snatches of his monologue because I was busy playing. Then, noticing his glazed eyes, I went to sit with him. I did not understand all he had said to me, but I understood the tears in his eyes. When I placed my palm on his knee, Bhau smiled and covered my tiny hand with his wrinkled one.

Just then a crow shrieked. Bhau looked at it, startled. Dusk had begun to set it. 'Oh, my god... I didn't realise I spent so much time talking. Come on, let me take you home.' Bhau held my hand and I ran as we rushed back home. The sky was blue-black by the time we reached my building. Mummy was standing at the entrance, rubbing her eyes with the edge of her sari while some neighbours stood talking among themselves nearby. Mummy let out a squeal when she saw me and rushed towards me. Bhau let go of my hand and I ran into her arms. She held me so tight, I felt suffocated. Just then Daddy came around the corner of the building.

I had never seen Daddy lose his temper that way before. He yelled at Bhau, asked him if he was about to kidnap me, and if his actions suited a man his age. Bhau, who stood silently taking in my father's anger, looked stricken when Daddy said that. He opened his mouth to respond. Then, obviously changing his mind, he stared at the ground while Daddy shouted. Asking Bhau to be more responsible, Daddy dragged me away by my hand. I turned to catch a glimpse of Bhau, guilt gnawing at my heart.

The next morning, Mummy and Daddy announced that I wasn't allowed to go to the library anymore. My pleas and screams had no effect. So, over the next two days, I ensured that no one at home could rest. As soon as mother turned her back after stacking books on my desk, they would be on the floor. Daddy's spectacles wound up in the refrigerator and Mummy's bedroom slippers were found wet and soggy in the bath. After I interchanged the labels on the salt and sugar bottles, Padma vowed to quit her job if I stayed home. Since there were just three more days left for school to begin, after many warnings I was allowed to go to the library again—but on the condition that I present myself in front of my father every hour. I hurried out of the door before mother could change her mind.

I ran to meet Bhau. I had to explain that I was scared and that's why I had not supported him when Daddy was shouting at him. Not that Daddy understood when I told him at home that I had gone with Bhau of my own volition. He didn't seem to understand how Bhau could be my friend.

Bhau saw me, but looked away as I walked inside the library gate. Seated on his stool, he drew patterns with his stick on the cracked tiles below. I was used to a Bhau who held up a hand to give me a high-five, the way I had taught him. 'Bhau, are you angry with me?' I asked, holding out a hibiscus flower I had plucked on the way. Taking it, Bhau asked me how I was doing. At the sound of his voice, I burst into tears. I placed my head on his knee and sobbed.

'That's enough, little one. Did your parents scold you a lot?'

'A little, but I am sorry for not standing up for you that evening.'

Bhau's cracked lips parted to reveal his broken teeth. 'Big words from a little girl,' he said, rolling the flower between his fingertips. Then he looked at me with an inexplicable expression. 'You are a child of the earth. Remain rooted to it and be who you are. Never let that connection with nature go away. It's that relationship which will teach you about relationships with people,' he said. His voice broke towards the end as he wiped his eyes with a tattered sleeve. He gave me a slight nudge to leave. 'Go inside to your father,' he urged. I went inside and spent the remainder of the afternoon amongst musty books.

The next day, as I neared the library, I noticed the empty seat outside. Hurrying inside, I asked Daddy about Bhau's whereabouts, since he usually never missed work. Getting up from his seat, Daddy took my hand and led me out. I was puzzled, but pleased with the attention. Walking down the road, I heard an Asian koel sing. I stopped and pointed it out to Daddy. Then I kept pointing out plants, birds and flowers to him, bombarding him with the information that Bhau had passed on to me. 'Who taught you so much about nature, Diya?'

'Bhau, when we went on our walks. Where is he, Daddy? Why didn't he come to work?'

'He has gone home, Diya,' Daddy said calmly. 'He won't be working here anymore.'

'But he didn't say anything yesterday. He didn't even say bye. How could he go like that?' I was angry and kicked a stone on the road. As we walked, I looked at my father's black shoes and remembered Bhau's cracked, brown feet and his mud-covered slippers. Why didn't Bhau tell me he was leaving? Wasn't I his friend? I told him everything.

'Bhau was old, Diya. He must have wanted to be with his family,' Daddy whispered. I remembered Bhau's smile the day he told me about his family. He always missed them and had now gone home to them. 'Bhau must be happy,' I said aloud to no one in particular. Holding Daddy's hand lightly, I walked back to the library.

'Song of the Summer Bird' is the Landmark pick from the short-listed stories in the Landmark Grey Oak Urban Stories Competition.

The Power Cut

MARYANN TAYLOR

Arun woke up feeling suffocated by the humidity in the air. His parents were shouting at each other in the distance. Glancing at the stationary ceiling fan, he realized that there had been a power cut. Arun's night suit felt damp against his skin as he rubbed off the sweat from the back of his neck. He looked at his alarm clock. There were still fifteen minutes for it to ring. Mornings in their South Delhi neighbourhood began with the sounds of domestic help ringing door bells to be let in to begin the day's chores, the thud of the newspaper on front verandas, and the clanging of pots and pans from the house next door. Rays of soft sunlight crept in through the window as he slipped out of the room and down the corridor towards the living room, where the voices seemed to be coming from. Peeping from behind the door, he saw his mother weeping hysterically, while his father looked disturbed and anxious.

'How could you, Subroto?' cried his mother. 'Didn't you for once think about Arun and me before doing something so selfish and pathetic?'

'Calm down, Indrani. Please take it easy. I'm sorry, it's not like

I planned whatever happened,' his father tried to pacify his mother.

'Calm down! You're asking me to calm down after what you've done?' yelled his mother, wiping away her tears with her dupatta.

'Indrani, you're overreacting. It was just one night, and I was drunk for god's sake. I hardly remember anything from that night!' stammered his father. 'I don't think I should have told you,' he sighed in exasperation, turning away from his wife to face the wall.

'Okay, that's it Subroto! I've had enough. I can't bear to look at your face for another minute, let alone live with a man like you,' sobbed his mother before she left, with a little black canvas bag in her hand, banging the door on her way out.

'Oh, Indrani,' groaned his father, cradling his head in his hands as he flopped down on the couch.

The shrill sound of the alarm pierced though the accusing silence of the house and Arun turned around and ran down the corridor, disappearing into the bathroom.

Arun's father was waiting for him at the door, holding his school bag while the school pickup van honked impatiently outside. Arun's strapped his dull green school bag—which proclaimed 'Arun Sengupta, Class 5B, St Michael's School'—onto his back and walked towards the van.

'Arun,' his father called out. 'I'm sorry but Mummy couldn't pack your tiffin box for you today. Here's some money—have something to eat from the canteen today. Okay?' His father smiled, pressing a fifty rupee note into his hand.

'Okay,' Arun mumbled as he climbed into the waiting van.

Inside the van, Arun's friends Sahil and Sameer were chatting excitedly amongst themselves about a surprise Maths test to take place that day. Arun squeezed into the window seat near Preeti, who was showing Aditi her new yellow pencil box filled with shiny slim pencils. Arun stared out of the window, his little forehead creased in a frown. He wasn't worried about the Maths test—he quite liked Maths and his Maths teacher told him he was good at it too. He wondered where his mother had gone and when she'd come back. One evening, a few weeks ago, Arun had heard their neighbours, the young Mr and Mrs Nair, having an argument. The following day, he had overheard their maid Sarita telling his mother that Mrs Nair had angrily broken lots of dishes—most of them, fine bone china. Arun quite liked Mrs Nair, or Kaveri as everyone called her. She was very pretty, wore very tight jeans and very high heels, and called Arun 'little mister handsome' whenever she would see him. It was difficult for Arun to imagine someone so pretty and so pleasant having such a nasty temper. He tried to remember if he had seen any broken dishes at home that morning.

All through his brief journey to school, Arun stared out of the window. Delhi's streets were a maze of traffic, which included cars, trucks, bicycles and bullock carts fighting for space. Arun's gaze followed the women he passed by on the road as he searched for someone resembling his mother. He looked at the way they were dressed, the way they smiled, or the way they walked hurriedly, taking short steps, an unknown sense of urgency clinging to each stride.

At school that morning, the Maths test did not take place, but an English one did. Arun spent the day staring at his desk, scribbling on it with his pencil. He loved the sound of its lead scratching against the wood. During lunch break, as he nibbled on a lukewarm samosa, he said to Sameer, 'My Mummy went somewhere this morning and I feel afraid.'

'Arey buddhu, she must have gone to office just like my

Mummy,' Sameer quipped. 'No, when she goes to office, she wears a sari and lipstick and looks very pretty. But today she wasn't wearing a sari and looked very sad.'

'Then ask your Papa. Grownups seem to know everything.'

Arun came home to find Sarita, the maid, sitting on the living room floor, fanning herself furiously with a newspaper. He looked up to see the ceiling fan as still as it was in the morning when he woke up.

'Arun beta, there has been no bijli the whole day. God knows when this damn electricity will come back,' she complained. 'I have been struggling in the kitchen. It's so dim there and so hot... Now hurry up and change your clothes. I have made rajma chawal and I know you like it.' She smiled at him indulgently.

After making sure that Arun had eaten, Sarita yawned, stretched out on the floor of the drawing room and was soon snoring gently. With nothing much to do and no cartoon watching possible, Arun made his way up to the terrace. He chose a shady spot and, resting his hands and chin on the parapet, began to look around. In the distance, he could see a sleek and shiny Delhi Metro train snaking its way across the vast sky on elevated tracks. He was amused and his gaze followed the train as far as possible. He had never been on one of those trains and wondered what it would be like. From where he stood, he could see into people's terraces, where women were putting out clothes to dry. Jars of pickle lined the terrace walls, and crows and pigeons sat on water tanks covered with their droppings. It was a humid afternoon and the street below was quieter than it would be in the evenings. There was a hawker selling jamuns, and a stray dog viciously chasing a bike rider down the street. Arun chuckled and longed to have some jamuns—he loved the way they stained his mouth a deep purple.

Arun was surprised to see his father come home earlier than

usual, and was pleasantly surprised when they both drove to India Gate. He was permitted to eat ice lollies and candy floss to his heart's content, and buy numerous balloons. He still wondered where his mother was and if she'd be home by the time they got back. They returned to a dark house. The electricity was still not back and his mother was not at home.

Arun's father lit candles around the house and warmed up some food. They ate in silence, watching the candles flickering cheerfully in the otherwise gloomy room, darkness seeping into every corner.

It came as a surprise to Arun when his father suggested that he sleep in his parents' bedroom that night. He had always slept in his own room for as long as he could remember. Many of his mother's friends had been horrified to learn that he slept alone even when he was little. His mother, however, had her own views on child-rearing. Arun refused and crept into his own bed silently. His father kissed him goodnight and walked out of the room, not shutting the door but leaving it ajar. Arun threw off the covers and rolled over in bed, feeling sweat gradually soak his clothes. As he stared at the boringly familiar pattern on the curtain in his room, highlighted by the pale glow of the streetlight falling upon it, he eventually drifted off to sleep dreaming that the electricity had been restored and that his mother had returned home where she stood in the kitchen humming tunelessly while she packed his tiffin for him to take to school.

Mervin

AHMED FAIYAZ

Vijay Kumar pompously strode out of the apartment building with a deep frown on his face. A sad-faced miniature look-alike of his walked reluctantly behind him. Vijay had been in a blue funk since his wife left town with a younger man after a quick divorce. She left their son, Rajiv, behind with him. He had heard that his ex-wife and her boyfriend had got married. She was now honeymooning in Malaysia while Vijay was sulking and fuming at every given opportunity, and playing babysitter to his son, of whom he knew nothing. He never had any time for the boy, who looked so much like him but infuriated him because of his laziness and lack of aptitude, or interest, in a sport.

'Watchman!' he barked, hearing which a puny old man in a khaki uniform limped across from his rickety chair outside the gate.

'Yes, saar?'

'Who is that fellow hanging around by my car? Why do you let strangers enter the building?' Vijay fumed and glared angrily at the dark-skinned, lanky lad who stood a hundred metres away with a confused smile on his face.

'Saar, he's your driver Thomas's son, Mervin. Thomas is sick today and he's sent him instead.'

'Harrumph…. you fellow, why can't you tell me, eh? Do you have a license?'

'Of course sir, shall I reverse your car? My father mentioned that you leave for the club at 6 pm.'

'Yes, let's go,' he said, tapping his feet on the ground.

'Dad, I don't want to go. I want to play *Need for Speed* on my Nintendo.'

'Shut up and get into the car. You spend your time sitting in front of the TV and getting fat. Come and play a sport at the club or work out in the gym.'

'Dad, I…' the boy said, grimacing slightly.

'Get in, I said. Get in now!'

Two hours later, Vijay found Mervin playing badminton with his son in the club room. 'Time to go,' Vijay said in his deep baritone. His voice slurred and he seemed a bit tipsy. It was his routine to come to the club every evening to play bridge and get drunk to forget his stressful day at work and his now-failed marriage.

'Dad, please… One more game. I'm winning against Mervin!'

Vijay sat down to see Mervin drop point after point that put Rajiv in a state of immense bliss. He hadn't seen his son laugh, let alone smile, after his mother left both of them and their army of servants. The kid moped around all evening, watching TV shows and playing on his gaming console.

'You can come and play *Need for Speed* with me. Will you come tomorrow?' a cherubic Rajiv asked Mervin, as he navigated the sedan through pouring rain and peak hour traffic on M.G. Road.

'Yes, I will try,' Mervin said in a friendly voice.

'So what do you do… err… Martin?' Vijay asked with a slur in his voice. His mind was on the presentation with the paper company in Singapore in a few days.

'His name is Mervin, Dad. He loves Batman comics and he was the fastest runner in school. He used to play for the cricket, football and basketball teams also. Right, Mervin?'

'Yes, sir,' Mervin smiled and turned slightly with a nod.

'Hmm… What do you do now?'

'I'm looking for a part-time job, sir. I failed my twelfth standard exams, so I'm preparing for them again. After that, papa is trying to send me away to the Gulf. My uncle, Tony, works for the dockyard in Dubai.'

'Hmm… Yes. Let me talk to your father. How does coming and spending time with Rajiv sound? I want you to come and play a sport with him. He needs someone around. I want someone who can be a friend, a mentor and a coach to him. He sits in front of the TV all day and doesn't get along with the other boys in the building. He needs to get out and be like the other boys. His grandmother is too old and his mother, well…' He stared at the seat in front of him with a pensive look on his face.

'The other boys call me fat-face, Dad. They don't let me bowl. They make me run for the ball all the time. Every time I bat, they bowl full toss and get me out on the first ball,' Rajiv complained looking downcast while Vijay looked at him with disappointment evident on his face.

'Yes sir, I wouldn't mind. It will be a pleasure to spend time with Rajiv Baba.' He turned to Rajiv and smiled.

'Yay!' Rajiv yelped.

'We'll smash sixes, Baba. Those fellows will be the ones who'll run to fetch the ball.'

'That settles it. Start tomorrow, 4 p.m. to 8 p.m. from Monday to Saturday. I'll pay you ₹3,000 a month.'

The next day, Rajiv reluctantly followed Mervin to the

basketball court with a bright orange Cosco ball with Chicago Bulls painted on it.

'But Mervin, I don't play basketball. The boys in my class don't let me. They say that I'm short and fat. My Mum used to say my Dad...'

'Dude, when you play basketball, you have a chance to be tall and thin. I used to be just like you.'

'Really?'

'Yup!'

'Okay, let's play one game. After that, we can go and play *Wrestlemania*. We can play a cage match...'

'Go on, first show me what you've got.' Rajiv flung the ball with all his strength towards the right. It rebounded after hitting the board, missing the ring completely, and came back to hit him in the face. 'Ow!' he yelped, given the force with which the rugged ball struck against his face.

'Dude, come here. Who asked you to throw the ball with such force? And you're taking a shot too close to the board. Everything is wrong. The way you threw the ball, your eyes were on the ground and not on the hoop. Come on, let me show you...'

Mervin took two pointers and three pointers, netting each of them through the hoops. He then proceeded to show Rajiv how to take a lay-up, while Rajiv, still wincing in pain, looked at him with awe.

'Come on, it's your turn now. Show me how it's done—first a two pointer and then a lay-up. Chalo Rajiv,' Mervin said with authority.

※

Rajiv, puffing and panting after a long game followed a sweaty

Mervin out of the basketball court behind the building. 'Do you know I failed Maths again? Dad is very angry with me. He's got this new tutor to come by and teach me three times a week. She starts this evening. I don't want to study,' he said, grimacing.

'It's important that you do. You don't want to fail a year, do you? I failed twice in the seventh standard. It's difficult to make new friends every year.'

'But I don't have any friends. You're my friend.'

'Thanks man, but let's go and do some Maths. You study while I play on your PSP.'

'That's not fair!'

'Haha!'

'This new tutor is Dad's accountant's daughter. She studies in some college and she's coming home to teach me.'

'Ah huh, nice.'

'Not nice. I don't like girls. They giggle and laugh at me in class when I eat the food that Dadi packs for me for lunch.'

'That's mean. They should focus on their own lunch. Why laugh at you?'

'Because I eat during class na! I get very hungry. At lunch, I buy dosas, samosas and a milkshake from the pocket money that Dad gives me.'

'How much does he give you?'

'A hundred rupees every day.'

'You rich boy. Give me fifty bucks and go upstairs to your Maths classes. I'll be back soon.'

Rajiv handed him the money and ran towards the elevator with his basketball in his hands.

Fifteen minutes later, Mervin walked into the room. He saw a petite girl, no older than him, stare at Rajiv's book with a stern expression on her face. He saw Rajiv looking completely baffled.

'Hi. I'm Mervin. You must be the tutor.'

'You must be the playmate...' she said with a wry smile.

'If you put it like that,' Mervin guffawed.

'Mr Kumar told me about you. I'm Sonam,' she said. She had a no-nonsense air about her.

'Nice to meet you,' Mervin said, taking a seat opposite her.

'Now, we need to work on simultaneous equations.'

'Sure,' he said, fixing his gaze on her with a charming smile on his face. 'Use examples. He relates to that and picks up things quickly.'

'Good luck, buddy,' he winked at Rajiv before walking out of the room.

An hour later, he felt a hand on his shoulder. 'I finished. I got two out of five sums correct.'

'Nice start.'

'Yes. Sonam Miss is very good.'

'Ah huh,' Mervin said, continuing his game.

'Will you take the car and drop her home?'

'Can't she go home on her own?'

'No. She stays close by, but it's a little late to walk, right?'

'Right you are,' Mervin said, getting up from the comfortable couch as he saw Sonam enter the room in her off-white salwar dress, carrying an old purse.

༄༅༅

'Big man, you're not into it today, are you?' Mervin asked as he dribbled the ball around the court, teasing Rajiv to tackle him.

'No, not really...' Rajiv said, looking aloof and disinterested.

'You've been like this for days. Come on, let's sit and talk...'

They went to a spot in a corner behind the basketball court

and sat with their backs against the wall. Mervin lit up a cigarette.

'What's happening? Why are you so troubled, big guy?'

'No, it's nothing,' Rajiv murmured, with a faraway look in his eyes.

'Okay, let's tell each other a secret. Let's tell each other three secrets,' Mervin said taking a drag.

'You go first.'

'Alright, here goes. I actually didn't win the interschool 100 meters dash. Or I shouldn't have won. I started five seconds too early. Yet, the records still have the fastest time in my name. I clocked two seconds faster than a man who won us a medal at the Commonwealth Games ten years ago and just three seconds faster than the guy I beat. Now it's your turn.'

'Really? So the record in your name isn't fair?'

'Let's move on with it—I won. Now you go…'

'I actually always wished that my mother would go away. She was interested in drinking and partying more than anything else. She brought her boyfriend home when Dad wasn't around. But I miss her now.'

'That's sad, man. I've come to blows with my Dad. He used to get drunk and attack my mother. One day, I leaped at him and punched him in the face. Since then, he doesn't lay his hands on her.'

'Wow! I didn't know he could be so bad. I always thought Thomas was the nicest person around.'

'Not when he's drunk like a fish. Well, your turn.'

'I feel upset about my Dad. I don't like his drinking and the women he brings over who spend a night in our apartment.'

'Hmm… Well, you have some help from me. I've been stealing his vodka, gin and whisky in small amounts. Last night, I took a swig from his precious bottle of wine from California.'

'Merv! What if he finds out?'

'Chillax, kiddo. It's so little that he won't notice. I keep adding back water and diluting it.'

'Haha... You're so funny,' Rajiv said, before he attempted a failed lay-up where he almost ran into the pole. 'Tell me one more...'

'Well, I flunked my twelfth on purpose. I didn't want to go to the Gulf. I want to stay right here and become a painter. I've been showing some of my work around.'

'Wow!' Rajiv said and attempted another lay-up where the ball just tossed in the air and missed the ring completely. 'So close!'

'Come here. You've got to tell me the last secret of the evening? What's getting you into low spirits?'

'You'll laugh at me. I can't tell...'

'Okay, let's go up to the terrace and chat. I need a smoke too.' Rajiv followed him into the building and headed towards the stairs.

'God Mervin, why do you have to make me climb so much?'

'You need exercise, man. Now, go on,' Mervin said, putting on a straight face.

Rajiv hesitated a bit and looked up at the setting sun that was disappearing behind the buildings a few streets away.

'I kind of like a girl...'

'Like?' Mervin asked, raising his eyebrows.

'I think I'm in love with her,' a sweaty Rajiv said. His cheeks turned red, partly due to the climb to the terrace on the third floor.

'And who is the lucky lady?'

'You can guess...'

'The Melwanis' daughter? The girl downstairs? Her dog chased you, remember?'

'No way! She's fat and wears these thick glasses. She has braces too,' Rajiv made a face like he wanted to retch.

'Have you seen yourself in the mirror? You'll make a nice couple. Okay, chill. So who is this mystery woman?'

'Don't laugh, okay? It's Miss Sonam. She is so beautiful and intelligent. She has such a sweet voice,' he said and averted his gaze from Mervin's, his face flushed with excitement.

'Aha! How interesting,' Mervin smirked.

'See? I knew it.'

'No, she's nice. And why not? You're a rich boy, with expensive toys and a taste for good food and music. She'd go for you.'

'Really? She's six years older than me. But I can't stop looking at her.'

'Don't worry, try and impress her a bit. Dress up for your tuitions, make her a mix-tape and, after some days, tell her what you feel,' Mervin grinned.

'I can't. I'm scared... Anyway, let's go. Dadi will send the watchman to look for me.'

Rajiv took his basketball and took the flight of stairs to the terrace. Sonam had smiled sweetly and complimented him on his new Nike basketball t-shirt during tuitions. He had also managed to give her a mix-tape of his favourite songs the day before. The plan seems to be working, he thought. It was a good idea to use Dad's Dolce & Gabbana body spray. He entered the terrace and heard voices from the other end. He quietly crept behind the water tank. He could make out two people sitting on the stone bench, their faces hidden by the dish antenna installed on the terrace. *Could it be?*

'Do you think it's safe here?'

'Yes it is. Kaun aayega? This building is filled with people with one foot in their graves.'

'Ha ha! What if Rajiv comes up? I'm scared.'

'No one comes up sweetheart. Fat boy must be making another

mix-tape or must be stuffing his face with burgers and pizzas. This time it will be a collection of songs by girl-bands. He has a super crush on you na? You're his new obsession,' Mervin hissed with a contemptuous laugh.

'You're mean! Is that why he gave me that mix-tape of songs by N'Sync and the Backstreet Boys?' he heard Miss Sonam say. His heart skipped a beat, and suddenly there were peals of laughter.

'Yeah, fat boy is in love. He can't take his eyes off you. He thinks that you're another toy his great father can get for him. Did you see his new orange Flintstones t-shirt? He'll wear another Bugs Bunny one tomorrow to impress you. I saw him empty half a bottle of his Dad's expensive perfume. I got the t-shirt for him. Told him it's an imported t-shirt from a designer. I took 500 bucks from him and picked it up for 50 bucks at Palace Talkies.'

'Ha ha, oh my God, Merv! You bad boy!'

'I'll take you for the new Spiderman movie tomorrow. It's playing at Rex. You'll bunk college na?'

'Hahaha! Of course, let's go.'

'The perks of playing bitch to fat face.'

'Don't be mean! He's sweet. I like him. I think you're jealous because of the amount of time he spends with me,' she said, looking at Mervin with laughter in her eyes.

'Jealous of that hippo? He eats seven meals a day! That kid is bloody spoilt. He's as lazy as a sloth. You don't know what I have to put up with. I have to bowl slowly to him, get out to his lollypop bowling and even miss my lay ups on the basketball court. Fat face has to win all the time… Even while playing video games as he stuffs his face with biryani.'

'He's a kid!'

'These are the kids that grow up with a sense of entitlement. Their fathers will send them to expensive schools, buy sports cars, set up businesses for them, make films for them... Bloody no good fools these rich kids are! Whatever they wish for, they get. People like me have to struggle for every dime. I play jester to a twelve-year-old to support my expenses.'

'Relax baba, I'm with you na,' she said softly and snuggled up to him. He saw them kissing passionately. He saw Mervin run his fingers down her cheeks and put his arms around her neck before he drew her lips into his. He turned around and crept out of the terrace as tears rolled down his cheeks.

⁂

'Here you go, man. That will be ₹500,' Mervin said as he handed a sketch to the customer.

'Thanks Merv, it's a nice one. Do you remember me?' a short, portly young man in a suit asked him as people moved around spiritedly in the newly opened shopping mall.

'Of course! How many giant pandas do I know? How's the love life? Still making mix-tapes? And how's your old man?' Mervin asked scornfully, with a hint of sarcasm in his voice.

'He's old and sick, due to liver failure. I don't see him too much. I took over his business but we live separately. I'm getting married in a few weeks.'

'It's a shame for him and good for you,' he said, looking at him with his piercing gaze that said, 'Now fuck off!'

Rajiv hesitated and stepped away, before turning around. 'I've thought of you often. What I did was wrong. I'm sorry,' Rajiv said as he took a few steps back.

Mervin looked at him and looked away. 'It was a long time ago and happened for the best. Thanks to you, I met the woman I married. I'm also an artist and I'm no chaperone to some fat kid.

That's progress, isn't it?'

'Sure is. I'm happy for you.'

'Take care, man. Have a good life,' he said, before turning to address a young couple who walked up to his little stand where he made portraits.

༺☙༻

Vijay Kumar opened the bedroom door and stormed into Rajiv's bedroom. 'Why weren't you opening the door? What the hell? What is that?'

'No Dad, nothing… I'm sorry.'

'What are you doing with my pack of cigarettes and what's in that plastic bottle?' he screamed, snatching at a lit cigarette in Rajiv's hands and indicating a plastic water bottle half filled with wine.

'It's your wine, Dad. I'm sorry…' He squirmed as Vijay rushed towards him and slapped him hard across his cheek. He snatched the cigarette from his hand and pushed him on to the bed.

'You're drunk! What the hell is going on here? How dare you?'

'Not me, Dad. It's not my fault. Mervin asked me to try it. He takes stuff from your bottles every day and replaces it with water. In fact, your new bottle of Merlot is half filled with Tropicana grape juice. He's finished your Bombay Gin and bottles of Chivas and Absolut Vodka, and filled those with cheap liquor. He also uses your perfume, Dad.'

'What? Why didn't you tell me earlier?' Vijay looked furious.

'He warned me not to. He said he'd stop playing with me. He even takes money from your wallet when he can. He told me that he's taking Miss Sonam to watch a film today. They keep kissing on the terrace and drink your wine in the evenings.'

Vijay's expression turned from irritation to deep outrage. He turned around and stormed out of the room. 'Thomas! Come here, you bloody fellow,' he yelled as Rajiv lay on the bed smiling to himself. *It was a good idea to drain the bottles of alcohol and pluck a 500 bucks note from Dad's wallet. I can buy a few more samosas and maybe a nice new t-shirt,* he thought. *Dad must be furious with Mervin. Serves him right! Just like Mum, who used to hit me. I got her caught red-handed, didn't I?*

Both Mervin and Thomas were abused and fired that evening and Vijay threatened them with police action and other dire consequences if they came near his son. Sonam's father was warned and asked to keep his daughter away from the alcoholic thief.

The next evening, a subdued and grief-stricken Sonam, with dark circles under her eyes, came over and taught an apologetic and tearful Rajiv his last class of algebra for an upcoming test, before she stopped coming to tutor him. She left silently and he watched her walking home from his balcony as he thought about how she would get a ride home with Mervin every day. Today, she'd have to walk all the way home.

She Got off Easy

SANCHARI SUR

'Do you remember Aalo?' Ma asked as I sat down to eat.

I hadn't thought of Aalo in the last eight years. Not since that thing happened.

'Yes. Aalo. What about her?'

'She was here to visit her parents earlier today. She has a son. They both looked well, especially her. Not the thin girl you probably remember. This was her first visit since... since she left.'

'Wasn't her husband with her?'

'I didn't see him. I think she just came with her boy. Also, I don't think she stayed for long. Mridula said that she saw them leaving around noon.'

We all knew about what had happened to Aalo. Of course, my earliest memory of Aalo dates all the way back to my childhood.

At that time, our family of six—consisting of my three brothers, Tarun, Varun and Subhrata, as well as Ma, Baba and me—lived on the second floor of the then fifty year old building on Bowbazar Street. The street was lined on both sides by jewellery shops. Our building could be accessed by a narrow alley tucked in between one such store, Nandi's Jewellery, and a paan shop.

The alley led to two four-storey buildings, Building A and Building B. When you entered our alley, the entrance to Building B would fall on your left. Further down, the alley turned a sharp left leading to the entrance to Building A, also on your left.

Ours was Building A. Our floor was occupied by three tenants: Nilkantha babu and his wife; Bhirendranath babu and his family of seven; and our family of six. We rented two of the four rooms on that floor. All of the three tenants shared a common toilet and a balcony. The balcony directly overlooked Nimai Mathor's house and their adjoining tube-well, both of which were located at the end of the alley, and in between the entrances of the two buildings.

Nimai was responsible for cleaning the stairwells, floors and toilets of both buildings. In exchange, Dhuri babu, the landlord, gave him the two-room tin-roofed house—well, a shack, really—as a place to stay.

Nimai had a large family, with at least eight or nine children. Aalo was one of them.

Every afternoon, around twelve-ish, Aalo would step outside to the hand pulled tube-well, and take a bath in her red checked gamcha. Although only eleven, the ritual attracted the attention of all the peeping toms in my building, including Tarun. He would come back and try to rattle me with minute details. When I threatened to tell on him, he would laugh and start singing a silly rhyme that he had made up:

'Aalo, Aalo,

Aruner jagater aalo.' (Aalo, Aalo, the light of Arun's life.)

Aalo may not have been the light of my life, but she was certainly different from the rest of her family. For one, she wasn't as dark as they were. Ma used to say that, if she didn't know better, then she could have easily mistaken Aalo for a good middle-class

Bengali girl. But Aalo's difference from her family went deeper than just the shade of her skin. She also carried herself in a different manner. Ma used to say that she had a 'middle-class air'. I think it was just Aalo's habit of keeping herself extremely tidy that made her stand out from others. Whenever I saw her, she was dressed in neatly-pressed, spotless clothes, with not a single hair out of place. I had never ever seen her in a dishevelled state.

Well... not never.

It was raining heavily that afternoon. I was a first year engineering student at Jadavpur University then. Having forgotten my umbrella, I was hurrying home from college. I had just passed the paan shop and entered the gulley, when someone darted in front of me from the entrance of Building B and ran towards the end of the alley, where Nimai Mathor's house was situated. For a second, I did not know who it was. But her yellow salwar gave her away, despite her half open hair. I did not give it much thought at that time and headed straight home. But a few days later, I saw her outside the alley, chatting with Ganesh. He was one of the young goldsmiths who worked on the mezzanine floor of Building B. Ganesh nodded at me, as I crossed them to get to the street. I did not know him, except in passing. I had given him a cigarette once.

Later, however, I overheard Bhirendranath babu's wife, Mridula Mashi, saying to Ma, 'You know that Aalo? Yes, Nimai Mathor's daughter. Yes, *that* one. She is going around with a goldsmith. Can you believe it? What is the world coming to these days? You would hardly think a goldsmith would willingly—and, openly—hobnob with a Mathor's daughter. To each his own, I suppose.'

'Yes,' Ma replied. 'I have heard other things too.'

What these other things were I did not find out, since Ma lowered her voice.

Now I would often see Aalo and Ganesh chatting at the gulley's entrance. Aalo's face grew animated when she was in Ganesh's company. I never even knew that girl could talk. Whenever we had crossed each other's paths, she had mumbled a quick 'hello' and averted her gaze. I had no idea her eyes could light up like that. But despite their 'differences', Aalo and Ganesh were often seen together.

I also sometimes heard her father shouting at Aalo to 'stick to their own kind'. This happened in the late evenings, when I would be returning from a night class at college or from an adda session at a friend's house. Since I had to pass Nimai Mathor's house on the way, and they did have very thin walls, the sweeper's raised voice inevitably reached my ears. I never once heard Aalo retort or defend her position. But, like clockwork, I would see her with Ganesh the following day in front of the alley, by the paan shop.

And then, after two months of this Aalo and Ganesh drama, I heard from someone that she was pregnant.

'Yes, pregnant! Imagine Nimai Mathor's state! Even his people must have concepts of honour and dishonour.' This was Mridula Mashi.

'Boudi, this had to happen. How can it not? She would visit him every afternoon at the workshop, when everyone else was at lunch,' Ma commiserated. 'Poor Aalo… All she did was fall in love.'

'Didi, love is for those who can afford it. Will this Ganesh boy marry a mathor's daughter, now that he has had his fun?'

But marry they did. And not too long after the scandal became public in the neighbourhood either. At some registry office, I heard later.

'So! Ganesh isn't so bad after all, is he?' I asked Mridula Mashi and Ma when I saw them next. I felt jubilant, even though it was Aalo's man who had come through for her.

'Hmph,' Mridula Mashi snorted. 'Of course, but only *after* his conditions!'

I looked at Ma, mystified.

'Ganesh made Nimai promise that Aalo would never ever visit her family again, nor would they keep in touch with her. The couple would also move to some place far, after the wedding—somewhere outside Calcutta. Only if Nimai agreed to these conditions, and only then, would Ganesh marry her and give his name to her child,' Ma offered an explanation.

'But, of course, Nimai agreed!' Mridula Mashi seemed triumphant. 'Who would want to keep an unmarried pregnant daughter at home, even if they are the sweeper class?'

'Yes,' Ma nodded. 'But at least she got off easy.'

The Gap

SARITHA RAO

Nita balanced a bag of groceries, a handbag, a Rexene-encased laptop and a dripping, unwieldy umbrella, as she tried to unlock the door.

The phone rang inside the house.

She frantically tried to insert the key into the keyhole. The laptop swung precariously from her shoulder. The frail handles of the laden shopping bag strained and finally snapped, spewing its contents onto the floor mat: deodorant cans, two cartons of fruit juice with '50 ml extra free' and two different varieties of breakfast cereal.

The phone was still ringing.

The grooves in the key probed those in the lock and fitted. After a click, the door swung open.

The ringing was now relentless.

Nita felt a moment's hesitation, then opened the door wider, dropped the bags on the sofa in a jumbled heap, scooped the cordless phone from its cradle and answered. 'Hello?'

The call was disconnected.

As she went back to gather the supplies that lay at the entrance to the flat, Nita thought about how Murphy's law was not only real, it actually worked in her life which was a medley of things going wrong. She knew, for instance, without even looking, that in her hurry to answer the phone she had left the wet umbrella on the sofa.

Nita put away the supplies and decided to pause a moment in the bedroom. She sat on the edge of the queen-sized bed, took off her kitten-heels and placed her sore feet on the cool tiles. Her eyes turned inevitably to the silver filigreed photo frame on her side table. Eight years. She felt a familiar sense of disbelief that the happy family in the picture didn't exist anymore.

Nita rose from the bed, and opened the wardrobe. Sameer's shirts still hung inside. She didn't know what to do with his things, but couldn't get herself to part with them. Every morning, when she opened the wardrobe to decide what to wear, the sight that greeted her was her yellow kurta nestling against the back of his favourite blue shirt.

'Where is the man when his family needs him the most?' she wondered.

And Zia—she just didn't know how to get through to her anymore. They had once shared a love for food, gamely trying out new flavours and heartily returning to old favourites. Now even that had ceased. When she packed Zia's lunch, she would invariably go out with friends for a pizza. The girl had given up all desserts—even the brownies that Nita used to bake for her every weekend. It was as though they lived in different orbits and only met at breakfast and dinner—that too, with her sitting at the dining table and Zia absently toying with the food on her plate, watching MTV in the living room. Neither Oprah Winfrey nor any of the imported parenting magazines had prepared her for this.

But Sameer would have known what to do.

As she had done countless times before, she now took the blue shirt from the hanger and, lifting it to her face, inhaled his smell, still fresh in her memory.

The phone rang. She left the shirt on the bed and returned to the living room to pick up the receiver. She was greeted with silence. Then, the call was disconnected.

It suddenly brought back memories of crank calls in her teens. 'Do people make crank calls at all these days?' she wondered. 'No, no, it can't be. It's probably just a problem with the phone line. But what if it was someone trying to... I must have that chat with Zia. It's high time.'

The phone rang again. She stiffened and picked up the receiver.

'Hello?' she said tentatively.

'Nitu, how are you beta?'

Thank god, she thought. 'I'm alright, Ma. Did you try calling a few minutes ago?'

'No, I just got back from Mrs Aggarwal's and called you.'

'Oh.'

'Are you alright? You don't sound very good. You work very hard, you know? Maybe you should take some time off...'

'Don't start, Ma. I'm fine, really. It's just that there have been some crank calls and I was worried that...'

'...that they'd be for Zia? Don't be silly! Zia is just a child. Who will make crank calls to her?'

'Ma, Zia is seventeen. She's not a child, and... you don't know the kind of things that happen these days.'

How does one explain stuff like lewd MMS clips and date-rape to one's mother? 'And', thought Nita, 'god knows what the guy at the other end was up to.'

'No, no. You don't worry now. Everything will be fine.'

Nita thought to herself, *that's what you said, Ma, when Sameer...*

That's exactly what you said. That everything will be fine.

'Ma, I'll see you Sunday as usual?' she said, as her eyes smarted with unshed tears.

'Alright, beta—should I make some rabdi for Zia?'

'I don't think she'll come, Ma. She probably has some movie planned with friends.'

'It's been a while since I saw her, you know.'

'I know, Ma. I'll try and bring her, okay? Bye.'

She hung up. The tears brimmed over and trickled down her cheeks.

Nobody said it would be easy being a single parent, but nobody said it would be this difficult either. The money decisions, the pressures of work, the constant juggling of time. The worry that gnawed at her insides when Zia was even a few minutes late. And doing it all by herself.

She made her way to the bathroom and washed her face. She used the face-wash that she reserved for days like this, days when she gave in to the single parent blues. The scent of berries emanated from the dispenser and, as she washed her face, she thought of how often she had used the face-wash in the recent past. It was as though she was gradually losing her ability to cope with challenges. All she wanted to do was curl up in bed and hope that she could rewind to an earlier, happier time.

The phone rang.

Spurred by a sudden anger, she wiped her face and decided to confront the caller. She picked up the receiver and, finding no response at the other end, said, 'Who is it? What do you want?'

No reply.

'I have caller ID, you creep!' she said. 'I know your number and I'll complain to the police.' And she hung up before the person at the other end could. She mentally kicked herself. She couldn't even threaten a crank caller properly. 'Creep' was the best she could come up with.

The doorbell rang.

Nita looked into the magic-eye and opened the door.

Zia walked in, dumped her bag on the already teetering pile on the sofa, picked up the TV remote and slumped into an empty chair.

'Well, hello to you too, Zia,' said Nita.

'Ma, don't. I'm very tired, okay?' said Zia without taking her eyes off the TV.

Nita thought, *and I'm not tired? What am I, the Energizer Bunny?* She made her way to the kitchen and returned a few minutes later with two steaming mugs of masala tea.

'Tea, Zia.'

'I don't want any, Ma.'

'But you said you were tired.'

'Yeah, but I'll get myself a Diet Coke or something.'

'Suit yourself,' said Nita. There was so much she wanted to tell her, especially about the crank calls. Sipping her tea, she tried once more. 'So, how was your day?'

'Okay.'

'Zia, I need to talk to you. Can you turn that thing off and listen?'

'Later, Ma.'

'Now, Zia—it's important. This won't take long.'

'But Ma...'

Nita took the remote from Zia's hand and switched the TV to sleep mode. Zia was every bit the picture of teenage defiance. She sat slumped, with arms crossed and a scowl on her face, staring at the intricate pattern on the carpet, her foot jiggling impatiently to some erratic inner beat.

Nita took a deep breath and began, 'There were a couple of crank calls today.'

'So what? It happened yesterday also.'

'And you didn't tell me? This could be serious, Zia. Do you know anyone who might be making these calls?'

'No. Besides, why are you getting all worked up about it? Just swear into the phone and whoever it is will stop bugging us.'

'That's hardly the way to deal with it,' said Nita, although she remembered doing the same a little while ago. 'What if it's some weirdo? He knows our home number, Zia. He might even know where we live. What if he…'

'Chill, Ma. Nothing's going to happen. Better still, just disconnect the phone for a while. Both of us have our cell-phones and those who need to call us know the numbers.'

'But Zia, what if he…'

'Ma, now stop, okay? Don't go on and on about it. It's not such a big deal!' With that, Zia wrenched the phone line from the base unit of the telephone. That done, she wrested the remote from Nita's fingers and focussed her attention on yet another reality show that flickered alive on the TV screen.

Nita didn't know what to do or how to react. On the one hand, she conceded that she was probably overreacting out of fear. On the other hand, she was angry with Zia for the way she had abruptly cut her off. It was disrespectful. What if they were being stalked? She didn't want to ever get to the point where something happened and she would blame herself for not taking these calls seriously.

All she wanted was someone to tell her it was going to be fine—that they would handle it together. They would play good parent-bad parent. They would take off on a holiday as a family. That he would be there for her. But he wasn't. It was up to her to be a double-duty parent. In the process, she had forgotten about being a woman with her own whims and gripes. Her own role in the family was to balance the boat when it rocked in a storm, not steer it.

If only Sameer... she thought.

Suddenly, she hated the wistfulness of that thought. A sliver of anger coursed through her.

Enough, she thought.

She entered the bedroom, and yanked open the wardrobe. She took out an old bed sheet and spread it on the floor. The blue shirt was the first to hit the sheet, followed by the many, many white shirts, suits, ties, jeans, kurtas, t-shirts and cuff links.

From the bookshelf, she pulled out Kafka, Pinter, Plath, Susskind and other authors whose names she couldn't pronounce. These joined the rapidly growing pile on the sheet.

She left the CDs alone. Zia liked some of them.

Nita bundled all these into the bed sheet, knotted it and dragged the lot into the living room.

Zia looked up. 'Ma, what on earth are you doing?'

Nita flipped open a telephone book and dialled a number on her cell-phone.

Remote in hand, Zia gingerly walked towards the bundle on the carpet. She pried open one of the knots.

Nita gave the person at the other end her address.

'But these are all... Ma, are you out of your mind?' Zia spluttered.

Nita hung up, then turned to Zia and said, 'These are only things, Zia. This is not him.'

Zia now had tears in her eyes. 'But Mama... Daddy...'

Nita softened. Zia called her 'Mama' only when she felt particularly vulnerable. She put her arms around Zia and said, 'I know you miss him. I miss him too. But look at what we're holding on to—things.' Tears streamed down Nita's face, but she continued.

'He is not here, Zia. He's gone. He doesn't know how old you are. He doesn't know what music you listen to. He doesn't know who your friends are. He doesn't know you have a huge crush on Kabir next door.' Zia, taken aback, was about to ask her how she knew. But Nita pressed on. 'He doesn't know that you've outgrown that mangy old stuffed toy that you used to carry even to the toilet… '

'Cheeku,' said Zia.

'Yes, Cheeku.' Nita continued, 'He doesn't know you had your appendix removed a year ago. He didn't hold your hand through it, sweetie. He is not here. And these are only things. Not him. He is gone. But you and I,' Nita pointed to the two of them, 'aren't we a family too?'

Zia didn't know when the transition happened. One minute, Nita was consoling her, the next, Zia was holding her mother who, finally, fully mourned the absence of her husband.

Zia held Nita through the waves of emotion that wracked her and gave her a glass of water to drink when she seemed a little better. Then, she led her to the bedroom and tucked her into bed. She switched the light off and shut the door silently behind her, carrying with her the silver filigreed photo frame.

When Nita awoke, it was past eleven on the bedside clock. The happy family picture on her side table was gone. She felt groggy and spent, but she also felt lighter. As though a storm had raged through her heart and cleansed her in the process.

Nita entered the living room. Sameer's things were gone. The telephone line was plugged back into the instrument, the sofa tidied and the TV off. She caught a chocolaty aroma wafting from the kitchen and found Zia slicing a fresh batch of brownies.

'I didn't know you could bake,' said Nita.

Zia turned around, relieved that Nita was indeed fine, and wordlessly gave her a hug.

'She's still my little girl,' thought Nita.
The telephone rang, startling her.
Zia handed Nita a brownie and said, 'I'll handle it, Mama.'

Pity

PARITOSH UTTAM

The wind soughed its way over the Bay of Bengal, rode the crests of the waves and skimmed the sands of the Marina beach to gently lift her tresses. It also seemed to have the effect of lifting their spirits. They giggled and guffawed, chuckled and chortled, their shoulders shook and heaved with laughter.

The wind bore the sound of their mirth to Dayakar, who sat on the sand fifteen yards behind them. To an extent, it also muffled the cacophony of the traffic on the busy Beach Road running a good hundred yards further behind him. It was only when their laughter was strong and the breeze was not that he could actually listen to their merriment. Their fervent gestures told him what he could not hear.

The girl laughed easily and naturally, but the boy's enjoyment appeared to depend on hers. The longer and more heartily she laughed, the more did he; when her evident joy eventually subsided, so did his.

Dayakar found it difficult to categorise his feelings. What was the emotion that was choking his heart now? Was it anger at the stupid play-acting they were indulging in? Or not something as strong as anger, but mere irritation? Or, perhaps, only detached bemusement at their childish antics?

The boy, Dayakar imagined, was pleasantly surprised by the heartiness of her laughter; never had anyone revelled in his jokes so much. The girl, of course, showered all her attention on him. And so the boy followed her laughter with his own, unsure of the route it would take, but deriving his enjoyment from hers. Dayakar could imagine all this lucidly as if he was there right with them, an invisible third companion. But he had been there, in that place, before. In the boy's place, that is. One year ago, two years, ten, twenty... It didn't matter now. But he had been there.

What was the boy saying, now that both their gazes were fixed on the horizon? Oh yes, he could as good as hear the boy saying, 'Isn't the sea-breeze so wonderfully refreshing? What an antidote the seaside is to the otherwise tormenting sultriness of Chennai!' She would agree with him earnestly and, in turn, ask whether he too didn't find the glint of orange reflected in the water fascinating. Then they would look at each other, eyes shining with the joyful belief of having discovered their soul mates.

All of a sudden, it became startlingly clear to Dayakar what he was feeling. He realized what was in his heart from the time he had begun observing the couple—pity. Not anger, or irritation or bemusement, but simple uncomplicated pity at their innocence. Innocence that would eventually be corrupted.

But for now, they thought... Oh god! To look at their faces now, suffused with delight, and their smug expressions broke his heart. Their faces, aglow with pleasure, as they looked around, made it apparent that they had unearthed a long-buried treasure of which they thought no one else was aware. They thought that what was happening to them was unique.

But it wasn't special. Dayakar felt an urge to cup his mouth with his hands and yell, 'A billion other people have also had such unique experiences. On beaches, in parks, in cars, in rooms, in movie halls, on the road. Morning, noon and night. Everywhere, all the time.'

He peered at them harder. They were teenagers. Probably still in school, or just out of it. Maybe they made excuses, told a pack of lies to their parents or teachers to come here. Dayakar wanted to walk over to them and say, 'Look, children.' But why did he feel so old that he wanted to call them children? He was, at most, fifteen years older than them. Anyway, he would say, 'Look children. How long do you think this is going to last? They lived happily ever after happens only in fairy tales. What next?'

They wouldn't be able to reply because they would not have thought of that. They would revel in each other for a few months, a year at the most. Then what? Perhaps their families would be against their being together. Maybe they would fight the world. Perhaps he would betray her, or she him, or both each other. Or maybe they were exceptionally mature and would fight together against that happening. All right, they battled the odds and prevailed. How would they fight against time?

Time would inexorably chip away at their blind love, make them get used to and tired of each other. One morning, they would wake up and wonder what had happened. Soulmates? They would laugh cynically, having learnt the futility of beginning all over again.

Oh, that would happen—sooner or later, but happen it would. As certain as death and taxes, and night following day. Nobody won against time. The same traits that they found endearing in each other now, would become sources of irritation later. 'I like his enthusiasm' and 'I like her carefree nature' would become 'When will he grow up?' and 'When will she show some responsibility?' Nagging and sarcasm would become the staple form of conversation, instead of silly baby talk. One day, one of them would even secretly wish that he or she could lose the other abruptly, so that he or she could remember and relive only their good times together, instead of helplessly witnessing their deterioration at their own hands.

'Children, listen to me,' Dayakar would say, 'I am talking to you from the other side of the passage of that corrosive time. I have been in the place you are, and I am in the place you will be.' But Dayakar also knew that there was no use telling them now. They wouldn't listen to him, or even try to understand. They would laugh at his fears, his pity. It could happen to others, not to them, not to their special love, their unique everlasting eternal love. They would march on the same trodden path, fighting their battles, winning and losing, until finally they would reach that morning when they would wake up and wonder what had happened. What a farce! Dayakar shook his head.

He watched the boy's arm hover uncertainly behind her shoulder. 'Go ahead,' he urged the boy telepathically. 'Put your arm over her shoulder. She won't mind. She's waiting for you to do it. She's only pretending to look hard at the sea. But before you do it, just know one thing. After this, you are never going to feel so innocently happy again. This will be the watershed in your life, your happiest moment ever. Do you understand? Not your child, not your job, not even she can bring back this moment again. When you wake up that morning and wonder, you will mark your downfall from this point. So remember the time, the place—everything—carefully. You will recall it again and again. I know.'

At last, the boy's arm fell clumsily over her shoulder and, not evoking a rebuff, settled itself comfortably and assuredly. Dayakar could not bear the painful pressure in his chest anymore. He suddenly felt old—very old—and weary. The sea had failed to work its magic. Whenever he found he could not take the mind-numbingly boring work at office or his wife's incessant nagging at home anymore, he turned to the sea. But the waves crashing onto the beach did not calm him today. The boy and the girl and their shy courting had triggered too many memories. He got to his feet, shook the sand off his trousers, and walked away.

'Honey?'

'Yes?'

'Did you notice the man behind us who was watching us all the time? He's going away finally.'

'Phew! Perhaps he couldn't bear to see our happiness anymore.'

'Oh! You mean he was jealous of us?'

'Of course. Anyone would be. Do you think anyone could be as happy as we are? No way!'

'That's true. Poor guy. I wish he could be happy like us.'

Pasta Lane

SIDDHARTHA BHASKAR

Holaram Chandwani started from his home, a place where he had lived all his life, first with his parents, then with his wife and children, and now alone. Every day he followed the same route to go out for dinner at nine in the evening. As he came out of his building that day, the Shalaka Apartments at Nariman Point, the black clouds over the Mumbai coastline started pouring. It seemed to him that his dark ambitions, which lay concealed within his heart, burst into life along with the rain.

He was fifty-eight years old, on the verge of retirement from the post of Head of Department, Chemistry at the University of Bombay. His wife, Delnaz, had died long ago and his two sons were well-settled in Mumbai. For the last six years he had lived alone without a companion. His sons were busy with their corporate jobs and they met only on birthdays and New Year's Eve. His job at the university gave him no joy, because good students no longer applied to the University of Mumbai to study science—they would rather join the IITs or engineering colleges. Nowadays, he had little to occupy his mind and his thoughts, good or bad, would keep popping out of his subconscious. As he stood at the traffic signal, he wondered to himself, 'Should I do it today? What would happen if I did?' If he took the road that went straight from the signal, he would reach his favourite restaurant near the Churchgate station. Or else he could eat at some restaurant at the Colaba causeway, which came to the right. He decided, 'Let me take a stroll on the Colaba causeway.'

Walking alongside Cooperage Park, he could see Azad Maidan across the street through the falling raindrops. Holaram had been a fast bowler when they used to play here. He continued to play till he was forty, which was quite remarkable keeping in mind the injury concerns of the pacers of the current generation. He was nicknamed The Nariman Express by his friends who were also his colleagues in the university. Most of them lived with their children now, happy amongst their families. 'Nothing untoward happened in their families. In fact they are much happier than I am!'

Ashok, his Bengali colleague, who now lived with his wife and children in Kolkata, had a long-standing affair with a woman professor, Miss Stevens, who taught English at Saint Xavier's College. They used to go to watch movies at the Sterling Cinema and spend nights together at her house. There were a lot of rumours then, about his leaving his wife for the professor. Holaram was somewhat infatuated with Ashok's wife, Hema. She was better-looking compared to Delnaz. When Hema learnt of her husband's affair, she left for her parents' home in Kolkata for two years. Many of them thought that the marriage was done for. 'At least I thought so. But didn't Hema come back after all? Ashok had to break up with Miss Stevens, who had befriended someone else by then. I never dared to have an extramarital affair or any physical intimacy with anyone else for the love of Delnaz. Love. Yes, it was love. Or was it fear?'

It had stopped raining and so he furled his umbrella. He had reached the other crossing, the one with the statue of B.R. Ambedkar. 'When we were young, he was just a great man who gave us the constitution. Now he is a god. His hands are pointing somewhere.'

He stopped at a small tea stall—four walls with a plastic roof—where some labourers sat huddled up to escape the rain and warm up with a glass of tea. He ordered tea and lit a cigarette. The labourers joked amongst themselves about an old man on his death bed who was suffering from lung cancer and whose last wish was to smoke a pack of cigarettes. Holaram had been smoking for twenty-five years now.

His thoughts went back to the first time he had smoked with Boman, the evil student, in his final year in college. It was the day when his appointment was confirmed by the University. Boman, a fellow student, met him at the university gates and demanded a party. When Holaram opened his wallet, he realised that the only option he had was to buy Boman a cigarette at the nearby paan shop. 'Then Boman forced me to light one for myself!'

As the first doses of nicotine ran through his blood, Holaram could hear Boman describing the other exciting avenues available to celebrate his success, one of which included the red light area of Grant Road. His first instinct had been to give it a try, but then the thought of Delnaz, his girlfriend then, cropped up in his mind and he answered with a firm 'no'. 'What would have happened if I had done it then? Delnaz would never have known. That Boman kept visiting these places even when he was married.'

A few years ago, he met Boman with his family at the Gateway of India. They had a chat and Boman looked changed and jolly. He did not talk of Grant Road then, but spoke of everyday things. 'He seemed to be set in his life, satisfied. There was no punishment whatsoever for his so-called dirty deeds. It's just a bodily need, that's all.'

After the last puff, he threw the cigarette butt into a pool of rainwater close by and crossed the road. A few steps ahead were the gates of the YWCA Women's Hostel. Many of his female students had lived there. He used to meet his male students at the nearby paan shop, where they waited with movie tickets in their hands for their girlfriends. Today there was no one. In fact, he had stopped seeing them there for quite some time. Probably the trend had stopped. 'Courtship methods have also been liberalised along with the economy. Nowadays, boys have their girlfriends' mobile numbers. They make a phone call and meet at the cinema theatre. Or they have their own cars with distinctive sounding horns which their girlfriends recognise instantly. A car is standing there along with a young man, maybe for the same purpose. She had a car too. Did she live here? Yes, I think she did.'

Holaram was now thinking of Sophia, the daughter of a chemical industry czar, who had fallen, or was pretending to have fallen, in love with him when he was still a young professor. He still had some of the love letters she had written during the first half of her final year. The lines were taken from Dev Anand's and Guru Dutt's romantic films, spiced with some imagination of her own. Since he was a shy man and a sincere husband, Holaram had developed a natural fear of her. It was even harder when he had to fail her in the chemistry paper, which was filled with references to Cupid rather than phenol or boric acid. It was worse when he was appointed to head a committee to probe allegations regarding the character of some students who were working as call girls for high society moguls living in South Bombay, and the first girl he'd interrogated was Sophia. 'She showed no guilt whatsoever, as if it was I who was responsible for not responding to her advances.'

When she was asked why she did it, because a lack of money did not seem to be her problem, she answered that it was fun and followed her words by unfastening the top two buttons of her shirt to show off her cleavage. 'I was shaking all over.' She then made the most business-like offer: first class pass marks in Chemistry and a recommendation letter for a Master of Science in the U.S. in return for her services during the period of her study at the University. So this was why she was chasing him—she hoped to entrap him into giving her high marks and a recommendation that would enable her to complete a Masters in Chemistry from the US, which is what her father wanted her to do. To be loved, however anti-social it might be, always inflates one's ego. So, even though Holaram feared Sophia, her love signals had boosted his ego and he kept all her letters. But when the true motives of her love were revealed, all that egoistic build-up crashed at once and took the form of bitterness. She was found guilty by the committee and given a strict warning, the lightness of the punishment owing to the interference of her father. 'I got nothing but respect out of the investigation!' Sophia gave up her studies after college and opted for modelling. She made a name for herself and was a regular feature in magazines and advertisements.

He was standing in front of Regal Cinema. He had seen many movies with Delnaz here. 'I think I saw *Ijaazat* with Delnaz here. Forget her, will you, you fat old scum? She is long gone. And after some time you will be gone too. It's time to have some fun. I have performed all my duties well. Why would anyone say anything to me? And who cares anyway?' Two attractive girls in miniskirts passed Holaram, and both of them smiled at him. A taxi was waiting at the signal. Its passengers were an old man and a young girl—the man had his arms around her and was trying to draw her closer to him. 'I am becoming corrupt! There is nothing to judge. The fear of others' judgement has been my enemy till date. What would Delnaz think in heaven? There is no heaven and no hell. Even if they exist, how do we know which activity would lead you to which place? One can see Ashok and Boman. They live as any other family. Sophia is famous too. I think I have been good till now. No. No. An idiot till now. An idiot for so long, missing all those years and those opportunities. And I still wish to remain one! Delnaz will hate me. Go to hell with her. She is dead. Should I make pasta from my memories of her? Pasta? Yes! It's Pasta Lane. That's it. I am going there.'

Holaram had known for quite some time now that Pasta Lane was a favourite with the sex-crazed people who came to Colaba. He had also heard of the recent police raids in some of the sex bars there. 'But who cares? The police know everything. They would have taken care of them if they really wanted to.'

He passed the Leopold Café. A few steps ahead, a small tree had been felled by the strong rain-bearing winds the previous night. It was lying dead, half on the road and half on the footpath. 'Does it symbolise my fall?' Walking quickly through the crowded shops, Holaram entered the first Pasta Lane confidently. He walked through the residential area looking for some mark, a sign board for a massage parlour, a lady combing her hair—something! But he found nothing. His excitement slowly waned and his pace slowed down. Then he passed a restaurant called Kailash Parbat. It served good food. He had been there before. The search continued in the second Pasta Lane and the third. 'These streets look decent. They have changed quite a bit. But how do I find the bars? Probably the bars are no longer there. So that's it. Let me have some food at Kailash Parbat. No. Wait. Maybe there is something in the fourth lane. Let me check it out.'

As Holaram was walking in the fourth Pasta Lane, he found

a small bar. 'Probably this is where I can get it.' He entered. A waiter was passing by. He inquired about the menu, the drinks and then the girls.

'Uncle, have you gone mad at this age?' the waiter asked him with a smile.

No one had ever spoken so rudely to Holaram after his father's death. He panicked, apologised and left the bar quickly. 'What stupid people and small time waiters. Delnaz would have given him a good thrashing had she been there. Delnaz—oh I miss her so much!'

A taxi driver who had seen Holaram coming out of the bar walked up to him. Holaram sat at the bench near the lamp post, putting his umbrella aside.

The taxi driver asked, 'Are you looking for something, uncle?'

'No. Nothing,' replied Holaram.

'I can get you whatever you want. All varieties—Indian, phoren, Chinese, American. Everything fresh.'

'What are you talking about?'

'Arey uncle, I know people like you need company. Come in my taxi. They are all good and cheap. No problem.'

Holaram felt confused—more confused than the time when he'd angrily refused to sell his father's home in Nariman Point to move to Bandra with his sons, after many days of discussions and fights.

'Come on quick, uncle. I have another passenger. There is no time. Huge demand. Less supply! So price increases,' the taxi driver tried to explain the economics of his trade in broken English.

'You come back after half an hour. I will eat something. Then we can go.'

'What airs, re! I will charge extra for coming back. Are you ready?'

'Okay, but please go for now.'

Half an hour later, the taxi driver came back. There was the lamp post and the bench with the umbrella on it. But there was no Holaram.

'Pasta Lane' *is the Dustbin Pick from the short-listed stories in the Landmark Grey Oak Urban Stories Competition.*

Mindgames

MANISHA DHINGRA

The whimpers were getting louder and louder. 'It's okay, it's okay,' he soothed her, patting her hair which was wet with sweat. The cabbie braked and turned around to give him a searching look.

'Sab theek hai. Aap hospital chalo,' he instructed the man calmly, the authority in his voice prompting the vehicle to lurch drunkenly and merge back into the flow of traffic. Seven years of painful experience had taught him to use his eyes, sometimes his voice, to good effect, shaming people into averting their curious gaze, cutting short their concerned questions. To them, his wife was nothing more than a freak show, a once-beautiful woman who now moaned, screamed and cried at the slightest provocation, mostly for no reason at all.

It hadn't always been like this. He remembered the time he had seen her, back in college. The first lecture of the year was well under way when she had knocked and asked permission to enter. Brash and insouciant, he had looked her up and down, a behenji in a salwar kameez trying to become invisible in a class full of spaghetti tops and neon bra-straps.

That first year, they had not even spoken to each other. At most, they had exchanged smiles if they happened to pass each other in the corridor. Within a few weeks, he had earned his reputation as the class Casanova, putting to good use his years of expertise with neon bras and short denim skirts. She, too, stayed true to her original self, only going so far as to experiment with loose, baggy jeans and long tops that went nearly all the way down to her knees.

He could not quite remember the first time they spoke to each other, but it must have been during that group project they worked on in the second year. They, along with four other people, had been assigned the task of studying any segment of contemporary society of their choice. They were given three weeks to complete their study and to present their research in the form of a written report, a class presentation and a five-minute-long documentary film.

'We can't study prostitutes!' He recalled the vehemence with which she had dismissed the idea put forth by one of the other girls in the group. 'Okay, how about gays, lesbians... sexual minorities?' he had asked, enjoying the colour that rose into her cheeks as she refused to entertain that idea as well.

In the end, it had come down to a vote: prostitutes versus slum-dwellers. The prostitutes had won, and they spent the next weeks discussing everything from condom use to AIDS to the problem of children born out of wedlock who then go on to become gangsters or bar dancers or follow their mothers' footsteps to form the next generation of prostitutes.

Difficult though the topic may have been for her, yet he soon came to respect her opinion on the project, from the methodology of research, to the way they should progress with the film shoot. Eventually, it was she who laid out the loose script for the film, who sat in as he edited the filmed material down to a manageable seven minutes, and who even drank a celebratory sip of wine with the team when their film was selected as being amongst the best of the lot.

But even as he grew to like her as a distant friend and a close colleague, the thought of being with her, of dating her, had never crossed his mind. Not until the last year of college when she took the initiative to ask him, as he came down the stairs one day, whether he would like to bunk the lecture and go grab a cup of coffee instead.

She told him later, many months after they'd been married, that she'd always intended to have him. 'I spent so many nights considering and comparing you with all my other options,' she said, 'but finally I figured I'd give my virginity to you.' He had responded in kind, laughing loudly at her description of the 'options' and mock-thanking her for selecting him.

'But what made you choose me?' he had asked later, this time seriously.

'You looked okay-ish,' she teased. 'Plus, I knew most of the girls you'd slept with in class, so there was no risk of performance failure either!' And she had laughed out loud again, amused at her own wit.

The first years of their marriage had been dotted with such incidents, like bright spots of dappled sunshine on the upholstery of a dirty old cab.

But marriage had not always been on her agenda, he knew. That had been entirely his idea, something he asked her to do on the spur of the moment, long after they'd passed out from college, broken up and moved on in life—she to a hectic professional career as a Hyderabad-based business consultant and he as a Mumbai-based film editor.

That day, that minute, when he bumped into her at the mall, would always be etched in his memory. He had known right away, even before pleasantries had been exchanged, that she was the answer, the one thing he had been waiting for to fill his full, vibrant life.

As he thought of the many years since that moment, he was somewhat surprised to discover that he could not remember how and when she had said yes. He wondered if that was of any consequence, whether his life would have been different had he not been saddled with the responsibility of a wife who was also a lunatic.

With this thought came the guilt. They loved each other, he reminded himself, clutching her tight, trying to shield her from the unseen demons that chased her. 'Kya hua?' he mouthed to the cabbie impatiently, catching his eye in the rear-view mirror. But it was the evening rush hour and he could understand how everyone wanted to get home quick, looking forward to a fun evening with a 'normal', loving spouse.

'I have never been a real wife to you, have I?' she said suddenly, sitting up against him, taking his hand into her own. They were back on the rollercoaster, he realised, this being one of the several times she emerged out of a fit of insanity, behaving as normally as possible, fooling everyone into believing that nothing was wrong with her at all. But this time, he would not turn the cab back. This time, he was determined to take her to the hospital.

He wondered why he hadn't done this before, why he had waited seven years to take her to a doctor—a psychiatrist, to be precise. After all, he had known about her problem for almost as long as they'd been married. It was he who had suggested she 'take a break' from her job when her madness had become uncontrollable, when she started losing control at any time, in any place. As in that song 'Iris', he hadn't wanted the world to see her, to ridicule her, or even for some well-meaning friend to tell her the truth about herself.

Of course, she had known it anyway. Long ago, she had told

him she knew there was something wrong with her. She wondered whether he had noticed at all. He had refused then, telling her she was perfectly fine. Even so, she was very grateful for his love. Every night, on days when she could understand these things, she would thank him for being with her, for holding on and supporting them through all the 'tough times'.

'I was hoping against hope,' he acknowledged to himself. 'I didn't want this to be real. Whenever she snapped out of it, I always thought it was the last episode. And now when I can't deal with it anymore, I am being a coward, ready to dump her in some mental asylum if only someone would give me permission to do it!'

Last night had been especially bad. In the middle of the night, she'd shaken him awake, put a finger to his lips and gestured to him to listen. For five long minutes, he had sat there like a fool, expecting any minute to hear a thief, a murderer, moving about in their living room.

He had only understood it when she turned to him, mouthing, 'See?' and pointing again in the direction of the living room.

'See what?' he had yelled, exasperated. He had had it with these nightmares. The next day she was seeing a psychiatrist and that was that, he'd thought, slumping face-first into his pillow.

So here they were, stuck in a cab in the middle of an ocean of honking cars. It took another hour before they made it to the hospital at last. He had called ahead but they were forty-five minutes late for their appointment and would have to wait. Meanwhile, he filled out the form handed to him. 'Medical Background', it said on top.

'What are you doing? Why are we here?' his wife asked. He did not answer, only indicated to her to be quiet. Dr Iyer had warned him not to tell her anything, not to let her panic before he had had a chance to examine her in this other, tranquil state of being.

Such a long form it was! Her medical history, family background, attitude towards life, their relationship... He was patient with it all.

'The doctor will see you now,' said the pleasant-faced assistant. They let themselves be led in and settled on the edge of the couch. 'Doctor, my wife has been having these wild dreams—uh, nightmares, fits...' he began, putting his arm around her shoulders, even as she looked away from him, hurt at this betrayal of their secret.

'Your what?'

The doctors at the asylum were very understanding, full of pity—but they couldn't let him leave yet, they told him, their voices full of regret.

They said later that he had always dreamt of marrying his college sweetheart, a big-shot consultant now married and settled in Hyderabad with her husband and two kids. From her, they learnt about his minor anxiety problem, about the way their relationship had to end when he had grown too possessive.

And this was even before his hallucinations first started.

Look How Far We've Come

SHREYA MAHESHWARI

Rishabh and I sat next to the floor-to-ceiling glass windows, on the top floor of Inorbit Mall, sipping chocolate shakes, watching Mumbai in the rains from above the clouds. Rishabh had asked to see the horizon, so we had gone to the highest floor of the mall, hoping to catch a glimpse of where the earth and sky met.

Puddles of water formed on the sidewalk and wet strangers jostled in the chaotic streets below—yelling, honking and fighting. Above the wet smoke of the traffic, above the towering buildings, the skies were pure, light and free of rain. How these two worlds, the calm sky and the chaotic earth, stayed together, where they met in space, I did not know, because I had hardly ever seen the horizon in Mumbai, locked in as I had always been here, amidst people, buildings and empty noise.

'Sorry buddy, but no horizon in sight,' I shrugged at Rishabh, who shrugged back at me.

Rishabh and I were meeting after two weeks. Every time I saw him, he looked taller and stronger. 'It's all the basketball he plays,' Rhea had told me. He was in the Junior School team and had practice early in the mornings, every weekend. 'All the stretching towards the hoop adds inches really fast,' Rhea had explained. I think it was just that I didn't see him that often. Ever since I'd moved to Bangalore, it had been difficult to spend time with him. Some weekends, I had to work and for most others, Rishabh moved between practice, his grandmother's place and tuitions. Sometimes, I didn't want to come to Mumbai because seeing Rishabh also meant seeing Rhea, and that was hard every time.

In the months leading up to our divorce, Rhea and I had thought about joint custody, but Rishabh had settled well into his school, so there was no question of moving him out. Rhea did ask me to stay back in Mumbai, but I had already accepted a job offer in Bangalore, and it would have been tough to renegotiate the place. It would have also been impossible for me to be happy in the same city as my former wife and permanent child, who had already started building their lives without me. So I moved to Bangalore and jetted into Mumbai every other weekend to catch a glimpse of what I had left behind.

Our divorce had been amicable in that we had both amicably concluded that we could not stand to stay in the same house any more. I was longing to get out of Mumbai and Rhea was longing to end our daily fights, and our longings eventually led us to want to get out of the marriage we had dragged along this far. Our marriage had fallen apart, day by excruciating day. When I first met Rhea, I thought that I had found a new joy; a heady state of being that I did not know was possible. We met after work, tired and exhausted after the day, but comforted by each other's presence. In this crazy, hard life of work, pay bills, fight with the maid, invest in pension plans, build a network, snatch away moments of time to pick up a long-forgotten hobby, I had found a constant source of warmth. In this exhilarating and exhausting city, I had found a way out. With

Rhea, the dirty sand strip of Juhu beach felt like the fine sands of Goa, and on some evenings, even Pattaya.

Of course, it all turned out to be an exaggeration. I knew that marriage would change things, but I had been sure that Rhea and I would be able to love our way through all our problems. It just didn't work out that way; it hardly ever does. I'll never know how and why our minds tricked us into believing that there was a new life possible, that someone else's presence in our lives could free us of the irritations of our own. We fought about the maid's carelessness, the society's dogs, the milk's watery taste, my compulsive smoking, the take-outs we ordered and never finished, our electricity bills, and my mother. Sometimes I think it was just the crazy traffic of this city that got us; driving in a trickle, crawling through the dark, narrow, packed streets of this city, dissatisfaction distilled within me, and I sensed it in Rhea too. Rishabh came along at the end of the first year of our marriage, and we, who had foolishly thought that a baby would bring us together, began drifting apart even faster. With both of us working full time, natural events like feeding the baby when he was younger, or attending his school concerts a few years later, became elaborate tasks that had to be pencilled into our daily planners.

We began to feel suffocated by the discontent of promises unfulfilled. We had both bought into a fairy tale; both of us had believed that together we could create a happy life, but we hadn't anticipated the reality of marriage. Sometimes I laugh about our naivety. Even Bollywood has changed—it has stopped making fairy tale romances, and has started making musical sagas about divorce and murder cases instead. How could our lives remain perfect then?

You know those advertisements for holiday packages—a family of three, a mother, father and child, posing for postcard photos, smiling and playing water sports on a sandy beach? I had hoped that we were on our way to becoming that. I had seen these fictional lives play out in the real world—there are happy families, I'd think to myself, and we could become one if we tried. But for every holiday-package-family, there are so many that aren't happy, so many whose lives devolve into a generic routine, so many families that sag under the weight of duties and compliance, strain at the seams with unrealistic hopes and crashed expectations. Rhea and I went down that way. We had suspended our differences, thinking and hoping that they would dissolve over time. But those differences lurked underneath the veneer of our supposedly postcard-perfect life, and in painful ways, broke us apart.

Rishabh and I played video games at the games arcade for over two hours after coffee. Seeing him laugh when I messed up my bowling shot or when he won nine pins, I felt as if a part of the holiday postcard was filling up. We joked about Manchester United losing and swapped statistics sitting on the bowling alley floor. We strolled through the shops in the malls and made fun of women buying cartloads of clothes. Then we went into a sports shop and bought Mumbai Indian IPL jerseys ourselves. We changed into our jerseys in the store itself, walking out laughing at our stupid boldness. We caught an evening show of *Iron Man 2* and gagged our way through it.

I knew that my time with him was running out: the last plane for Bangalore left at nine and it was already six thirty. I had an important client visit early the next day and Mumbai traffic would not allow me to linger any longer. I turned to ask Rishabh if he was ready to call it a day but he had walked up to the photo booth under the atrium of the mall and was looking at me with mischievous eyes. We had countless Polaroids at home, taken at photo booths in malls, with Rishabh and me making funny faces at the camera. It took me a moment to consider, but I decided that my Kingfisher flight would have to leave without me in it tonight.

Sitting inside the photo booth, my arms around his shoulders, I looked at him make crazy faces, his solid white teeth glistening in the darkness of the camera booth. I thought of all the dentist appointments he had to go to when he chipped his teeth falling on the floor years ago, and how I had complained all the way through them. Now, he went to the dentist on his own, or with his mother, and I had nothing left to complain about.

I could not stop feeling guilty, could not keep from second-guessing myself: had we done the right thing? When we had first broken the news of our separation to Rishabh, he had been upset, but Rhea and I had talked him into seeing how we could be happier that way. How Rhea and I both still loved him, but had to build separate lives for ourselves. How we would always remain a family, albeit one that would spend more time talking on the phone, texting, chatting, Skypeing and Facebooking each other, than staying together in person. It had mostly worked out well. Rhea and I had developed a cordial relationship and exchanged regular notes on Rishabh's life. Our families had outgrown their initial horror at the news of our divorce and had come to a loving acceptance of our choices, happy that Rishabh would not have to endure any more fights between us. I had taken up a high-paying, demanding job in Bangalore and was glad to have the distraction of work to make up for the loneliness of post-divorce existence. Rhea and I both thought that it was too soon to have other relationships, but we put no restrictions on each other. On our weekly calls, Rhea would assure me that Rishabh was fine. He was enjoying school, getting good grades, had a lot of friends and seemed happy to talk to me on the phone every day. Everything seemed just fine after twelve long years of enduring anguish, but I still could not shake off an anxiety about Rishabh. Was he really okay with it all?

❦

'Dad, you were looking at me in all these pics! You were not making goofy faces!' Rishabh cried out in mock anger.

'Next time we'll paint our faces and do crazy stuff, okay?' I said, appealing hopefully.

'Okay, that'll be cool,' Rishabh smiled.

My phone rang and 'Rhea Cell' flashed on the screen.

'It's your Mom.'

'Let me talk to her.'

Rishabh grabbed my Blackberry eagerly. I knew it was getting late, and I had told Rhea I'd have him back by seven. Maybe Rishabh was tired too, and wanted to go home.

'Hey Mom, we're having so much fun. We'll get dinner here, okay? Dad's flight?' He looked at me quizzically, and I mouthed, 'We have plenty of time'. 'No, he says there's plenty of time. Okay. See you soon, Mom.'

'Let's get some KFC chicken!' I proclaimed loudly. I'd felt happy when I heard Rishabh say that we had had fun together—that he had fun with me.

'Yes!' Rishabh jumped up and wrapped his arms around me. I knew he would be excited, since Rhea was a vegetarian and Rishabh was not allowed non-vegetarian food at home. During our marriage, I would sneak Rishabh out to restaurants and order non-veg dishes, secretly indoctrinating him in my chicken-loving ways.

'Can we order a large bucket?'

'Sure, we can.'

Finally, something he needed me for! It felt like a foolish victory, but Rhea had been so efficient in taking care of Rishabh after I moved out, that it seemed that there was nothing he lacked. I spent our weekends together always searching for the missing pieces in Rishabh's life, things only his father could provide, even if it was just fried chicken.

I rang the bell at the apartment and Rhea opened the door, wearing a new pink chiffon salwar kurta. I knew all the clothes she had; had seen them all and had felt them against my skin. Seeing her in her new clothes, outfits I couldn't identify, felt like another fresh stab at an unknown wound. I wasn't sure why I felt sadness, even betrayal, on seeing her in unfamiliar clothes. Was it because I felt that she was moving on too easily after our divorce? At least it seemed that she was doing it more gracefully than I was. I still wore the same clothes I had before our divorce, and my life was just about working through the week so that I could come and see Rishabh on weekends.

Was divorce a competition? Was it about who moved on faster, who was emotionally stronger, whose life improved afterwards? Sometimes I felt as if it was; that I should be stronger; that we had taken the decision after so many long nights of talking; that going back to the anger and unhappiness of our previous lives would not be a good idea. But most of the time, I did not know what this new life meant. I was trying to seek answers from her, from Rishabh, hoping maybe they knew.

Rishabh was the only strand still holding together the memories of the marriage we'd had. I had moved to Bangalore, to a city with worse traffic but, somehow, knowing I didn't have anyone waiting for me when I reached home made me appreciate the prolonged activity that was driving. It gave me something to do, some place to be, even if that place was on the roads, as opposed to reassembling the picture of my life again in my empty new apartment.

'Hey,' I said to Rhea and smiled.

'Hi.' She smiled back at me.

'Hey baby,' she hugged Rishabh. 'New jerseys, huh?'

Rishabh grinned.

'Still supporting Mumbai?' she turned to me.

'For life!' I high-fived Rishabh.

'What about your flight?' she asked.

'It got delayed. I'll go to the airport now.' I felt a sudden urge to leave, but had nowhere to go. 'You take care, buddy. You're doing great, right?' I asked, looking at Rishabh.

'He's doing great.' Rhea smiled and ruffled Rishabh's hair.

'Sure?' I asked again, frowning. Now I was just shooting blindly. Maybe because I was tired; maybe because I didn't have another flight till the next day; maybe because I didn't want to spend another night alone; but I was hoping that Rishabh would say that he wasn't okay, and maybe he would ask me to stay.

Rishabh saw the seriousness in my eyes and reached for my hand. 'Yes,' he looked into my eyes with an equanimity that surprised me. 'I'm good. At least you guys are not fighting any more, like most of my friends' parents. This is so much better than staying unhappy together. Most of my friends hate their homes because their parents keep fighting. And three people in my class have divorced parents, fighting over their kids. But I get to have both my Mom and my Dad. So this is cool.'

I looked at his porcelain face, this eleven-year-old standing in his IPL Jersey, sweaty and thin. Rhea looked at me and smiled wryly, both of us stupefied by the irony of our child dealing with our divorce better than we were.

'Okay then, Mr Smarty pants!' I said. 'You take care and get ready for next weekend because it'll be crazy!' I hugged Rishabh hard. 'Now I'm going to run and try and catch my flight, okay?' I smiled at Rhea. 'Bye.'

'Bye. Have a safe flight home,' she said warmly, and I pushed the elevator button.

When Rhea and I had first begun thinking of getting divorced, we had met with Rishabh's school counsellor who had assured us that divorce and marital problems were commonplace in Mumbai. 'Children today are better equipped at dealing with it than you think,' she had said. I hadn't believed her until today.

I walked out of the building where we had lived for twelve years, stood on the wet, muddy road outside and lit a cigarette. It was still drizzling lightly, and I wanted to go back and hug Rishabh, hold Rhea's hand and hear from them again that everything was really okay. As I looked into the distance, it struck me that in Mumbai, with all the space, buildings and smog in between, even though I could not see the horizon, I knew it existed; I knew that the earth and the sky met somewhere. I felt it somewhere I could not quite place.

I wanted to run back and tell Rishabh that, but it felt odd. It felt odd to go back to tell him about a trivial epiphany when I had just run out pretending that I was getting late for my flight. It felt odd, wanting to make him feel the invisible horizon that I felt. It felt odd, realizing that it wasn't so much that my eleven-year-old son needed me, but that I needed him.

Paradise

ANITHA MURTHY

I lie awake, deep in the shadow of the night.

'Remember: between one and two.'

That's what Hari had whispered to me in the morning. I was going to the street-side vendor to buy vegetables and he was washing the silver Toyota Innova. I had looked straight ahead, my heart beating too fast and too loud.

It had been a crisp December morning. The morning mist had disappeared, leaving a nip in the air, but that was not the only reason I had pulled my sari closer. The wide street, lined with tabebuia trees bleeding purple blooms, had been empty. But when I returned with my purchases, I had almost been hit by a scooter driver, who then zoomed off like a bullet.

The fright had paralyzed me, and an unbidden thought had entered my mind: I could be dead by tomorrow, between one and two.

I turn in my narrow bed, longing for warmth, for the feel of fingers squeezing and kneading my flesh.

A bird-like cry sounds in the adjoining room. It is little Kiran calling out in his sleep. I get up to check on him. My own room is a converted walk-in closet, just large enough to contain a steel bed, an old wooden cupboard, and a small oil-stained table that holds a photo of Lord Shiva and sundry puja items. I wake up at four o'clock every morning and have my bath in Kiran's bathroom, which is not used by anyone else. I do my puja and then begin my day in the kitchen with a strong cup of tea, with lots of milk and sugar.

Kiran looks like an angel in repose in the moonlight filtering through the curtains. His eyelashes cast long shadows on his fair cheeks, his mouth is just a little open, and his chest gently rises and falls.

'My precious darling,' I whisper. 'May Shiva protect you from the evil eye.'

I wait for a few seconds before I return to my bed. I sit and stare into the darkness. Hari, my Hari. Will the morning never come?

I did not know that he was the driver for the new Toyota Innova that Ashok Sir and Geetha Madam had bought. I first saw him cleaning the car, when I went out to hang the clothes to dry, and he made no impression on me. But he told me he saw me, and he knew. Hari is like that: his instinct drives him, and he believes his instinct is never wrong. I fervently hope that his instinct is right for tomorrow too.

I cannot fathom what it was that drove me into his arms. He did not pursue me, I did not seduce him. We found ourselves thrown into each other's company every day—to pick up Kiran from his pre-school, to assist Geetha Madam in her shopping, to run general household errands.

I told him everything about myself. I don't remember much about my early childhood. I was abandoned in a railway station, I was put into an orphanage, I had sporadic education and some vocational training and, finally, after working as a maid and cook in a couple of places, I was picked up by Geetha Madam.

Geetha Madam sometimes jokes that I am her mother-in-law. I smile when I think of what she says to her friends. She loves to pretend that she doesn't do anything, that I run the entire house like clockwork. The truth is that she is supremely efficient. She bustles about in her crisp designer dresses fresh from her boutique, her earrings swinging like pendulums, her eagle eye never missing a thing. She is the one who persuaded me to complete my tenth standard. 'What will you do if I kick you out,' she would ask me with a smile. But six years have passed and I have never given her cause for complaint. Till tomorrow.

A rasping cough disturbs the night that breathes like a monster. It is from the master bedroom. Anil Sir has been trying to give up smoking. He has multiple health problems. He likes my samosas and I make them whenever Geetha Madam is away on a business trip. I buy Bhagatram's jalebis for him every other week though he has sugarless tea. He is glued to his laptop and I know he is home when I hear the CNBC channel on in his room. He has never spoken to me directly, always preferring to talk through Geetha, Kiran, or addressing the wall.

I often wonder how they are in bed. I never hear anything, the slightest moan, the faintest squeak. How did they make Kiran? During their twice-a-year vacation?

Will we have vacations, Hari and I? Will we make little Kirans, little rays of sunshine that will light up our lives? It seems a dream so far away, yet so close! I only have to wait till tomorrow.

I shiver, the air suddenly cold. Why do these fingers of darkness caress me with their deception, draining my warmth, my confidence? I feel sick in my stomach. The taste of bile floods my mouth. Should I not believe in my instinct too, my sixth sense that tells me everything is wrong, everything is so horribly wrong?

I have seen Hari drive, and his hands move over my body in the same way. His intense gaze never leaves the road, just as it never leaves my face. He is brutal on the road and in bed. When he talks, his words tear the air with their precision. His dreams are big, passionate. His garage will be the biggest, the best. His vision is unclouded by the doubt and despair that have tinged my past.

His plan is simple.

Tomorrow, Ashok Sir will leave for Delhi in the morning on a business trip. Geetha Madam and Kiran will also leave for her mother's house in Kolkata. At the stroke of one, Ganapati, the security guard will have his lunch and settle down for a snooze. That is when Hari will come—between one and two. I have the keys to the safe. We will clean out the house. Then we will drive away fast and far. That is all I know.

All I have to do is to open the door and let him in.

I look around, dark guilt already staining the walls. Does the butterfly not destroy the cocoon to emerge stronger, more beautiful?

But the morning is still hours away, and the door is still shut.

Crossroads

AHMED FAIYAZ

Sahil Seth wakes up with a start at the sound of the door being shut. He had fallen asleep at noon on the couch in the living room. He sits up and rubs his eyes, watching his wife walking in after a long drive from her office in Colaba, Mumbai. She is vice-president, marketing at Maxis, a large apparel retailer with stores across major cities in India.

'What time is it?' he asks sleepily.

'It's half past six. Didn't Savita come in to cook dinner? How long have you been asleep?' Ruchika asks with a hint of irritation.

'I don't know. I passed out soon after lunch. I'm not sure if she rang the bell while I was sleeping.'

'Come on Sahil. You've done this for two days in a row! I am sure not much writing has happened today either. How long do you believe the publishers will wait? You've put off your deadline three times and your manuscript is overdue by eight months.'

'Stop nagging me. I cannot force myself to write! You know I have been working at it. It's difficult to move forward when I'm confused. The story can move in three different directions from where it is right now.'

'Well that's what I've been hearing for the past two months. You spent the advance you received from the publisher months ago. We bought this plush apartment and your expensive SUV. Now, I have to pay for everything—the servants, the food and the electricity bills! Do you even think about the responsibilities that are on my head?' She flings her handbag on the couch and plonks herself down.

'Come on Ruchika, quit the drama. The folks at Flamingo will send in my royalty cheque for *No Other Way* next week. Let me know what you've spent and you can take your money. Just stop nagging me now. I'm really not in the mood,' he says, turning his gaze away from her and lighting a cigarette.

Sahil a former Wealth Manager at SDG Bank was the best-selling author of *No Other Way*, which sold over a million copies in India and abroad. He quit his bank job after the success of his debut novel and signed a three-book deal with Flamingo Books. He was given an unprecedented advance of 500,000 dollars and enjoyed the status of being the poster boy of Indian fiction. Ruchika and he had moved from their small one-bedroom flat in Mulund to this plush sea-facing apartment on Bandstand in Bandra soon after he'd signed the multi-book deal.

'Yes, all you want to do these days is to sit and smoke in the balcony and gaze out into the distance, as if you are waiting for the arrival of some ship from across the sea,' she says, heading for the kitchen in a huff.

'For God's sake, cut it out will you!' He goes into the bedroom, banging the door shut behind him. 'I'm off for a run, I will be back in an hour,' he says in the direction of the kitchen a while later, grabbing his iPod and storming out of the apartment looking annoyed.

Yes, run, sleep and smoke this is all you can do apart from shouting. Our life in Mulund was better than this pretentious existence! At least we didn't argue and fight like we do every other day here.

⁂

Meanwhile, in the apartment next door…

Reha walks into the living room in a pair of shorts and an old top, a fashion magazine in hand. She sits down on the divan with a bored look on her face and begins flipping through the magazine while Farookh is busy responding to messages on his Blackberry.

'Why aren't you getting ready?' Farookh asks with a hint of irritation in his voice. They had agreed to go out for dinner to Samunder with a couple of his friends in the city. She had been on edge with him for the past few weeks and didn't seem to care whether he was coming or going.

'I'm not in the mood. Why don't you go ahead? I don't particularly want to socialise with these people tonight. It's going to be another night discussing politics and real estate. I'm not up to it,' she says firmly.

Reha was a recently failed film actress whose career nosedived after her last two movies sank without a trace. At 36, she was still single. Despite twelve years in the industry, she had only three hit films among many unforgettable ones to her name. After a year of struggle and being out of circulation, she had got into a relationship with a much-married Farookh Mirza, the head of M-Polyester and Modern Paints, whom she met at a friend's party a few months ago.

The press had a field day printing angry quotes laden with unthinkable profanities which Farookh's otherwise dignified wife showered on Reha. Despite this, Farookh carried on the affair in the open and even bought Reha a sea-facing apartment. He often came over from Delhi and spent two or three days a week in Mumbai with her. He had also offered to take her as his second wife, an offer she had seriously considered till some time back, as it sounded better than being called his mistress.

'It's an important dinner, Reha. The suppliers from Malaysia will be there. They are quite keen to meet the glamorous Reha Kothari,' he says with a wry smile, trying to persuade her.

'Yes, now I go from being your mistress to being your trophy showgirl. Stop trying to take me around like some prized exotic monkey! Go for dinner with them if you want to, Farookh. I'm not coming.'

'You made a choice when you decided to get into a relationship with me. I told you I cannot leave Tasneem. I offered to marry you…' he says, raising his voice.

'Yes, from the husband-stealing bitch to the second wife! What after that? Why do the tabloids call *me* names? Why aren't they saying that you are an adulterer and are sleeping with women a little older than your daughter?'

'Reha, stop! Don't bring my daughter into this!' he screams angrily. An intoxicated Farookh grabs her by her arm and raises his hand to strike her.

'Don't try intimidating me like you intimidate your wife! I'm not the kind of woman who will take this lying down,' she says, pushing his hand away and looking him in the eye.

'Yes, you're the kind of woman who'll sleep with anyone if it serves her interest. The whole world knows what you did with that married actor and how you ended up doing six movies with him. They also know about you playing muse to that director who is older than your dead father! Don't get me started…' he stutters, outraged. He realises he's had one peg of whisky too many. He tries to retain his composure for he does not want to end up hitting her.

'If that's what I am, what are you doing here? Cleaning up the remains of what is left of my reputation? Why don't you leave, Farookh? Just go away from here! Go and stay at the Bay Continental where you have a suite booked and where you and your son ravage groups of young girls,' she says spitefully.

'Stop this nonsense! What has gotten into you? You think I've taken a flight from Delhi and come out here to deal with your frustrations in life? I don't need this and I can find a dozen women who would be happy to marry me, you wretch! My office will be in touch with you. Please vacate this apartment by the end of the month,' Farookh screams, out of control now.

'Oh, poor baby. What happened to my good old lover boy Farookh? Upset that your bird in a cage can talk back to you? Find someone who cannot stand up for herself next time! I'm Reha Kothari. I can sign two films right now. I don't need your small mercies!'

'You wait you filthy slut. I'll fix you. I don't believe you've realised who you're dealing with!'

Farookh takes his coat and walks out, seething with rage. He takes the elevator down to the basement and gets into his steel black Skoda Laura. He had decided against a driver in Mumbai as it would be difficult to find a man he could trust, given the nature of his dalliances and the many lives he led outside Delhi.

Meanwhile at the promenade at Bandstand…

Sahil finishes his run starting opposite his apartment to the end of the promenade. He decides to walk back towards his house and take in some fresh air and think about what he is going to do. He feels out of breath and unfit and realises that he has gained a lot of weight in the past couple of months.

His thoughts go back to this morning when he went knocking at Reha's door to have breakfast with her. Reha and he had gotten to know each other and were having an affair over the past few months. They had met at a book reading of his bestseller and realised that they lived two doors apart. After Ruchika left for work, and if Farookh was not in town, they spent most of the day in each other's company.

He recalls the conversation they had this morning.

'So what do you plan to do about us? Don't you realise that I'm five years older than you?' she asked, running her fingers over his bare torso, looking at him playfully.

He kissed her on her neck and wrapped his arms around her. 'It doesn't matter if you're older. I have feelings for you. I've never felt this way before. I certainly haven't felt this way about Ruchika, even though I went out with her for three years before we got married.'

'So what are you going to do about Ruchika?' she asked teasingly, sitting up and wrapping the sheet around her still luscious and well-maintained figure.

'Will you leave Farookh for me?' he asked, sitting up and gazing intently into her eyes.

'Yes, tonight I will. It won't be difficult. Can you leave Ruchika after all these years?'

'You know I've been so confused about this since the day we began... you know... three months ago. I haven't written a word for weeks. Yes, I have decided to leave her. I will speak to her over the weekend.'

He stops jogging and takes a deep breath before he steps onto the street lost in thought.

Should I leave Ruchika? She has been with me through the ups and downs in life. We're married for God's sake! Or should I end this affair with Reha? No, Reha is beautiful and someone like her by my side is what I need. But do I love her? Or do I love Ruchika? She is ill at ease with my success. She nags me a lot, but cares about me in a way Reha might not. Will Reha stay committed, given her chequered past? What should I do?

With music blaring on his iPod he does not notice the manically speeding steel black Skoda Laura coming at him from the opposite direction...

Virtual Reality

VRINDA BALIGA

Bangalore. To some, an ever-expanding metropolis, to others, a city bursting at its seams. Whichever way you look at it, it's a city that refuses to stay still, even as its infrastructure huffs and puffs to keep pace. A city is said to lend its character to its population, and nowhere is this truer than in Bangalore. The citizens of Bangalore, when they're not busy planning their next move, are busy making it. The graphs of their lives are plotted in terms of the milestones to be reached at appropriate junctures.

The Deshpande family—Lalit, Simi, and their thirteen-year-old daughter Raima—was no different. Like most other people in the city, they were very busy and reasonably happy. During the day, they gave the city its due by playing their respective roles in it to the best of their abilities, and in the evenings, they worshipped at the altar of the television, once the dispute over the remote control was settled. And like most other people, they had stuck, more or less, to the average curve in the milestone graph.

The latest milestone had recently been reached when Lalit and Simi had bought a townhouse in a gated community on the outskirts of the city. This was, they promised themselves, the culmination of all the acquisition they had practically been forced into, one way or the other, over the years. The bike that proved to be of no use, given the pollution and the potholed roads. The hatchback car that became cramped with Raima's arrival, what with her car-seat, pram and all the other baby paraphernalia that had to be lugged around wherever they went. The rented house where the owners grumbled every time their toddler daughter took a crayon to the wall, or when an extra nail had to be tacked somewhere. And then, their own little no-frills apartment.

With each purchase, they had intended to make things better, simpler and more organized, but somehow their lives only seemed to get more and more complicated and cluttered. In short, the city had them firmly in its grip, even as it allowed them the occasional delusion of being in control.

Thus, after a while, even their apartment, of which they had hitherto been quite proud, began to pale in the face of the blitzkrieg of ads announcing new gated communities. Giant billboards beckoned to them. Full page inserts fell out of the morning newspaper—pictures of smiling parents, prancing kids, happy families; names that suggested peace, quiet, serenity, tranquillity; twenty-four-hour security, power back-up, swimming pool, children's play area, herbal garden, meditation hall… the works. And the questions started once again. Didn't Raima deserve the same facilities that every other child at her school seemed to be enjoying? Besides, they—Lalit and Simi—weren't getting any younger, it was high time they started paying more attention to their health; if there was a gym right where they lived, there would be no excuse, really, not to go, would there? And so it went. Before they knew it, they were the proud possessors of a home on the outskirts, and a huge loan to go with it.

When they bought the townhouse, they had hoped to occupy it within a few months, and they had been assured with great certainty by a smooth-talking marketing executive that this would indeed be possible. But, as such things went, they had been able to move in only a year later, just in the nick of time before Raima's summer vacations ended and the new school term started. The project was still only three-quarters complete, and only a half dozen or so families had moved in. Many of the promised amenities were not in place, and there was constant noise and dust from the houses still under construction. So, it was with some difficulty that they finally settled in. Lalit made the arduous daily commute to work. They enrolled Raima in a school that was closer by, though still at a considerable distance from their home, and a school van came to the gate to collect Raima and another girl from the community who went to the same school. Simi, too, went back to her work.

Simi was a software professional. After Raima was born, she had quit working full-time, and now had a part-time job with a start-up. The nature of her work was fairly independent so, for the most part, she worked from home, going to the office only when she had to attend a meeting or make a presentation. She liked the flexibility the job offered—she didn't have to scramble to make alternate day-care arrangements for Raima whenever there was a holiday at school. But it also had its disadvantages. Working part-time was apparently defined in her employer's dictionary as working full-time, but at half the pay. And 'work from home' was all too often taken to mean 'not working at all' by her family, neighbours, visiting in-laws and various other assorted people who supplied a near-continuous source of interruption.

Thus, it was with a sense of resignation that Simi rose to answer the doorbell one Thursday afternoon, when she had been sitting in her study, trying to get some work done. Raima usually got home from school by three in the afternoon. But she was taking part in a school play that was scheduled for that weekend. Simi was glad for the couple of extra hours she got to herself thanks to the rehearsals Raima had after school hours. She had a deadline to meet, and she was hard-pressed for time. She had tried to ignore the bell, hoping that whoever it was would go away. No such luck. The visitor was persistent. It could only be Kirtana, Simi thought glumly. Kirtana Rao, a neighbour who lived two houses away, had taken it upon herself to follow up with the builder on the quick delivery of all the promised amenities, and because Simi was one of the few other residents, she often dropped by to discuss one issue or the other. And issues there were aplenty—the pool was not ready as promised, the intercom system was not up, the security arrangements left much to be desired, and so on. While Simi appreciated Kirtana's good intentions and enthusiasm, a visit from her could easily take up an hour, and that was being optimistic.

The visitor at the door, however, was not Kirtana, but a young man she had never met before. He wore a loose t-shirt and jeans frayed at the knees.

'Yes?' she said, a little curtly.

'Mrs Deshpande?'

She nodded.

'Hi, I'm Maya's brother.'

'Maya?'

He seemed flustered, but plodded on nevertheless.

'Uh... Maya. Your daughter's friend at school.'

Simi stared at him, confused. Now that Raima had changed schools, Simi didn't know the names of all her classmates. Raima was growing up and, nowadays, it seemed she was telling Simi things strictly on a need-to-know basis. But, now that he mentioned it, yes, Simi did recall Raima mentioning Maya's name.

'The Maya who celebrated her birthday last week?'

His face lit up. 'Yup. At Pizza Corner.'

'What's this about? Is everything alright?' she asked, suddenly concerned about Raima.

He held out a bag. 'I just came to give these to Raima. Maya was supposed to lend Raima her shoes for the play on Saturday. But she's not well. She won't be going to school tomorrow. So, she asked me to bring them over. Also, there is this assignment of Maya's that had to be handed in by tomorrow. She asked if Raima could submit it for her.'

Simi glanced into the bag. A pair of black heels, and a notebook covered with brown paper.

'Uh, ma'am, could I have a glass of water please? It's very hot and I rode out here on my bike.'

Simi felt ashamed at what must have seemed very boorish behaviour on her part.

'Of course,' she said, stepping aside. 'Please come in.'

She showed him to the sofa in the drawing room and went to the kitchen to fetch him something to drink. When she returned with glasses and a pitcher of orange juice, she found him walking around the room, examining the photo frames on the walls.

'It was nice of you to come with the shoes,' she said, placing the tray on the table. 'Did you have to come a long way? I think I recall Raima mentioning that Maya lives close to school.'

He shrugged and waved a hand dismissively without turning. The gesture struck her as odd, especially since he had been so polite and almost shy up to that point. And now that she was paying attention, he seemed a little too old to be a thirteen-year-old's brother. Was he in college?

Before she could ask, however, the bell rang again. She went to the door. This time, it *was* Kirtana Rao.

'Hello, Simi,' she said. 'Do you have a minute?'

Simi sighed inwardly and stepped aside. With Kirtana, it always started like this.

'It's about the so-called *gym*,' Kirtana began, making vehement little quotes in the air around the offending word. 'Put in a couple of rickety treadmills, one measly exercise bike, some odds and ends, and it's supposed to become a gym? I want to make a representation…' She stopped short as she noticed the young man's presence. She raised her eyebrows questioningly.

'Kirtana, this is… the brother of Raima's friend at school.' Simi turned to him. 'I'm afraid I didn't catch your name.'

'Uh… Sandeep.'

'Hello, Sandeep,' Kirtana said, sitting down. 'Well, like I was saying, Simi, I'm conducting a signature campaign to demand better gym facilities from the builder… oh, thank you.' She accepted a glass of juice and turned to Sandeep. 'By the way, Sandeep, if you don't mind my asking, did the security guard at the gate stop you and note your vehicle number?'

'Uh… No, I don't think so…' Sandeep looked bashful as ever. Perhaps she had imagined the aberration, Simi thought.

Kirtana turned to Simi with a martyred expression. 'There you have it. I just instructed them last week about maintaining a log of visitors' vehicles. I'll have to speak to them again.'

'I have to leave now, ma'am,' Sandeep said, addressing Simi. 'I just realized there's some place I have to be right now.'

It was only after he left that Simi noticed that his glass of juice was untouched. Kirtana followed her gaze.

'I hope I didn't scare him off,' she said.

'I think you did,' Simi laughed, and then said, 'No, he was a bit shy—came to drop off some things for Raima's play.'

'Oh, Raima's taking part in a play? Isn't that lovely? Is this at school? We must organize such activities for kids here also...'

Half an hour later, Kirtana left and Simi could finally return to her work. She opened her laptop and brought up the design document she had been working on. She had typed only a couple of lines when she stopped short. She sat still for a long moment.

For the past half hour, she had been fighting a growing sense of unease. And now that the distraction posed by having to chat with Kirtana was gone, it hit her with full force. Questions came flooding to her mind. If Maya stayed near the school, why would her brother come all the way here? Why couldn't he just hand over the things at the school gates for someone to take to the classroom? And why would Raima need to borrow black heels when she owned a pair herself?

She went to the living room and retrieved the bag that she had dumped on the sofa on her way to the kitchen. The shoes were new. They looked like they had never been used. Even before Simi opened the notebook and flipped through it, she knew that it would be empty. Just as she knew that Maya had no elder brother or, if she did, he was not the fellow who had shown up at her doorstep.

She went upstairs to Raima's room in a daze. Who was this chap? How did he know so much about Raima? Did Raima know him? Simi was in completely unfamiliar territory. What should she be looking for? A diary? As far as she knew, Raima had never kept a diary. Then, her gaze fell on the computer.

In their earlier home, the computer had been in an alcove off the dining area, which had originally been meant to be a puja room. Raima had used the computer for her school assignments and e-mail, but it had been out in the open and, even without intending to, Simi could keep an eye on her. When they moved, they had decided to put the computer in Raima's room. A long time back, when Raima had first started using the computer, Simi had installed some child-protection software on it that blocked any sites with adult content and also maintained a record of activity including mail and chat conversations by taking periodic screenshots. She had checked the records initially, but there was nothing untoward in them and, after a while, she had stopped. It had felt too much like snooping.

Now, she started the software program and examined the records for the last couple of months. There was still nothing improper. The chats and emails had increased, but that was understandable since she had just changed schools and probably wanted to stay in touch with her friends from the previous school. However, for the last few weeks, one name popped up with unnerving regularity. Sandy_123. Sandy. Sandeep? Except that it was a Sandhya in the chat conversations. Simi traced the conversation back to the first communication.

It was Sandhya who had initiated it.

'Hi, want to chat?' she had said, pinging Raima.

'Who're you?'

'My name is Sandhya. You're Raima?' Raima's ID was raima_deshpande.

'I'm not supposed to chat with strangers.'

'Oh? Did your parents say so?'

Raima had ignored this. And so, there was a conciliatory message.

'I'm not supposed to either. But it's a lot of fun to get to know someone like this. I have a lot of online friends whom I've never met. It's just like having pen pals.'

With a few more blithe statements, she had soon convinced Raima to let down her guard and talk about herself. Simi read on with a sinking feeling. She could see how information had been cleverly drawn out of her unsuspecting daughter over the course of the next few weeks.

On one occasion, Sandhya had deftly steered the conversation to books and claimed to be a Nancy Drew fan. Let's play detective, she had suggested, let's see how much we can guess about each other—Raima's school, her class (and, hence, her age), her interests.

More conversations, more questions. Raima's friends? She had had plenty in their previous apartment complex, Raima had said, but now they had moved to this remote place where there was hardly anybody, just one more girl of her age.

Didn't she feel lonely then, until her parents returned from work? Raima had replied casually that no, her mother worked from home.

There were other questions, slipped in casually, totally innocent in the context in which they were asked. Now, they sent shivers down Simi's spine.

'I have this cute Hannah Montana nightdress,' Sandhya had said when they were talking about TV shows. 'What do you wear at night?'

Maya. The birthday party. Pizza Corner. The play. The rehearsals. Everything was right there in the chat transcripts.

The main gate was visible from the window in Raima's room. Simi looked up at the sound of the loud honk and saw the school bus pulling up to the gate. Raima and her friend, Preeti, got off. They walked hand in hand towards the house. Simi saw that they were playing that game popular among school-girls—three steps forwards, one step back, all to the rhythm of some song or rhyme whose words Simi couldn't recollect. Giggles when one or the other misstepped.

Raima would have to be confronted. Simi could already hear her protesting: 'Why're you *spying* on me?' And later, when she was told, when it sank in: 'But she *said* she was a *girl*.' She would perhaps lose some of her innocence, some of her naiveté. She would perhaps stop taking things at face value, stop blindly trusting people (quite possibly, this would include her parents). She would grow up overnight into the real world. It would be a steep price to pay. But Simi would pay it if it meant keeping her daughter safe.

Simi couldn't even think of what else would have to be done. There was a stranger who knew their address, their daughter's name, her school, her class, the names of her friends, the fact that Simi was alone at home all day, and god knew what else. What hadn't happened today could easily happen on some other day. Should they inform the police? The school?

But for now, watching her daughter skip merrily down the road safe and sound, Simi could only feel an enormous sense of relief.

Footsteps in the Dark

MINI MENON

The loud click of stilettos on the polished granite floor sent a shiver down her spine as always. Alice could feel her heart pounding and the pink folder that she had in her hands fell down.

Was there a word for 'fear of footsteps'? Something like footstepophobia, perhaps?

They were Merlyn's four-inch heels, she knew, and that did nothing to slow down her heartbeat. Merlyn was the big boss's personal secretary, though she did the job sitting in a cabin that, for reasons Alice couldn't comprehend, bore the nameplate 'Merlyn Fernandes, Manager, Market Research'. Barely five feet tall, Merlyn was loud, rude and had no sense of humour. She also made no pretence of trying to hide the unreasonable animosity that she had for Alice.

As she bent to pick up the folder that had fallen from her hands, the door opened. Alice grabbed the folder and straightened herself and, in doing so, her elbow hit the edge of the desk. She winced in pain and her eyes smarted.

'Don't tell me you're crying, Alice! Three months in the city and you're still homesick?' Merlyn's loud voice was mocking. 'Did you manage to finish the report?' Merlyn, as usual, was accompanied by her ever-faithful lackey, the oily Raj.

Oily? As in slippery? Maybe—or maybe just oily, as in dripping oil. Alice suppressed a smile.

'No, ma'am—Ms Fernandes—ma'am, yes, I did, Merlyn—' In this place, everybody seemed to think that being addressed by their first name made them younger.

'Is that a yes or a no?'

Alice cursed herself for stammering like an idiot. The inner Alice was smart, witty and very voluble. Unfortunately, the Alice as seen from outside was not so.

She silently held out the pink folder with the typed report in it.

The older woman took it without a word of thanks and flipped through the pages. She turned to leave and, as if she had suddenly remembered, said coldly, 'Mr Kelkar wants to meet you in his cabin. He wants you to write a speech… Though I wonder what makes you so qualified to write a speech. What did you graduate in? Speech writing?'

Raj laughed loudly as if Merlyn had just cracked a brilliant joke.

'No, ma'am—Ms—Merlyn. English—and then a PG in Mass Communication.' Alice did not add that her post-graduation was incomplete. There was no need. She had heard that neither Merlyn nor Raj was very literate in the conservative sense of the word.

Merlyn rolled her eyes and looked at Raj. They smirked as if sharing a private joke. Alice continued to look naïve. She could slip in and out of such roles with extreme ease. The duo left after another smart remark or two that they thought were at her expense.

For a fleeting moment, Alice recalled the various comments about the two that her fellow trainees chewed upon, along with their roti, at lunchtime. 'Raj and his mother-hen' was the kindest.

The ones that started with 'Merlyn and her...' were more vicious.

The heavy crunch of shoes told her of Mr Rai's arrival. Mr Rai was her immediate boss and liked to be addressed as Mr Rai. His balding head and rounded body did not bother him much and he seemed supremely unaware of the undercurrents running through the institution.

That's the only way you could have survived here, right?

Alice informed him about Mr Kelkar wanting her in his cabin, picked up her notepad and pencil and left. Arjun Kelkar—she knew precisely why he was calling her into the cabin. It was not as much to write the speech as to get her alone in his presence. There was little choice—as long as she was here, she had to deal with the situation.

And I will, in my own way, as I have always done.

She hesitated at the door of the cabin. More footsteps—this time muffled by the thick carpet that lined the room. Her heart started beating loudly once again. Her fear of the sound had been with her for as long as she could remember. She recalled the silent sunsets of her lonely childhood, sitting in a large darkening room reading, a part of her waiting for the sound of her father's sandals on the gravel as he returned from work. That was the sound that determined how the rest of their evening would transpire. A steady crunch meant saner nights, and unsteady shuffles turned into nightmares.

Silence was her mother's defence—a deep silence in which a million screams had given their lives. Even her footsteps had been apologetic—muffled sounds that had somehow worried Alice more than her father's drunken loudness.

Life, which had been nothing great to start with, became unliveable for Alice and her mother after her father's death about six months ago. Two women living by themselves in an old house was an open invitation to disaster, especially when the dead man had accumulated enough debts to ensure that anybody could walk into their lives and claim their right.

From behind locked doors, the mother and daughter had listened to the loud footsteps of the men who came to collect debts. They came in the daytime, initially all sweetness and understanding, later with innuendos and subtle invitations, and finally with threats and warnings. At night, the footsteps were different—they were muffled and stealthy, followed by subdued raps at the door or window, whispers and muttered threats. The two of them sat behind the door, terrified, sleep a forgotten luxury.

There were times when the mother and daughter had discussed quite matter-of-factly the relative advantages of a piece of rope from the ceiling over a razor blade or a bottle of sleeping pills. Finally, her mother, who had been silently flirting with insanity for a long time, had given in to sleeping pills, and now existed in an asylum run by some nuns. The first look she had given Alice after waking up from her drug-induced sleep had been an uncomprehending stare. Virginia Peters had finally managed to escape from the real world into a more bearable one. *Good for you, Mom.*

Alice knew that she herself walked a thin line—sanity was something she was barely clinging to. Good looks, a high level of intelligence and borderline schizophrenia were her parents' legacy.

But I'm not going to give in that easily, not if I can help it.

When she had finally come back home alone, her father's so-called best friend had assured her that she could stay with him, gratis, and he would look after her. Alice had listened, subdued, apparently compliant with whatever he said. After he had left, she quietly took the very few pieces of jewellery her mother had given her, her certificates and a change of clothes in a shopping bag. The only extra item she had taken with her was the six-inch ornate knife with its razor-sharp blade, the one heirloom of any value that was left.

She had latched the front door of her house, boarded a bus to the town, and then a train to Mumbai. Her unannounced appearance at her friend's hostel had caused mild panic, but eventually, the elderly matron had been reluctant to leave a lone, good-looking girl from a small town at the mercy of the wolves in the big bad city. Luckily, in less than a week, Alice had landed this job.

Life was easy enough when one had nothing to lose.

She knocked on the door. Silence. She knocked again. 'Come in.' Kelkar's voice sounded distant.

He was sitting at the computer, engrossed in whatever was on it. He waved a hand casually without looking up, indicating that she sit down.

I know you'd been pacing the carpet all this time. I know you just sat down when I knocked.

She waited patiently until he looked up. 'Ah, it's you. What did you say your name was?'

I didn't, but I know that you know. 'Alice, sir. Alice Peters.' 'Yes, Ms Peters. I'd like you to write out a little speech for me. You see, I have to speak at the inaugural function of...' Kelkar was speaking and she was writing, but Alice was aware of his eyes caressing her. Alice continued to pretend that she was completely unaware of anything.

After all we're two adults holding a mature conversation.

'Ms Peters, there is this conference in Pune the day after tomorrow. I'd like you to come with me to take down notes. My secretary, unfortunately, is tied up with other things.'

Other things like Raj? 'What time do we leave, sir?'

'Please don't call me sir, Alice. Call me Mr Kelkar—or better still, Arjun. Sir makes me feel old.' Kelkar laughed loudly.

Alice smiled. *Just who do you think I am? Your best friend?*

'The conference begins at ten—that means we leave early in the morning. My driver will come and pick you up at the hostel at six.'

You didn't know my name, but you know where I live.

'It continues up to six in the evening. At eight there's a party. We'll return only the next day.' *I'm sure.*

'Yes sir—Mr Kelkar.' *The moment of truth is near.*

'Arjun, not Mr Kelkar. That's it, then. You can speak to Merlyn—she'll help you with other details.' *I'm sure she will—she's helpfulness personified.*

'Thank you, sir—Arjun.' She closed the door behind her.

The time has come.

'The time has come,' the Walrus said,
'To talk of many things:
Of shoes—and ships—and sealing-wax—
Of cabbages—and kings…'

Alice realised that she was actually muttering the lines out loud in the silent room.

Have I finally crossed that line between sanity and insanity?

This turn of events was not unexpected, but it had happened sooner than she had anticipated. There was no one to speak to. Her friend had married and moved to Delhi with her husband just the week before. Moreover, Alice had always been her own best friend, advisor and confidante. No one knew her as well as she did herself.

Self-awareness is a psychological state in which one takes oneself as the object of attention…

Her little hostel room seemed too large and empty with Sukanya gone. Loneliness, which had loyally followed her all her life, was now beginning to turn around and bite her. The warden had informed her that her new roommate would arrive by Sunday.

She dreaded the prospect as much as she dreaded the silent nights that her friend had left behind when she went. Alice sat in her bed and weighed her choices. She could pack and leave—but where to? Delhi? That wouldn't be fair. Troubling a newly married Sukanya once again was not an option.

For a moment she thought of going back to her mother. *I can take her back with me to the house and—And?* And what? The nun who ran the ashram had made it clear that they were going out of their way, taking in a refugee with no means of living and no hope of returning to normal life. Upsetting the equation even slightly would mean that she and her mother would be, literally, on the streets. That door was permanently sealed, unless a miracle happened.

And we lived happily ever after…

Arjun Kelkar thought of her as a naïve small-town girl—easy prey. She was, in fact, one. But she was also more than that. What is the worst that can happen if I play along? She thought of Merlyn who, according to the office grapevine, had been Mr Kelkar's prime entertainment for a very long time. *I can certainly do better than her.* After all, she had nothing to lose—except a misplaced sense of right and wrong that was another one of her congenital flaws.

I am sure there's a way out of this… There always is.

Alice walked to the cupboard and sifted through her meagre belongings. She took out her best clothes, a nightdress and some innerwear and folded them. Let's do it in style, baby! She placed them neatly in a small overnight bag and opened the old chocolate box that contained her jewellery. There was a pair of ruby earrings and a thin chain with a matching pendant—the remains of her mother's once-ample inheritance. That, and the ornate knife. She opened the sheath of the knife and ran her finger tip over the edge of the blade. She winced as it drew blood.

The tiny drop of blood fascinated Alice. It glittered in the feeble light of the naked bulb that hung from the ceiling. This blood—this was what life was all about. This entire struggle was just to keep it running in the veins. What if it flows out? The thought seemed to hold her in a spell as she lightly pressed the edge on the blue vein of her wrist.

Footsteps. Girls from rooms beyond were moving in batches toward the dining hall. Dinner times had been bearable as long as Sukanya was around. Alone, the prospect of dinner was a daunting one. Ever since her friend had left, she had avoided going to the dining room at night when it was crowded, making do with a banana or an apple. Tonight, she had nothing with her. But then, she was not feeling hungry.

Who was it that said something like, 'Where hunger reigns, strength abstains'?

Thud, thud… There was something different about this sound—a muted, tinny sound that seemed vaguely alien. No, they were not footsteps, Alice was sure. It took her a moment to realise that it was the sound of drops of blood falling on the open lid of the chocolate box. There was a tiny pool forming there, a tiny deep red pool on the old faded gold. Like ruby on antique gold. Beautiful!

Death was so easy when you had nothing to lose.

Footsteps, again. This time they stopped by her door. Knuckles rapped on the door. 'Alice, Warden Ma'am wants you to come down.' It was Geet, the girl who lived in the room opposite. There was somebody else with her. 'Alice, your new roommate has come. The warden is calling you. Alice!'

Alice slowly opened the door. Somebody screamed.

There has to be a way out…

Footsteps running….

The phone rang just as Arjun Kelkar was falling asleep. He cursed under his breath and leaned over to pick it up. It must be for Priya. It was for her that these untimely calls usually came.

The caller at the other end did not wait for him to answer. 'Priya Ma'am? This is Brinda.'

'Hold on.' He handed the receiver to his wife who was already up. She spoke for a while, put the receiver down, and got up to change.

'Do you have to go? Can't Brinda handle it for once?'

'Arjun, this is a strange case. The girl has slit her wrist but claims that she was not trying to kill herself. And her wound is not deep enough to retain her at the hospital. She has nowhere to go. They would have called the police, except that the duty doctor took pity on her—such a young girl, obviously educated, who did not seem to be quite in her senses—and decided to call Sahay.'

Arjun was not interested. In Priya's life, there was a similar story every other day. Sahay was Priya's brainchild, an institution that took in abused and helpless women and rehabilitated them. Brinda, Priya's assistant, too was an equally committed social activist.

'I must see what I can do. Brinda is on her way to pick me up. See you in a while, then. Go to sleep—you have a long day tomorrow and you have to start early.'

Arjun smiled into the darkness. *You are right, tomorrow is going to be a long day...*

Mini's debut novel, Lesser Lives, *comes to bookstores nationwide in December 2012.*

Gautam Gargoyle

SHAILADITYA CHAKRABORTY

It was a cruel name, no doubt coined by an undergraduate straight out of college for all the wrong reasons. There were many such on the office floor. But Gautam Gargoyle didn't seem to mind. He responded to it every time, usually with a tired grin and a hunched nod. His face, when he did so, pulled at its flaccid edges and bunched up in little rolls of fat around his hook nose and glassy eyes. Gautam Gargoyle was grotesque.

To British callers, he was Greg or Gregory and they knew nothing of his thick tongue, slithering nervously over his dry lips as he took call after call through the night. They did not see the bony hands that hung limp by his sides as he spoke relentlessly into the microphone, or the misshapen hump on his back grow larger as his head bent close to the computer screen to compensate for his weak vision. That suited Gautam Gargoyle just fine.

His colleagues did see him, though. And when they thought he wasn't looking, they pointed at him. Often, they asked him where he lived and snickered when he said, 'VT.' 'On the roof of the railway station building, I bet,' they would say to each other amidst guffaws and giggles. Over post-dinner breaks and coffee and cigarettes at the stairwell, they laughed at the shabbiness of his shirts and the flabbiness of his belly. Gautam didn't take any breaks. He manned his desk like a—well, like a gargoyle, and stayed rooted to his responsibilities. That suited him fine, too.

It was no surprise that he performed better than the rest. After three years of supplying insurance advice to strangers, the management saw it fit to move Gautam to the less taxing job of floor manager. Gautam politely refused. He would do far better behind the desk, he said, and bared his jagged teeth in a crooked grin. Management quickly agreed and averted their eyes.

A week later, Malini was recruited as his boss.

Malini was an MBA, and as such was brimming with ideas for the reorganisation of the workforce and the reallocation of resources. The management would have none of it. Neither would the team she had been assigned to handle. Her job, in no uncertain terms, was to ensure deliveries on deadline, coax productivity out of veterans younger than her and wine and dine with the gora clients when they came down every six months or so.

After a flabbergasted few days spent trying to make a noticeable difference, Malini sought advice from her peers. There was none. 'It's only a job,' they said. 'Punch in, punch out.' Some were bold enough to suggest discussing ideas over breakfast, others sneered behind her back. 'MBAs,' they scoffed. 'What do they think of themselves?'

At her wit's end, Malini scoured the charts and found that there was one employee whose performance was head and shoulders above the rest, and consistently so. She knew from experience and a hard life wrought out of middle-class values that it was no accident. Here, finally, was a kindred soul with a spirit devoted to labour. And so it was that, in the middle of the night, she summoned

Gautam Gargoyle to her cabin.

Anybody could have told her that it was a mistake, but nobody did. They were far too busy swivelling agape on their seats as Gautam gingerly took off his headset, tucked his shabby shirt in, and walked the gangway with his chin held close to his chest all the way to the end of the room, where he disappeared behind the dark film on her glass door.

Malini had rocked the boat. She had miscalculated the hysterical effect an unusual spectacle can have on a frustrated group high-strung on caffeine, nicotine and nocturnal work hours. And it was an unusual spectacle indeed. Gautam had never, in the three years he had spent at McCann's, taken his headset off before the appointed eight hours of his night shift. He had never even taken a sick leave. For all that mattered, Gautam *was* the gargoyle of the office floor, watching dispassionately over all that happened without moving an inch, ever.

What Malini didn't know was that she had disrupted the balance that reigned over the entire floor. She had shattered the shackles beneath the feet of their stony mascot. She had set him free.

The question was why, and nobody desisted from asking it of themselves and others. When an answer lies behind closed doors, conjectures can be several and fanciful. They grow in series, like the many heads of a hydra. One is decapitated only to make way for three others. Before long, rumours began to surface. Ten-minute coffee breaks extended into two-hour gossip sessions, while performance suffered.

But Gautam Gargoyle stayed, as he was destined to, at his desk and at the top of the roster.

Malini could not rein in her team and she could not understand why. This wasn't a textbook situation at all. She decided to rely on Gautam instead, who seemed to have a good head on his shoulders, though terribly hunched. She picked his brain over tea and discussed plans to bring in new clients and hire fresh blood.

At his behest, Malini attempted to fraternise with the team. She repeated to them all the lessons she had learned about leadership and teamwork. She urged them on with promises of appraisals and threats of expulsion. Nothing worked. All she got in response were tittering whispers and bitter glances down her blouse. With pressure from her superiors steadily mounting, she began to demand more time with Gautam, her only flickering flame of hope in what was increasingly growing into a nightmarish world of rejection.

It only made matters worse. Her collusion with the office gargoyle had corrupted her image. The very sight of her, once deemed able to motivate the faint-hearted to action, now appeared distasteful to her staff. Where she once had smooth skin, they now imagined warts. What was once enigmatic and unattainable turned vulgar and available. Her authority corroded further.

Phones went unanswered. Senior citizens from the UK complained about the customer service, or the lack thereof. The clients felt terribly 'Bangalored'. That it was Mumbai made no difference. Nor was it of any consequence that it was a simple human drama that had derailed their iron-clad systems. The numbers said it all. And if the numbers didn't improve, the process would be given to someone else. The entire team would be sacked.

Management was not impressed. It was one thing for a new recruit not to effect an immediate improvement to the bottom-line—it might even be expected. But to single-handedly sabotage a functioning unit within a month or two merited investigation. Since they were not the kind blessed with mature deductive prowess, they did the next best thing. They issued ultimatums and kept their ears to the ground.

The ground had much to say in those days, as did the walls

of the men's urinals. They spewed graphic details of a strange relationship between a monster and its mistress. They spelled out hours of unproductive gossip and misdirected creativity. The office floor said more. People were rarely to be found at their station, and more so each time Gautam plucked the headset off his pointed ears and shambled up to Malini's cabin. They milled about their cubicles and discussed with vehemence the utter forwardness of the illicit relationship that was blossoming behind the closed door.

With each passing day, the rumours grew bolder. The whispers grew louder. The nudging and winking became more exaggerated than in ribald comedies. The management saw it all.

A board of bosses with BlackBerries and Bluetooth earpieces summoned them both. First, they spoke to Gautam. Malini waited outside with mixed feelings. It was true that her figures had been dismal, and that they might all be pink-slipped at the drop of a decimal. But why would they want to speak to Gautam? He was the flag-bearer for the entire floor. He was the only one who could not be blamed. In fact, if she let herself believe so, he was the only one who showed even the slightest glimmer of hope. If he was involved, surely, it was for a positive end. It seemed farfetched that the super-bosses would seek his advice as she had. But there was hope. With Gautam, there was always hope.

But when Gautam walked out, he seemed unsure. He avoided her eyes and tripped over his own feet. His face carried the faint afterglow of an inward smile, but the outside was all stone. Gautam Gargoyle was unusually grim as he held open the door for her.

Malini walked in to an inquisition. The bosses looked at her from over their spectacles and offered her a seat with raised eyebrows. 'So, it's true,' they said.

'I'm sorry?' she said.

'Yes, you should be,' they said, pleased with themselves.

'No, I'm afraid I don't understand. What's true?'

'About you and Gautam.'

And there it was. For a moment, Malini assumed that they were referring to the plans they had been working on all week. She had been considering shuffling the night-shift employees to a time better suited for them. It was Gautam who had worked out how to categorise them by the distance they had to travel from home, the traffic at that time of day, the responsibilities they had to compromise on, the accents they were most comfortable with and the hours at which they were most naturally productive. But that moment passed.

And then the matter-of-fact turn of phrase began to take root in a field that had already been prepared over the past weeks of hushed ridicule and gesticulation. 'You and Gautam.' It finally made sense. Those three words summed up what she had been trying to read in the averted eyes of her team all along—horror and revulsion. They made her hair stand on end.

'What exactly do you mean, "me and Gautam"?' she asked anyway.

'Well, he has confessed to it already. Though I must say it's not really news. Everybody seems to be talking about it.'

Malini bit down on her anger as her brief tenure, the way the others had seen it, played itself out in her head. She closed her eyes against it and composed herself.

'It's against company policy, you know,' they went on. 'Seeing each other in a workspace. Very bad for group dynamics.'

'But it's not true,' she cried out. 'It's not true at all. Why would you think something like that?'

They looked puzzled at that. 'But he confessed,' they said. 'Said he, um, loves you.'

Malini drew herself up and mustered the coldest voice she

could. 'Well, I certainly do not reciprocate.' She spent the next few minutes signing declarations to that effect. Each dotted line bled holes in her otherwise well-meaning self. When the formalities were done, she stormed out of the office and headed straight for Gautam's desk.

The workstations were empty again. People had gathered in the shadows of their cubicles, waiting for the drama to unfold. She was happy to comply. When Gautam looked up with a sheepish grin that that drew dark lines beneath his eyes, she reached out and slapped his face. The sound echoed through a roomful of people that was uncharacteristically silent.

'How dare you,' she spat out. 'Who the hell do you think you are, you filthy piece of work? What made you think you could take that kind of liberty with me? I'm your boss, you fucking idiot. Where's your sense of professionalism? What have you been telling all these people? That I'm easy? Is that it? One woman decides to talk to you and you think you're some kind of Casanova? This is why everybody makes fun of you, you fucking loser.'

Gautam Gargoyle sat silent through it all, an uncomfortable smile etched in stone across his face. When Malini had stomped back to her cabin, he pulled his headset off for the last time. He cleared his spartan desk, put his pens and Post-Its in his bag, slung it over his hunched shoulders and walked quietly out.

In the silence that followed, the other employees went back nimbly to their desks. They put their headsets on without complaint. The next sound to be heard was, 'Hi, you've reached United Banking and Insurance. This is Mike. How may I help you?'

In her cabin, Malini fumed. Gradually, her anger turned inward. She had ventured too far beyond the person she knew herself to be, and the time it took to get back to her own self caused her much pain. She didn't leave the cabin for her break. It was dawn and the end of the shift by the time she saw the letter of resignation on her table.

Gautam had known what was coming all along.

Over the next few days, matters quietened. Her team began to treat her with respect, and a little misplaced fear. It was good for business, and for 'group dynamics' as the management had said. The numbers turned themselves around and the employees were again working at a steady average.

Malini was made permanent at the end of three months. Her appraisal was handled by the same row of bosses that had once almost fired her. 'Funny thing,' they said. 'Remember Gautam?' Of course, she did. 'Not that it's worth mentioning, but we had already decided to fire you that day. I mean, not that we had anything against you—just company policy, you see. Remarkable, how things fall into place.'

'Yes,' she said morosely. 'That it is.'

'And, to think, the only person in the whole damn team worth retaining fashioned a bloody noose for himself. I mean, no offense, but you were still green. And you were not really performing—not like now. Things have changed.'

Malini got a raise. But she wasn't happy about it.

That night, she went through the records to track down an address. She followed it to VT, shorthand for Victoria Terminus. It wasn't called that any more, though. It was now Chhatrapati Shivaji Terminus, the last halt in the dark city of Mumbai. She walked past the gothic arches of the railway station that housed it and on by the silent statues of Flora Fountain. She walked through prehistoric lanes into the shadows of the past till she was lost, hurt, angry and helpless.

Beneath the crumbling pillars of a Victorian bungalow, far too dilapidated to be awarded a heritage status, she broke down and cried into her palms. 'I'm sorry,' she said to the chipped cherubs and angels carved on the pillars. 'I'm so sorry.'

There was a flapping of wings overhead. Birds, no doubt, disturbed from their rest. As she cried, the flapping grew closer and came to a halt behind her. From the darkness emerged Gautam Gargoyle, his bony hands clasped behind his hunched back, his smile still crookedly in place.

'It's okay,' he said, and reached out to hold her. 'Just close your eyes,' he whispered, as she sobbed gratefully into his chest. He wrapped himself around her. A leathery warmth came over her heart. She closed her eyes. She held him tight.

And her feet left the ground.

'Gautam Gargoyle' *is the Editor's pick from the short listed stories in the Landmark Grey Oak Urban Stories Competition.*

Baba Premanand's Yoga Class

PARITOSH UTTAM

Dr Basu had never thought he would feature on national television. If at all that came about, he imagined it would be a matter of pride. His wife, friends and sundry neighbours would pile into the sitting room and cheer as he disseminated words of wisdom and expertise that he had painstakingly acquired through four decades of practice as an obstetrician.

Instead, here he was, closeted in his room, as lonely as a Himalayan ascetic. Where he ought to be covered with pride and glory, he was buried under layers of mortification, watching himself on TV, holding his ears and performing penitential squats before a jeering mob. The TV channel played the clip endlessly in a loop, until it appeared he had done not ten, but hundreds of squats. To ensure he could not get away unrecognized, they drew a red circle around his head on the screen, captioned 'Doctor'. Another red circle identified the young woman next to him as the 'Victim'. A thoughtful viewer might wonder why the purported victim looked so triumphant while he, the alleged oppressor, looked utterly defeated.

Pulled along by an inexplicable sense of masochism, he could not get himself to switch off the TV. Finally, tiring of the scoop, the channel turned to the next controversy surrounding the Indian cricket team. Dr Basu snapped out of his trance. He had been hypnotised by his own humiliation.

It had to be the Fates, he concluded, swallowing the spontaneous protest that rose in his throat. He had never believed in destiny or fortune, had always fought against his family's village-rooted superstition and fatalism. In fact, he had chosen his career in medicine for that very reason—to prove the supremacy of science and logic. A man's destiny, he was fond of saying, lies in his hands alone. But not one scientific fact came to his aid now, or even came close to explaining what had happened the previous day.

Like dominoes falling, so many events had occurred one after the other, in just the right sequence and manner to make the next one possible: The traffic light had turned red, forcing him to halt at the junction. He thought of the yoga exercise demonstrated by Baba Premanand on TV, which was a hatha yoga mudra that involved encircling the fingers of one hand with the other. The woman stopped her Kinetic scooter alongside his car window. She looked in, and misconstrued his gestures as lewd signals.

The unfortunate train of events did not stop there. She created a commotion, and he chose not to speed away but to attempt to clear the misunderstanding. A crowd collected within minutes and threatened to beat him up. Someone in that crowd possessed a mobile phone with a camera and recorded his humiliation for posterity and sold the damning video clip to a TV channel.

That this impossibly long chain of events had unfolded uninterrupted, only pointed to the conspiracy of the Fates against him for the cavalier attitude he had shown them lifelong. But was this long drawn out revenge, culminating at the sunset of his life, justified? He had as good as retired from active practice, reducing the opening hours of his clinic until he had left himself a window of just a couple of hours to advise and refer patients who flocked to him on the basis of his reputation. Another one hour as a consultant in the big multi-speciality hospital near his home. One or two years more, and he would have shut shop altogether, living out the rest of his life on his retirement kitty, or going on long-due vacations with his wife that he had always put off to some other time, just because he had been too busy with work. Or, going to Chicago to visit his son and grandson who, by now, must be prattling with an American accent.

He could still have avoided the disaster had he managed to convince her of his innocence. But back then, in the heat of the sun—and of her anger—it was impossible to make her see that it was a laughable misunderstanding. Her frenzied screaming had collected a crowd within no time—all too eager to relish someone else's discomfort. So self-righteous was her wrath that she did not pay the slightest heed to his vehement insistence that it was Baba Premanand's hatha yoga he was trying out in the privacy of his car. Everything he said was immediately turned against him.

'I am a doctor. An obstetrician. I would never insult a woman. My patients are all women.'

'An obstetrician? Aren't you ashamed? See a young woman and...'

There was no doubting which side the crowd was on. He was in a car, she was on a scooter. A man versus a young woman—he had no chance. If he were on a two-wheeler or on foot, and a young man in a car had knocked him down, then he would have had the crowd's sympathies. But in the existing circumstances, there was nothing or no one he could appeal to.

There seemed no staunching her tirade. 'Don't you have a

daughter my age? How would you feel if some man teased and molested her?'

'Molest! I didn't touch you, or even look at you!'

'Oh right. You thought you could get away in your car, making those dirty signs at me. You thought I would be quiet... afraid like other women. You've done this before, haven't you?'

'I did not. I was practising Baba Premanand's yoga while the light was red. I...'

'I am a working woman. I face people like you all the time in my office, in buses and trains, in bazaars, and now on the roads. And I have taught all of them a lesson.'

'Look, this is a misunderstanding.'

'You think there is no one to defend me? I am married. If I tell my husband, you see what happens.'

'But I was... Baba Premanand...'

The crowd had burgeoned, and an enterprising man stepped forward to play the role of the defender of virtues. He caught Dr Basu's collar.

'Apologize to the lady or I will teach you a lesson right here.'

'Let go of my collar,' Dr Basu said, shaken.

'Apologize, or else.'

Dr Basu finally saw discretion as the best part of valour. 'Sorry, Madam,' he said, without looking at her.

'Will you ever do it again to any woman?' she asked.

'I didn't do anything!'

'Again?' The man, who had let go of his collar, gripped it again. 'Hold your ears and do ten squats, and say aloud each time that you will never trouble a woman again. Either we hand you over to the police, or you take our justice.'

He never saw anyone capturing his compliance with that instruction on camera. But by then his vision was blurred. The crowd was a sea of anonymous faces, like dots on a TV screen without any reception. The only thought that he clung to was that he should somehow get away from that place in one piece, with the vague notion that, in a couple of days, everything would blow over. If he didn't go by that road for a few days, everybody would forget about the piece of entertainment he had unwittingly provided them. A stupid misunderstanding, maybe even laughable a year later but, as long as no one who knew him had witnessed his humiliation, nothing was lost. But that, he realized, as the channel abruptly switched back to replaying his video, wasn't the way it had turned out. The Fates...

Dr Basu badly underestimated the power and reach of television. He seldom watched it, wholeheartedly agreeing with the description of it as the Idiot Box. When he watched his wife surfing laughter and dance and reality shows, not to mention the unbearably melodramatic soap operas and no less dramatic news channels, he considered the Idiot Box too flattering a description.

He could turn off the TV in his house in disgust, but he had no control over what the world outside chose to watch. After his wife had had the shock of her life finding him on TV, cowering at the mercy of a mob, he had made it clear that the TV should not be switched on for at least a week.

But the next day, as he honked his car impatiently, waiting for the watchman to open the gates of the building to let him out, he realised that the matter was not destined for a quiet burial. The watchman could barely keep the grin off his face as he lazily and insolently got up from his chair, instead of the alacrity and smart salute he usually did it with.

At his clinic, most of the calls he received were from friends or colleagues, more or less along the same lines: 'Was that really you on TV, Basu? Is it true?'

At first, he laughed it off. 'Stupid misunderstanding, you know. And then there was the crowd. You can't argue with it. I was lucky to get away in one piece.'

'Yes, but the woman. Did you really...?'

The first few times, he answered patiently, narrating the entire story in good humour, showing that he could take a joke at his expense. But when caller after caller asked the same questions, he found it difficult to retain his humour. He sensed that all his explanations and justification were accepted with a pinch of salt— the imagery of the television was too strong to be overturned by mere words and hearsay.

He turned abrupt in his replies, putting the onus of his guiltlessness on their conscience. 'Look, do you believe I was harassing a woman on the streets? For how many years have you known me? Will you believe your friend or colleague or doctor, or will you believe an unethical TV channel that will go to any length to boost its TRP?'

'I believe you, but...'

'Either you believe me, or not. There's no but.'

What rattled him most, however, was when a woman, obviously pregnant, accompanied by her husband, walked into his clinic for a consultation. Her eyes, glued to his face, were clouded with hesitation until suddenly, with a yelp of recognition, she got up while he was speaking.

'You are that doctor, that eve-teaser who was caught on TV?'

'That was a horrible misunderstanding, madam. I could never...'

'Get up!' she yelled at her bewildered husband. 'I cannot dream of being examined by this man.'

Too shocked to continue sitting in the clinic after this fallout, Dr Basu left for home. As soon as he reached his building, the gardener's kids began doing squats energetically, holding their ears and giggling. He yelled at them and immediately felt ashamed—he could not recall the last time he had shouted at a kid.

He heaved a sigh of relief on reaching the asylum of his home and related to his wife the events of the day. She was not surprised. She had her own story to tell—the phone calls from both genuinely solicitous relatives and friends, and those who simply called to savour their discomfiture. One of their neighbours had even shut the door hurriedly on catching sight of her, as though she couldn't bear to be associated with the family of such a criminal.

Dr Basu threw his hands up in despair. He imagined and dreaded the embarrassment his fifteen minutes of fame—or notoriety, rather—could have caused his son, had he been here, and not on the other side of the globe, thankfully insulated from this madness. No, he had to get a grip on himself and think this out rationally, just as he had all his life, and succeeded so far.

All he had to do, he decided, was to lie low and let the brouhaha blow over. The next scandalous clip the TV channel came across would ensure that. He had to do precisely nothing. Their limited attention span and the search for something juicier all the time, made both the TV channel and its viewers suffer from amnesia.

Didn't the TV channel, however, have more important things to show and talk about? Crime, corruption, the economy, politics, foreign policy, terrorism? Policemen being blown up by Naxalites, or floods ravaging Bihar got a barely passing mention, while his alleged outraging of the modesty of a woman was repeated ad nauseam by excited and breathless anchors. Where was the sense of perspective?

Having milked the item dry, the TV channel expectedly dropped the item in a day or two. But the people around him, Dr Basu soon discovered, did not drop it as easily from their memory. Those who used to accord him so much respect now greeted him with insolent sniggers and ill-concealed laughter.

The word of mouth began to tell—his practice suffered. Most of the entries in his appointment diary had lines struck through them. A few tried to be diplomatic about the cancellation—the busyness of life, unavoidable and unforeseen circumstances that arose mysteriously. He understood he would not get a straight answer if he asked about rescheduling their appointments, so he stopped asking. Others were more forthcoming about the reason. 'We can't come to you now, doctor. My wife is not comfortable.'

Whereas, earlier, he had to put off appointments by a week in order to accommodate them, now people could saunter in as they liked. The few who did drop in were strangers in the locality and rarely ever returned.

The multi-speciality hospital that he visited for an hour a day as a consultant informed him politely that his services were no longer required. At home, the president of the apartment society hinted that he should resign from the secretaryship of that body, in keeping with the wishes of other members. Dr Basu complied immediately, having no heart to protest the forced ostracisation.

Every day, he went straight home from his clinic. For shopping and other essentials, he took a circuitous route to go to localities where he was not known.

The last straw fell, however, when his son called from Chicago and said, anxiety killing his voice, 'What's this I hear, Papa? Is it true...?'

Dr Basu, broken-hearted, handed the phone over to his wife without a word.

The flood of maternity-bound ladies to his clinic first abated, then reduced to a trickle, and finally sputtered to the occasional drop. He still kept going to his clinic, more out of habit than anything else. His heart thudded with a dull ache as he took out his car every morning, like that of a reluctant child forced to go to school. He missed the camaraderie and banter he'd enjoyed with his patients—the nervous first-timers whom he put at ease, or the weary second or third-timers he tried to enthuse.

In the clinic, lonely and idle, he brooded. He seriously considered advancing his retirement. But he abhorred the idea of staying cooped up at home all the time, reading newspapers or novels, and pottering around the garden, when his hands and mind itched for activity. Yet again, going out of the house had stopped appealing to him. He mulled over his son's proposal that he shut his clinic, rent out their flat and come to the US to begin a new life where no one knew him and he could forget his past. Aghast initially, that he should think of a new beginning at his stage of life when he ought to be tying up loose ends, he had gradually veered around to the suggestion. Besides, it was unfair to inflict his punishment on his wife too.

A knock intruded into his reverie, followed immediately by a woman pushing open the door. He felt a violent twisting in his insides as he recognized her as the woman on the Kinetic. He stared at her, too dumbstruck to react. She, on the other hand, showed no signs of surprise or shock. She expected him.

'What do you want now?' he said in a hoarse whisper, recovering his voice marginally.

'Nothing,' she said, and then added softly, 'I only came to say sorry.'

He was too old to jump around shrieking, but for a moment he did feel the ground sway. 'Why the change of heart?' he asked after the woman sat on the chair, unbidden.

She did not look up. 'I saw that... that same yoga exercise by Baba Premanand on TV.'

He would have laughed aloud had he not been seized by both anger and relief at the same time. Do what he might, he could not shake off the overarching sense of futility, of waste, of the absurdity of it all.

'It's no use now. I have lost all that was dear to me—my reputation, my character, my...' he spread his arms, taking in his room and the empty waiting room beyond, 'my work.'

'I cannot undo the past, but I can help restore what you have lost,' she said quickly.

'I don't want money. How can you restore my character? How did you find me, by the way?'

She had noted his car number at that time, perhaps with the intention of tracking him down if he proved to be reprobate and unrepentant and in need of further lessons. Later, when she realised her mistake, she had gone to the RTO and ferreted out his address from their records.

'I was on TV,' he said, burning with shame at mentioning it. 'Did you watch that?'

'I am sorry. I will call the channel and tell them. I will publish a public apology in the newspaper.'

'I don't know if all that will work. It's not a switch you can flick off and on.' Maybe he should simply accept her apology and move on, he thought, instead of acting like a petulant child refusing to be pacified.

'There's one more thing I can do.'

He looked at her quizzically.

'I am expecting. Will you be my obstetrician?'

The surge of joy made him feel half a century younger. 'And I can tell all my earlier patients that you are consulting me?'

She nodded.

He held out his hand and shook hers. 'Thank you, and congratulations,' he said. He opened his appointment diary and reached for the phone. There was a long, long list to go through.

The TV channel was not interested. Restoration of character, they said, did not make for good TRP. People would have forgotten about the incident by now, and they would have to air the old clip again to refresh their memories. Besides, there could be no video clip certifying his bona fides. 'Idiots in the Idiot-Box,' Dr Basu muttered and shrugged it off—his patients had begun coming back to him.

Wrong Strokes

FOR DEEPALAYA

Sandeep Sinha strode into the lounge area with Ashmita, his wife of six months, by his side. She looked beautiful in her cream top and light blue jeans. Both wore stylish pairs of Oakleys, a brand that Sandeep had been signed up to endorse at an unheard-of fee. They were followed by two security guards and his man Friday.

He took off his shades and sat back in a contemplative mood. Dark circles were clearly visible under his eyes. All the partying and drinking over the past few weeks wasn't doing his form any good. Two days ago, he had pulled out from the ongoing test series against Sri Lanka, citing a hamstring injury. The team had a tour of New Zealand lined up in the week. The Entertainment Cricket League wasn't far away, and he was the captain of one of the franchises.

The ECL had revved things up for him. He returned in style after being dropped from the test team after a poor season. It had also brought Ashmita, a struggling Bollywood actress he met at an after-party during the previous ECL season, into his life. After a very public affair and amid much media frenzy, they had decided to tie the knot. Endorsement deals from leading sportswear and lifestyle brands flowed in. He was now the face of a number of popular brands, a regular in the celebrity party circuit and the hero of middle-class India. He was himself hardly middle-class anymore though with one villa in South Delhi, another in Bangalore, where his parents lived, a penthouse in Bandra and a fleet of six sedans, which included a BMW 7 series, a Hummer, and his Yamaha 500 cc sports bike. He was also touted to be the next captain of the Indian cricket team.

The two remained silent for a while, she toying with the five-carat solitaire on her finger, he hooked to his Blackberry. They averted their gaze from each other. Ashmita looked forlorn and bored. She rose from her seat to pick up a croissant and a cup of coffee. They'd had an argument last night after returning from a party; he had accused her of flirting and being frivolous with Ashmit Singh, a famous model. She had responded in a fit of rage as she always did, breaking the lamp in their hotel room and yet another cell phone. She was the victim in the relationship, Ashmita believed, given that she'd had to give up her career to follow him around the world and be a sideshow while he lived his dreams.

Sandeep's phone rang; it was his mother at the other end. 'Where are you?' she asked.

'I'm in Jaipur, Ma. We were invited here for a wedding—the Railway Minister's son with a girl from the royal family. We are flying back to Delhi in a short while...'

'Akshay passed away... yesterday,' his mother said, struggling to bring the words out of her mouth.

'What?'

'He was engaged in crossfire with militants near the Siachen glacier... There was an explosion. I don't know the details now. The army is flying in his body from Delhi in a short while... Oh beta, it's terrible!' She broke down. 'Such a wonderful boy he was!

His parents... What will they do now?'

'I can't believe this, Ma,' Sandeep was incredulous. Ashmita looked at him, but turned her attention back to *Jaipur Times*. She pushed the paper in his face and pointed at a picture of both of them from the party. He pushed her hand away, at which she recoiled and turned to look away from him.

'Come home now. Come for the funeral.'

'Oh, Ma. I don't know... I'll call later, I have to board my flight,' he said, before he saw a staff member from the airline standing in front of him, almost bowing in reverence. He hung up, his mind a muddle of thoughts, and drifted back to the time when he was just Sandy.

'Come, Sandy. What a knock yesterday! You scored a century again. What strokes—superb yaar!' exclaimed the well-built Akshay, lying in bed, a copy of *Teens Today* in hand.

'Thanks, Akshay bhaiyya,' Sandeep said, smiling. Akshay was the big brother Sandeep never had. Two years older, he was the one who had encouraged Sandeep to pursue cricket and take it up professionally.

Akshay's father was Sandeep's father's supervisor, a foreman at the factory, though the families lived as close friends in the same compound. Sandeep was always over at Akshay's house. He looked up to him as a role model, imitated his hairstyle, his manners, and often borrowed his things. Akshay was a feared fast bowler in the school cricket team, and Sandeep was the only one who could put him away for boundaries with ease.

'So, what's happening with the team selection?' Akshay asked.

'Tomorrow, bhaiyya. I hope I get the chance to bat for a while...'

'Sandy, this is the National Junior Team selection. What are you doing here? Let's go and practice, I'll bowl to you. Let's work on your strokes, they're your biggest strength.'

'Okay, let's go. That's a good idea,' Sandeep said enthusiastically. 'I'll go and get my bat. Can I borrow your pads and gloves?'

'You don't have to ask, Sandy. Take my bat. You prefer using it anyway. It's better to use this instead of yours,' he said, pulling it out from where it lay—on top of the almirah—and handing it to Sandeep. 'You can also take my Adidas shoes,' he added, before he put on his own. Ready, the boys left to practise in the ground nearby.

The next day was a turning point in Sandeep's life. He picked the bowling with ease, putting on display spectacular strokes and driving every second ball over the boundary. At fourteen, he was picked to tour England as a member of the Indian under-18 team. There had been no looking back since. Two years later, he played for Karnataka, taking the team to victory in the Ranji Trophy. After a year, he was included in the national team to tour Sri Lanka.

He saw little of Akshay after that. He had left for the National Defence Academy a few months before Sandeep made it to the national team. Akshay, till then, had been his pillar of support. He would cheer for him during matches, bowl to him in the nets and help him train and remain fit every day.

He saw him last in Delhi, a few years later. Akshay had come to visit him during a test match. He had taken special leave for the event. They spent some time over dinner, discussing their starkly different lives and plans for the future. Akshay had always wanted to be in the army, to be in the middle of combat, to 'save the good guys'. Sandeep had noticed then how Akshay looked a lot more sober than he used to in his younger days. He had a crew cut, had put on muscle and looked intimidating. 'Fighting at the border is more about saving your own life and the lives of the members of your regiment. I don't know who the good guys are anymore. We all think we are good,' he had said with a faraway look in his eyes—eyes that had seen life, death and survival despite all odds. Sandeep could never agree with Akshay's choice of working for a mere eight thousand rupees in conditions where the temperature hovered around minus twenty degrees, with no guarantee of coming back. He had tried to reason with him, but Akshay seemed self-assured.

That was three years ago, Sandeep recalled.

After that, it was only the occasional text message or call on his birthday or festivals. He hadn't remembered Akshay's birthday in the last two years. He had even forgotten to invite him for his lavish birthday parties or his four-day wedding celebration across Bangalore, Delhi and Goa, though his parents had kept in touch with Akshay's family and tried to include them in the celebrations. He had received a text message from Akshay six months ago, a day after his wedding: 'Sandy mere hero, congratulations! Bhabhi is very beautiful, lucky hai tu. I saw her pictures on the net. Everyone here is talking about your wedding. It's freezing here and I can't wait to meet both of you when I come to Delhi.'

'Thanks,' he had messaged back. He never went to meet him though, as he was busy moving from one shindig to another. As far as he knew, Akshay was still in love with Priya, a girl who was a fellow student of theirs in school. He had plans to marry her and settle down. Now, Major Akshay Bhisht was dead.

'Give me your BlackBerry, I'll put it in my bag,' Ashmita said as they walked with their entourage towards the security check.

He handed it to her quietly, his mind whirling up a tornado of emotions, struggling to bring words out of his mouth on Akshay's demise. 'The funeral is tomorrow morning,' his father had messaged before Sandeep had handed the phone to her.

'I need to go and pick up a new outfit for Shamita's party tonight. What are you going to wear?' Ashmita asked, turning her gaze towards him as she zipped up her Chanel handbag.

'I... I don't know yet. Ma just called to...' he stuttered, still gasping to find the right words and remain composed.

'Maybe you should come with me. I can pick something from Deepika Gujral's store for you.'

I do not want to go to a fucking party, he wanted to say, but managed a nod. He had been paid to make an appearance. It was a wine and cheese soirée to celebrate Shamita Khanna's new paintings.

'I don't like Shamita, she's such a slut! Her paintings are so down market. If I want to see a village or a bazaar I'll go to one. Why would I want to see it in a painting?' she said, before turning away with a frown. Sandeep didn't respond.

After passing through the security amid prying eyes and a cricket-crazy crowd that cheered and smiled and showed thumbs-up signs, they walked past the boarding gate towards the aerobridge. Ashmita handed him his phone, which was ringing. It was his manager at the other end.

'I'm boarding, Sumit. Anything important?'

'You'll have to be at Saxena's brunch tomorrow morning. The old man has invited a few friends over...'

'I'm not sure. I might fly to Bangalore tonight for a funeral.' Ashmita turned to him with a frown.

'The Saxenas are close to signing you up for a multi-year deal to launch your designer label, your own line of fashion wear, and bring your wife on board to run it!' That will keep this damn woman out of my hair,' Sandeep thought. 'You don't want to upset them, do you? They've decided on brunch as you're busy. You're dining with the Home Minister and his family tomorrow evening.' Sumit was relentless.

'Can we... maybe... put off the dinner?'

'The minister's son loves you, and we need the father to support the extra security for you. He has cancelled a trip to Agartala after your confirmation of the dinner plans.'

'Hmm... I'm just boarding the flight.'

'I've confirmed you and Ashmita for brunch with the Saxenas,' Sumit said and hung up.

Sandeep had received a message on his phone in the meanwhile: 'Getting into Delhi for Shamita's blast tonight, dude. Let's take our beauties and hit the streets after the party.' It was Zubair Mirza, the popular Bollywood star he often partied with in Mumbai. They both shared a love for sports bikes and the fast life. The popular perception was that they were best friends. In fact, he had first met Ashmita at Zubair's party—she was doing a cameo in his movie back then.

'I feel bad, but can't make it. Sorry,' he typed, and sent the SMS to his father. His entourage moved stealthily down the aisle to take their seats at the back of the aircraft. No piña coladas served by the prettier and more cheerful crew for them.

'Switch off your damn phone!' Ashmita scoffed at him with a frown as she strapped on her seatbelt. She rattled off about how she was again without a phone because of him.

'Oh my God! I can't believe it is *the* Sandeep Sinha. You are great, saar,' said a portly south Indian man, dressed in a business suit, taking his hand and shaking it vigorously. He flashed his crooked teeth and continued standing there as the flight attendant, with a plastic smile on her face, wondered what to tell him. She couldn't be rude to the business class passenger—he was special, as opposed to the coolies on the other side of the drapes separating the rows of passengers in economy from business class.

'I have never seen such a stylish stroke player. A Don Bradman reincarnated in India. I was there when you hit a century in sixty balls against Pakistan in Eden Gardens. Saar, waat ya innings! fantastic, too good! You hit that mad man Aslam out of the grounds three times! Such effortless strokes, so much class! Wonderful! You are a National Hero, saar,' he gesticulated, almost frothing at the mouth. Sandeep closed his eyes and felt an arrow pierce his heart.

A Grey Oak Foundation initiative. For the many soldiers who man our borders despite the looming threat to their own lives.

The Last Week

VENKATARAGHAVAN SRINIVASAN

Silence greeted Ramesh when he opened his front door. There were no sounds of children playing; no delighted yells of 'Papa' to greet his arrival. He missed the sizzle of spices frying in the pan and felt its absence acutely. He looked into the kitchen, half-expecting to see Aarti standing over the stove, her back to him and face in profile, flushed with the heat, turning to pick up a wooden ladle. He draped his arms around her midriff and kissed the hair at the top of her head. She lifted her shoulders, screwed her neck and looked up for a quick peck on the lips. His twins dragged him to their room, eager to show him some monstrously important result. Ashok raced ahead, unable to contain himself. Nandini's tiny pink fingers, with their dewdrop nails, curled tightly around his own wrinkled forefinger. He filed this image away in his mind. His daughter was laying out, in a very serious voice, the menu for the dinner she had prepared for him. She led him to her little table on which plastic plates and utensils were arranged neatly. His son appeared by his elbow with his toy train and excitedly told him how the special train left the Mumbai railway station and took off to go to outer space because he was the train driver and decided that he wanted to go see how the Earth looked from the moon; all his passengers had bought tickets.

That night, Ramesh could not sleep until he threw back the blankets and found his laptop in the darkness to which his eyes had adjusted. He put on soft music to fill in the vacuum created by the absence of Aarti's breathing.

As Ramesh walked into office, he nodded greetings all around. Jayaram pushed back his chair and leaned over the cubicle wall.

'So, the wife and kids have left, have they?' he asked.

'Yup,' said Ramesh, 'I put them on a flight yesterday to New York.'

'They're not flying alone, are they?'

'No, Aarti's parents are flying with her,' said Ramesh. 'There's no way she can do such a long flight with two young kids all by herself.'

Jayaram nodded and asked, 'So, when do you fly out?'

'In a week,' said Ramesh, switching on his computer. 'I need to wrap things up here, get the movers to come in and pack everything up, and pack a couple of suitcases myself.'

'You know you will be missed around here, right?' Jayaram said and clapped him on the back.

'How was your day?' Aarti asked. She clicked her tongue when Ramesh recounted Jayaram's questioning. 'I think it's the office. You speak in questions too, you know.'

'Do I?' he asked, his eyebrows pressing towards each other.

'You're doing it right now,' she laughed.

Ramesh speared a piece of penne along with half a black olive. He loved the silence in Aarti's laughter. He got up from the sofa and headed to the kitchen to clear up. Aarti would have been cross with him for not eating at the table and for watching television while he ate, no matter if it was on mute. Why was it on mute? There were no children sleeping in their bunk bed, Ashok in the upper with his mouth open on his Lightning McQueen pillowcase and Nandini in the lower with one arm around a pink elephant and the thumb of the other in her mouth.

In bed that night, Ramesh threw back his blanket and sought his laptop.

At a little after noon, Ramesh leaned back satisfied. He marvelled at how de-stressing it was to bring an end to his work. He had expected to feel morose, but instead, he found he was energised and enthused.

Ramesh's reverie was broken by a cheery 'Hi' that was more sung than said. He swivelled his chair and was blinded by a flash of red.

'Hi, Joanna,' he said, massaging his eye sockets with his thumb and forefinger. 'Boss not keeping you busy?'

'Humph!' she snorted. 'He needs two secretaries.'

'Ah, but you're as good as two secretaries,' said Ramesh.

'Aww, that's so sweet,' sang Joanna, tilting her head. Her straight black hair rested on her shoulder. Ramesh gazed at the neckline of her deep red top.

'I was wondering,' said Joanna, 'if you would like to join us for lunch. Some of us are going out.'

'Sure,' he said. She smiled and turned to go. Ramesh watched her knee-length dark grey skirt stretch over the curves of her hips.

Ramesh didn't remember much about lunch, except that Joanna had sat next to him. They had been the largest group in the restaurant--about eight people--and consequently, the noisiest. He did recall everybody singing 'For He's a Jolly Good Fellow' after dessert. Some of them had hugged him after that.

'What's the matter?' asked Aarti as Ramesh picked at his macaroni-and-cheese. 'I thought you'd have been pleased with the lunch. Singing for you was really sweet.'

'It was,' replied Ramesh.

'Anyway,' said Aarti, 'the kids really missed you today. They were playing with the hose in the backyard, all giggly and wet, when Ashok suddenly stopped and stood still, with water dripping off every part of him, and said, 'I wish Papa was here.' And then, just as abruptly, he went back to hosing his sister, who was screaming with glee.'

Ramesh willed a tear to cloud his eyes, but none appeared. Instead, he switched channels on the television and settled down to watch a sitcom, un-muted. He wanted to pick up the phone and find Aarti at the other end, closer than she'd been the last week. He wanted to tell her that he too missed her and the kids, more than they could imagine.

Before settling in between the sheets, Ramesh switched on the music, but he still tossed and turned for two hours. Just as he drifted off to sleep, he realised that the battery on his laptop needed to be charged and the music had stopped.

Ramesh walked into office feeling like a marked man. Everybody looked at him as if he had a terminal disease. He glared like a cornered big cat when Jayaram asked him, 'So, last day today, huh?' Tension hung in the air, over his head and behind his chair, as he spent the day closing everything and clearing out his desk and drawers. He felt like everybody was holding their breath and waiting for him to die so they could exhale him and continue.

That moment came a little after four. Joanna glided across the floor asking people to congregate in the conference room. Ramesh noted some relieved expressions. The strain was being lifted. He was being put to sleep. Jayaram placed a heavy arm around his shoulder and said softly, 'This is it, buddy.' Ramesh felt like Julius Caesar.

The boss congratulated Ramesh on his move and assured him that he would be sorely missed. A couple of colleagues said something along similar lines. Everything sounded like a eulogy. Samosas were passed around on paper plates. For the next ten minutes, buffeted by the sounds of munching, he stood by the door trying to smile sadly as people came up to him, said a commiseration or two, gripped his shoulder and shook his hand, and walked back to their lives. Ramesh felt like the Godfather at his son's funeral.

He slung his bag over his shoulder and began to walk out. The enthusiasm of moving into a new life had been replaced by a terrifying sense of loneliness. Where was he going? Whom to? There was nobody waiting for him. People stood up to peer over their cubicle walls and called out goodbyes and good wishes. Ramesh's eyes met Joanna's. He numbly waited for the elevator to take him into infinity.

❧

'Why didn't I come with you?' Ramesh asked, though he already knew the answer. 'If you'd stayed another week, we could have flown together.'

'You said that if you had the kids and me out of the way, then you could get everything sorted out and done,' replied Aarti.

'I know what I said.' Ramesh wiped his brow. 'I'm just saying it would have been nice to have you guys here. I miss you.'

Aarti's jaw relaxed and her gaze softened. 'Why don't you go out tomorrow and meet up with some friends?'

'The movers are coming tomorrow to denude our home,' Ramesh gave a forced laugh. 'I'll have to pack before they get here.'

'I mean after that,' said Aarti. Then, in a softer tone, she said, 'Are you going to be all right?'

Ramesh ate his dinner in silence, staring forlornly into the middle distance. After dinner, he switched on the lights in every room and ran his hand over his pieces of furniture. He already missed seeing the dinner cabinet lean against the lime green wall. He couldn't imagine looking up from his writing desk and seeing a cold New York street instead of a bustling Mumbai one.

'Don't jump on the bed, kids.'

'Ramesh, there's a lizard here! Come quick!'

'Aarti, are you going for a shower now?'

'Papa, come see this!'

Ramesh fell asleep listening to his family.

❧

The movers descended like a school of piranhas at a quarter to eleven and left before it was five, with a forty-minute break for lunch, barely leaving the four walls standing. Everything was dismantled, packed and shipped: the Sony 42' flat-screen television; Aarti's upright Kawai piano; the kids' bunk bed (w/ ladder); two double beds; the teakwood dinner cabinet and writing desk; the dressers in matching oak brown; the antique dinner table with cushioned chairs and the brownish-black sofa that Aarti had ordered online.

Ramesh walked around the empty house, his footsteps ricocheting off painted bricks and cement, and was reminded of that day seven years ago when he and Aarti first came house-hunting. They were young and childless, no longer newly-wed but still in the giddy first years of marriage. They fell in love with the house, with its spacious rooms and large windows. They dreamed of and lived memories: sweeping a surprised Aarti off her feet on the first day and carrying her laughing over the threshold; waking up to sunlight streaming through white cotton curtains; painstakingly searching for the right furniture to build a home together; Aarti's pregnancy followed by the madcap dash to the hospital; coming back with a baby each; bawling in each other's arms outside the nursery school on the first day they handed the children over to the teacher.

Ramesh checked into a hotel for the night. His phone chimed.

'Hi,' a voice sang.

'Who is this?'

'Joanna, from the office.'

'Hi, Joanna,' he said. 'This is a pleasant surprise.'

'I'm glad,' she said. 'I know you're flying to New York tomorrow. I was hoping we could go out tonight to, you know, celebrate your last night in Mumbai.'

At that moment, everything that had happened in the past week came surging back to Ramesh: returning home to utter silence; desperately seeking his wife's warmth and finding cold machinery instead; walking out of his office into a cavernous emptiness; seeing his possessions being carted off; closing the front door to an empty house to never open it again.

'Sure,' he croaked.

Ramesh drank too quickly. He thought Joanna's flattering black dress was cut too low as well as too high. When she leaned across the table, he saw deep cleavage and wondered if she was wearing a bra. After dessert, she excused herself and made her way through the tables to the restroom. Ramesh gazed at her bare back, her swaying hips and her naked legs. He felt a rush of blood and his mouth went dry. He drained his glass and called for the check.

In the cab, Joanna put her hand on his thigh and sighed, 'I'm really going to miss you, Ramesh.' She left her hand there for the rest of the ride. Ramesh couldn't take his eyes off it. His racing, swirling brain implored that dainty, manicured hand with its red painted nails to move.

When they reached her place, Ramesh began to make noises about taking the cab home, but Joanna cut him short.

'Don't be silly, Ramesh,' she said. 'I'm not going to say goodbye to you in the back of a cab. Come on upstairs.'

Ramesh paid and followed her upstairs. She unlocked the door to her apartment and walked in. He stood in the middle of her living room on a rug of some sort, unaware of the details around him. They both stood there, looking at each other.

'Would you like something to drink?' asked Joanna.

Ramesh shook his head and mumbled.

'So, I guess this is it, then,' she said.

'I guess it is,' he said. 'Actually, I think I'll have a glass of water, if you don't mind.'

'Sure,' she said, kicking off her heels. 'Why don't you sit down and make yourself comfortable?'

Ramesh glanced at the sofa and decided he wouldn't. His head was starting to settle a bit, though he still felt very foggy. He turned to see Joanna bending over, reaching into the refrigerator. She brought him a glass of water which he drained. He noticed that one of the straps of her dress had slipped off her shoulder.

'Wow! That thirsty, huh?' said Joanna with a smile. 'Would you like some more?'

'No, thanks,' said Ramesh and put the glass on a side table.

'Well, I guess this is it,' she said, opening her arms and advancing to hug him.

Ramesh was taken by surprise. He wrapped his arms around her back while she clasped his neck. He smelt her perfume with a hint of fruit and felt the softness of her hair on his cheek. He rearranged his hands so that there was one hand on her lower back as well. She fanned out her hands and started exploring his back. He felt her press into him--he thought back to her bending over to reach into the refrigerator --and began to pull away, but she held him close. She lifted her head and looked up at him. Then, still looking into his eyes, she grabbed his bottom and thrust their hips together. She stretched up and kissed him on the mouth. Ramesh reacted without thinking; he kissed her back. They kissed fervently until the inevitable first break appeared. Both of them leaned their heads back and opened their eyes. Ramesh looked at Joanna, and didn't see Aarti. Joanna pounced on him with renewed vigour. He buckled under the rush and both of them fell on the sofa. She quickly straddled him and continued trying to kiss him while her hands went to work on his shirt buttons. Ramesh caught her by the shoulders and pushed her off. He got up and straightened out his rumpled shirt.

'What happened?' panted Joanna.

Ramesh looked away from her, lying across the sofa, her chest heaving, her lipstick smudged, and her dress riding up her splayed-out legs. 'I think I should leave, Joanna,' he said in as normal a voice as he could muster.

'You don't have to,' she said, standing up and reaching for him. 'It's your last night here, with me. Why don't you stay just for a little while?'

'No, I really don't think I should,' he said, pushing her away and making for the door. 'It's not right.'

Ramesh had his hand on the door knob when Joanna said simply, 'Look.'

He turned and saw her slip her arms out from under the thin straps. The dress slid to the floor around her ankles and she stood in black lace underwear. Ramesh smiled.

'No bra,' he thought.

Then, he turned the door knob and walked out.

'Sweetheart, are you boarding the flight?'
'I am, my love.'
'Have a safe flight. I'll see you soon.'

The Pink Slip

MALCOLM CARVALHO

Shankar leaned back in his chair, tossing the paperweight from one hand to the other. He had to do it again today. There was no escape. How he hated his job now.

This was due to the darned recession. He had already fired a dozen employees in the last two weeks. Like most other IT companies, his organization too had been severely hit by the economic slowdown. What else could it do, other than sending employees on six-month long, unpaid holidays? Or even worse, handing a worker the pink slip?

He thought of the experience he had had doing the dreaded job of firing people in the last two weeks. His day would begin with going through a list of employees, then letting each one on the list know that the organization no longer needed their services. The management had told him to do this in the mildest possible manner. 'It's a difficult time for everyone. Let's ensure the exit is smooth,' a senior manager had told him. Yeah, right! The top-level management decided who was to be fired and yet they did not even have the courage to have a word with the employee. So almost every other day, for the last two months, Shankar would call a few people to his cabin and somehow summon the courage to tell them they had been fired.

By now, he was being called names behind his back—The Messenger of Death, Encounter Specialist. Some even called him Sharpshooter. He had shrugged uneasily when he overheard the titles in canteen conversations. He himself did not like the organization's strategy of dealing with the recession. They could have introduced pay cuts across all hierarchies. Even that would cause resentment among the employees, but at least it would not polarise the environment as it did now. There were already questions being asked in water cooler conversations—Why isn't anyone from the top management being sacked? After all, firing a senior manager would save the company's coffers much more than packing off an entry- or mid-level programmer. But strange were the ways of the management. Maybe they wanted to save their ilk first. If others had to face the brunt of it, let them be damned. Shankar remembered what one of his senior managers had said at a meeting over tea with a few developers: 'We created the recession, so we need to face the consequences.' When a programmer asked how he had created the recession, Mr Manager had simply shrugged off his question and said, 'Well, you need to have greater maturity to understand this.'

Maturity, bull! They were all like that—thick-skinned, smooth-tongued, management-quote-mouthing assholes. Firing those at the lower levels was just a ploy to keep their jobs safe and their pay cheques as large as ever. And the dirty job of firing employees was assigned to him.

Enough of ranting, he thought. He needed to get going with today's candidates. He opened his diary, flipped over a few pages, and read the list of people who were to be fired that day.

Picking up the phone, he called the first person on the list. 'Rahul, I need to talk to you for a few minutes. Can you come over now?'

'Yeah, sure.'

'Okay,' he grunted before hanging up.

Rahul, the man who could solve most problems at work with his skill and ingenuity. Rahul, who always had a witty rejoinder to any remark thrown at him, whether it came from a new teammate or from his team leader. Rahul, who could make work seem like a breeze, yet make things difficult for himself with his candour and occasional blunt words. He was a livewire, but it was a shame he did not know how to rein himself in.

The portly figure of Rahul Dhende appeared just as Shankar was drifting further into his thoughts.

'What's up Shankar?' he asked in his inimitably friendly tone. Shankar found it even more difficult to break the news now.

Try as he did, he could not help meandering away from the matter. 'So Rahul, how's the project going? I heard you guys have been working long hours these days.'

'Yeah, demanding client, challenging work, and uncompromising bosses,' Rahul winked. 'Not quite in that order though. Nevertheless, we should be done before this weekend. By the way Shankar, I hope you are free this Saturday.'

'Why?'

'It's my son's first birthday. Veena thought it would be a nice occasion to meet up with you and the other office guys. It's been a long time since we last met over dinner.'

Shankar's heart sank further. How could he get himself to tell Rahul about his sacking now?

'Well, I might be out of the city,' he looked away and said. 'Anyway, let's get back to what I was saying. Rahul, you know the organization's going through a rough phase. We've had to take some drastic measures, and even though it's not what I prefer, I have to do a job. You understand right?'

'I understand, Shankar. So is it my turn to receive a sending off?'

'Yes,' Shankar nodded. Rahul's straightforward question made it easier for him to talk now. 'Sorry to give you the news today. I wish I could have averted it. At least till your son's birthday had passed.'

'That's a professional's life, I guess. One can't guarantee job security these days. Do I get a notice period?'

'Two weeks.' Shankar could not look him in the eye.

'Okay, I need to get going quickly then.' Rahul's cheerfulness was gone, his voice sounded dry and stoic now.

As the programmer walked out, Shankar felt a twinge of helplessness. How could the organization let go of him? He felt worse because he could not do anything to prevent his termination. He had known Rahul for the last three years. In this period, they had developed a friendship beyond work, thanks to the common interests they shared—movies, football, trekking. He had found Rahul to be extremely well-read and friendly, albeit a little volatile. Conversations at lunch had ranged from Rahul's hilarious mimicry of the client's accent to insightful analyses of the stock market. With Rahul around, there was never a dull moment, and an unbiased opinion, if there was need for it, was always lurking around the corner.

How could he help Rahul now? His contacts in other organizations could help. Recession had hit them as well, but who knows, an opening may come up somewhere. Yes, he would try to get Rahul a new job. He launched a new mail message on his desktop, and selected a few friends in the *To* field. He typed in the subject: 'Any openings for C++ programmer?'

He began the email: 'Guys, a friend and colleague of...'

'Shankar, I need to have a chat again.'

It was Rahul peeking through the door held only a little ajar.

'What is it? You need to extend the notice period?'

'Not at all. Actually, even the two weeks are not needed. Tomorrow can be my last working day.'

'I hope you are not making this decision under stress. Take your time.'

Rahul flashed his mischievous smile. 'Not stress, Shankar. I have got another job. I knew the organization was not doing well. So I had started searching for options a few months ago. Got a couple of offers last week. They were not really interesting, so I'd decided to stay back here. But obviously, this organization does not have the same affinity for me.' He held out an envelope. 'Here's my resignation letter.'

Shankar did not know how to respond. He felt happy for Rahul, but also felt embarrassed by the irony of the situation. 'All the best, Rahul,' was all he could mutter as he picked the envelope.

'And yes, see you for dinner on Saturday,' Rahul said.

As Rahul walked out, Shankar smiled at the turn of events. He stared at his computer screen. The email he was typing was no longer needed. Just then, the phone rang.

'Hello... Yes, Sachin... What? But we had decided there'd be no more layoffs... So that decision has been reversed as well... Whatever is the management coming to?'

He slammed the phone and held his head in his hands. Perhaps this was inevitable. What went around came around, he told himself. I've got to deal with it. Regaining his composure, he got back to his desktop and changed the subject of the email to 'Any openings for a project manager?'

Plummet

AVNEE RAJESH & PRANAV MUKUL

'I lifted my foot off the parapet. The cool breeze seemed to promise freedom. I took the leap.'

It is now five hours and twenty-one minutes since I lost my son. I have been counting the minutes ever since I came to know the news. I walked into his room, hesitating at first—he had never liked my entering his space. Savita wasn't taking it too well. Her sobbing could be heard across the passage, in the bedrooms, to the back of the house. It wasn't like Kaushik, she tried to convince others. He always seemed to enjoy life! I couldn't take it, the crying and the lamenting. I walked into his room and sat by his bed. Under the pillow was a leather-bound book with the words *Diary 2009* etched in gold. I remember when I had given him this book, but I thought he would have thrown it away or lost it. As I flipped through the pages, I could see he had confided his words and thoughts to this book rather than to us, his family. His sketches filled other pages. He always did have a passion for drawing. I skimmed through the diary, till I reached 14 May 2009—which was when I saw him last.

'The door slammed shut. It was an odd alarm to wake up to, but

I was used to it. It was the same old ritual. My days never changed. I knew he'd be livid, so I decided to stay away from him. Breakfast was being made. I could hear the sound of the tawa sizzling as Ma poured the batter. As I looked at her, I could see her face. Tired. Not from this ordeal of cooking, but from this daily tussle between my father and my sister. It was unbearable for me, but it was draining her. No wonder she'd lose her cool with me. I guess that explained Papa's anger as well.

'My days never changed, like I said. But today, I felt numb—I could not react. So when my mother shouted, "Idiot! Study every once in a while!" and my father bellowed, "Fool! I don't know why we didn't enrol you in a hostel!" it just didn't affect me. I had decided and I knew that my way was the only way.

'When I thought of death, my death at least, I always thought I'd die with a smile on my face and happy thoughts in my mind, but I can't stop thinking of all the reasons why I have decided to do this. Of course, I'm worried about the kind of expression on my face when I reach the ground floor. Visions of my classroom invade my thoughts. I recall my classmates pointing and laughing at me in Class II because I had glasses. Fast forward to Class IV when I wet my pants. And throughout every games period, never being able to shoot a goal or go beyond five runs in cricket! Oh the smirks that came back to haunt me in Class IX! She had asked me out—ME! Naturally I was bewildered, but I thought that the time we'd spent in the physics lab as partners meant something to her too. So the next day, as asked, I came and told her how I felt. She did not apologize but said rudely, "Ha, you dweeb, that was just a dare! You think I'd like YOU of all people?" Taunting laughs, shouts of "Dumbfuck", "Retard" and "Pant wetter" rained down on me then.

'From Class VII to X, tuitions meant only one thing for me—

torture. Late to class? Sit-ups. No homework? Sit-ups. Untidy graphs? Torn and thrown in your face. Then sit ups. The girls would laugh, the boys would glow. I'd be mocked for my inability to speak Sanskrit and poor marks meant hanging about in the witch's lair for another four hours. The cycle of one bad tuition teacher after another continued. Come home late, be shouted at for that. The day we were given our report cards, I faced a double threat—that of a beating from my father, while I heard the neighbour's son being praised for passing. If I cheated and sucked up to the teachers as he did, maybe I'd manage to pass as well, I thought.

'When I became an adolescent, my life changed at home—I began to feel I was a burden for my family. I longed to change the situation. However, my best was not good enough. They were right after all—I was good for nothing. And I was always compared to my younger sister. Her mere presence would annoy me, despite her not being at fault. She won medals and certificates so often, and I watched as my parents gushed about her to their friends and relatives. But when they asked about me, it was evident from the expressions on their faces that they were pained and embarrassed. I always thought they would rather not talk about me. They covered up for me unhappily when I failed a year and lied about my age to people. They put up a façade of optimism for our neighbours, friends and relatives, but I always saw through it.

'Yesterday, when we returned from my cousin Anita's wedding reception, I knew the ride back would be far from pleasant. Rahul Uncle's son had just cleared the IIT entrance test and would join next month. He'd proudly proclaimed to my mother how much his son would earn—"Close to 1 crore as soon as he graduates." "That's if he passes from there," I said. "It's one thing getting in, but to stay in, that's another matter." "Since when have you learnt to talk like this? You talk to us like this, but when you are with outsiders, it's as if you suddenly transform into a mute object!" Ma shouted. It's true, I realised. I was just all pomp and no show. What had I ever done to be worth so much trouble? Why should anyone ever listen to me? How had I ever been able to prove myself to them? As I thought of all this, my father's anger at what I had said only grew. I'm sure he must have compared me with his nephew—his brother's son had cleared the IIT entrance, whereas I kept failing year after year. I'm sure he must have wanted to send me away somewhere. I had been spoilt at home—so spoilt that I never bothered to apply myself. All I had learnt was to question authority and act as though I was answerable to no one. He must have thought I had become arrogant. I went into my room when we reached home and locked the door. This always upset my father, and he banged on the door. I wasn't calm either—I glowered at him when I opened the door. I kept wondering if some of the failure was also his responsibility—if I had failed as a son, he must also have failed as a father. So we fought verbally. Then, in a fit of rage, he grabbed the encyclopaedia. I always knew keeping the encyclopaedia within reach was a bad idea. That bruise only seems to be getting worse now.

'This day was inevitable—with my self-confidence beaten to the ground, it only meant that this day would come sooner rather than later. I don't know how I will die—with a smile on my face and happy thoughts in my mind, or otherwise. But I've always thought it to be something like this. I lifted my foot off the parapet. The cool breeze seemed to promise freedom. I took the leap.'

Tainted Love

ROHAN SWAMY

I struggle to find an apt description for the place. Sandwiched between Grant Road and the lesser known suburbs of Byculla - Mazgaon Docks, the forgotten stretch known as Kamathipura is unlike the brightly lit streets of De Wallen in Amsterdam or the Reeperbahn of Hamburg. It feels more like wasteland. The infamous red light district of Mumbai, the biggest in Asia, and one of the oldest, is not the best description that a place deserves. Endless lanes merge into one another as I walk through the evening shadows. On one side is the bustling Grant Road suburb, where life hurries on at its usual fast pace, while on the other is Byculla, which harbours one of the most famous chor bazaars of Mumbai.

But Kamathipura is different. Seeing an unknown man carrying a dusty duffel bag and walking down the street, girls stare wide-eyed. Some glance at me fleetingly as I walk by. A flat-faced girl with big eyes and a lot of garish make-up gives me a flirtatious smile, and this time I smile back. Emboldened by my response, she beckons me to come into a small shack, barely big enough to hold an old iron cot. I shake my head indicating otherwise. To tempt me further she lifts her short skirt, revealing a dark patch of hair between her legs. I shudder at the cheery smile with which she does that. I shake my head more vigorously, indicating a firm no. Her skirt drops down, along with her smile and face. Dejected, she looks at me, indifferent again. I walk on, and she finds a fresh pair of eyes staring at her. The routine is repeated, and Kerry King screams 'God hates us all' in my ears.

Joan has actually asked me a million times about this visit of mine to this godforsaken place. Sitting in the comforts of a cosy four-room apartment that overlooks the St. Charles Bridge, where I had kissed her for the first time, she still does not understand why the magazine has sent me so far to this ghetto. And yet, when I tell her the story of Chanda, she understands why I have come this far. As I finish speaking to her on the phone, I find myself again in the company of a new girl. She is pretty, or had been at one time. She wraps herself around me, much to my surprise. I have been told by Khan, my local guide in this suburb, that these girls always try to fleece outsiders, and there is a good chance that I might get robbed of even my clothes if I am not careful with them. As I struggle to untangle her from me, another girl comes and offers me her services. Seeing that her charm is fast fading and that a prospective customer is going, the girl unwraps herself from around me and starts yelling at the other girl, telling her to back off, along with the choicest abuses hinting at her parentage. I just gently push them aside and reach Khan's little liquor den a few paces away. Khan, as I have known him through my friend Marty, a photographer who had done some stories here, is a hustler in the true sense of the word. He sells bootlegged alcohol, to sordid looking customers and has a melange of supplies for everyone. Right from condom packs, to pornographic movies and old copies of *Hustler* and *Playboy*, he supplies them all—for a price, that is. Seeing me enter, he welcomes me with a warm smile which displays his tobacco-stained teeth. He takes me to the rear of the little shanty of his, seats me on a charpoy and offers me a very warm cola to drink. The humidity in this area is at an all-time high, and my thin white shirt and faded brown trousers do little to alleviate the heat and the hatred of this hostile land. Trying to be as courteous as possible, Khan offers me advice in the very famous Mumbai dialect of Hindi. I have not told him that I am here to capture Chanda's life. Instead, as Marty had advised me, I got to him through a shady restaurant in Byculla saying that I wanted to have a good time here. And I also showed him a picture of Chanda, saying that this was given to me by a friend who insisted that I contact him and get to her. He bought it, and here I was.

'Chanda is not very pretty,' he warns me. 'She is almost twenty-eight years old, very big for you, no?' He continues laughing as he spits out a betel leaf that he has been chewing. I don't reply but smile back. 'Why don't you look at Sameera?' he asks, simultaneously yelling out to his minion to fetch her. A while later, she walks in. I am guessing she is not more than twelve years old. Her swollen eyes tell a story as they meet mine. Filled with shame, I look away, unable to meet her gaze. A minute later, after Khan's careful scrutiny and my subsequent rejection, he dismisses her, quietly asking his minion to save her for late evening. I don't really know how to react to this. Sometime later, after the girl is long gone and the warm cola drink finished, through bits and pieces of my own accented Hindi I learn that every vile desire a man could dream of is for sale here. And ironically, child virgins are the region's most noted delicacies. I look at the IWC strapped to my pale white wrists bearing the scars of a forgotten past, and signal to Khan that I need to get going. He smirks and says that I am getting impatient. Then, after what feels like a decade, he takes me to a falling, old English-style building that proudly displays a license from the year 1929, showing that it is a brothel where prostitutes can work. Having shown me the place where Chanda does her business, Khan, with his characteristic tobacco-stained smile, goes back to his shanty.

The room is modest and clean. Chanda, dressed in a bright red sari, ushers me in with a warm smile. She shows me a picture of her along with Marty, and even boasts about a battered old mobile phone that has his number stored on it. Barely five feet in height, her blouse and sari wrap around her giving her the appearance of an Egyptian sarcophagus. A red bindi, red bangles and flowing black curly hair complete the image of a fluorescent fakir. Her charm and grace has been fading away slowly. Through her frail smile, the disinterestedness of human life peeks out. The thin wrists have quiet burn marks that show through the bangles, and her gait has lost the poise that one would normally associate with someone her age. And yet it is the expression in her eyes that speaks volumes. It is somewhere between hoping for a different world and the fact that this is her world and everything that she can associate with it. Noise, silence, the words reverberate through my ears. And I hear someone deep within me screaming, 'Noise... noise... my kingdom for some noise.'

There is a cot in the room, a cupboard on one side, a small table and a chair on the other. I wonder about her religion and her ideals, and how, despite having being mocked by the gods, her faith in them continues to be strong. I marvel at it, staring at my pale white wrists occasionally. Her smile however is unending. She has time for it always. 'It makes more sense to be a little happy doesn't it?' she asks. 'It could have been a lot worse. I could be on the streets, maybe even dying of AIDS... Who knows? At least here I have a roof over my head. And I even have a bank account with money for myself. That is reassurance enough for me,' she says.

Sometime later, as a heavy storm begins to blow outside, she goes out quickly to take a look and comes back in. Her walk is definitely unique. I really think one cannot miss it. You can actually hear it. Her dark hair with flowers in it reminds me of something. I struggle to remember what. Then I remember. She has a quality similar to that of those Matryoshka dolls, which I had seen when I was doing a story in Khabarovsk, Russia. The gait, clumsy as it is, has its own charm. And I realise that when I hear her giggling and gesticulating. It's like when she is in the vicinity, it gathers you in the eye of the storm.

I struggle to begin the conversation. Looking at my unsure face, she begins it herself. 'I am sure even you have problems. We all have them, don't we? I am here doing this, you might have had your own. It is the essence of our existence,' she says.

She begins telling me her story. Born in a small town in Andhra Pradesh, Chanda was married off when she was barely a young girl. Her only memories of her birth are the fact that her grandmother used to tell her that she was born on a very rainy day. 'But the night sky was clear, with a bright moon in the sky. That's how they named me,' she says, her face lighting up suddenly. I smile. The rain beats the tin covered window pane harder. A voice on the Murphy radio set hanging on the wall sings an old Hindi song about blowing off one's troubles in a cloud of smoke. My hare lipped smile breaks up again. 'If only it were that easy,' something within me says.

After having lost her husband within three years of her marriage, with two kids to support and no job to pursue, she found her way to the chawls of Kamathipura. And now, ten years later, with two sons aged thirteen and twelve, she still continues to search for the light and still continues to search for a better existence.

Chanda speaks to me about her family now. Her father was a farmer who died many moons back and her mother, frail and blind, is still alive. Chanda looks after her too. There are siblings but they have been separated from one another by the wiles of time and circumstance. Chanda has memories of her childhood too. But they don't come along as easily as her laughter does. She doesn't know where her other siblings are. And she doesn't want to talk about the details of growing up in penury and want under the scorching southern sun. Maybe she just doesn't want to remember the pain. And I have wondered, ever since I tried to obliterate myself, how to define pain. But when I see her talk in such a calm manner about a life that has dealt her nothing but blows, I understand her sense of immunity. Even though she stops occasionally to glance into the distance, where she seems to lose herself, there are the remains of a little girl in her eyes. Of a childhood raped. Of a girl smothered. Of a set of memories systematically killed.

The dial on the IWC points to half past twelve. She gets up, dusts the front of her sari and offers me food. 'You must eat. You have come a long way just to hear my story. The least I can do is offer you food,' she insists as she offers me a plate full of rice and curried chicken which she had ordered from a small roadside joint a long time back. I do not say anything. I switch the tape into record mode again and hear her talk as I take occasional spoonfuls of food—she has got a spoon for me too, so that my hands do not get dirty.

I have realized that the manner in which people talk of adolescence differs across the world. For most girls that age, when I was growing up, it was all about wearing pretty dresses, smearing make up and ensuring that they got to roam around with the coolest boys in class, so that they could boast of it to their girlfriends. Chanda didn't have any of that. 'The men,' as she still refers to them, with haunted eyes, gang-raped several times.

It resulted in her having repeated abortions and several venereal diseases long before she was eighteen. For the girls I knew or had grown up with, this was a stark reality of which they were oblivious. I know for a fact that Joan was. And yet, they used to be lost in utopian dreams of finding a prince charming riding on a white horse and taking them to kingdoms far beyond.

Chanda on the other hand found Bada Tamma, the local agent who helped her finally find deliverance in a brothel where she was sold by her family. 'It is the destiny of many girls from my village. Middlemen habitually make the rounds for girls like us,' she says. These middlemen bet on poverty—poor farmers are unwilling to care for their girl children. They are desperate because they till land made barren by the heat and dust, repeated monsoon failures and over cropping. All this ensures that Chanda and the other girls from her village, like the stars on a clear night sky, will continue to light up the shabby little rooms in Kamathipura for the dregs of society.

But there is something spectral about her. There are scars on her body, knife wounds and burn marks, but Chanda refuses to stop smiling and offers me tea. It is almost three in the morning. 'If you stay longer, I will cook for you,' she says happily. 'That is, if you feel like eating with me,' she adds as an understandable afterthought.

I sip from a small steel tumbler full of black tea and a withered piece of lemon to go with it. Chanda offers me black tea citing the truth—that there is no milk in the room. As we continue talking about her life here in this little cubicle of a room, she tells me stories. Some painful, some that depict the horror of the atrocities inflicted on her. To illustrate the point further, she lifts her sari and shows me her arms and legs. I can see knife and burn marks. Chanda's body has withstood other unimaginable violence. She talks about these injuries in a matter-of-fact voice, as though reading out a child's report card. There's no drama, no tears, no self-pity. 'How's the tea?' she asks, smiling, trying to cheer me up.

Chanda is in her late twenties and wants to live in the brothel till the last ebb of life. 'I can't go anywhere now. This is my home. I go to my village whenever I want, send money every month for my children's education and hope they will do well in life,' she says. My eyes whirl around the little room again. It is a clean room. It's about the size of the pantry back home in Prague. But it's clean, cool and optimistic. There are shadows lounging around and geckos are mating on the wall. The barebones of human civility are evident.

'There is nothing else in my life,' she continues. 'I am a prostitute. It is my job.' What the scum of the world does. The garbage can. Born to be used. They are all random phrases that dart across my mind. But they hold promise, especially in her case. I have no words, just as I always never had them. Her bright cheery smile comes back again. Through an impish grin, like long lost gossip cousins, she nudges me about my life. 'Are you married? I am sure your wife must be very pretty. Not like me. And your children? How many do you have? I think you have three children. Two daughters and one son? Hai na?' she asks it all in a flourish. I nod, blushing, and show her Joan's picture along with me in front of St. Vitus' Cathedral. I tell her we got married recently. With childlike innocence she says, 'Your country is very beautiful. Do you have women there who live and do jobs like me?' I nod a sad yes to her. But I tell her that life is not easy for them either. 'Maybe God doesn't love us a lot, that's why we do these things,' she muses as I give her a pensive smile. The storm has long since died down. The time on the IWC shows a ghostly 4.30 in the morning. I change the tapes on the recorder as I continue to make small talk about Joan and myself. She listens in quiet amusement, taking swigs of the last remaining tea.

A look into her daily life reveals her profession in placid terms to me. Chanda charges ₹300 for a session. A portion is handed to the madam. She usually has four or five customers a night. Occasionally, she gets one customer for a night, whom she charges between ₹1,500 and ₹2,000.

As the warm humidity of the early hours of Mumbai start filtering in, Chanda says, 'I have customers I have known for years. I have loved too, but now I don't love like that. I think I have grown up. That mad, desperate love is over, thank god. My mind doesn't connect to the body. It's just a job. I guess love now is just a tainted emotion for me.'

She says that there are many customers who just want to talk and tell her their problems. 'They pay me because I listen. No one listens to anyone in the big city. No one has time. Everyone has problems. When I hear them, I feel my problems are nothing,' she says with deep insight.

I have gauged that she is a believer in karma. She says that it's absolutely true. Otherwise how can I explain her life to her, she asks. 'I haven't even had the chance to be a bad person. I was raped as a child. So there must be something I did in a previous life and this is my punishment. When I die, my punishment will be over. My next life will be good. I have done nothing wrong in this life. It is destiny, nothing else.' I look for answers in the room. The brown bed sheet, the green pillows and the thin mattress that have seen her struggle a million times offer me none.

I ask her about God, religion, about her spirituality. Her room has several pictures of deities. In a world distraught by the rape of their souls, it is the only soothing balm that they have, for themselves, and for one another.

'I am born a Hindu and I pray to all the gods and goddesses. Religion doesn't matter to me. I feel happy when I pray. So I pray. I don't know anything else. Maybe there is no God. I don't know. Maybe is not kind, maybe is not just, maybe is. But praying makes me feel happy and strong, so I do it,' she continues to speak into my tape recorder as I listen dumbstruck.

It's early morning now. The silver beams of light come through the tin panes of the room. The rooms adjacent to it, however, are full. Business is good like it always is. The cubicle's door is shut and there is no noise intruding in our space. A long triangular stretch of light seeps in from under the door. Some girls, who have not been taken for the night, sleep on charpoys in the hall outside. Chanda keeps talking and giggling like a schoolgirl. She is kind and loving and wants to pamper me. To the extent that she gets some more rice and heats some dal for me. 'Your journey has been long. Eat as much as you can. Who knows what tomorrow will bring? We haven't seen it,' she says.

Finishing our early morning snack, Chanda who has become a gossip colleague, as I have christened her, shows me a picture of her two sons. Two little boys, frail, tanned, well-oiled hair and powdered up, in matching blue shirts with white stripes, grinning away. It is a studio shot taken in her village. There is a world apart from her own, a world unlike the ghetto where she lives—a world where it is okay to be born again.

'When I meet my mother, I wonder what dreams she had for me. She must have had some dreams at least. I have dreams for my boys too, and I hope they will live their lives well. Luckily, my mother is blind and can't hear or speak too well. If she knew what I have gone through, her heart would ache,' she says. She tells me that there are stories here too. The girls have their crushes. Sometimes they squabble over who had a more handsome customer, but then again, it's in good spirit. Occasionally the fights are bitter, when they have to fight for the customer's attention. But it's all normal here. Having experienced that a few hours ago, I am inclined to believe every word she says.

Chanda however tells me that the girls don't entertain customers during their menstrual cycle, but hang around and chat. 'It's holiday time then,' she says with a laugh. They also eat out with customers. Vendors come to the brothel with fruits, vegetables, flowers, clothes, utensils and jewellery—almost everything the girls and the brothel needs. So there is no need to shop unless they need the colours, smells and noises of the bazaar.

The brothel here, unlike the street smart women who spread out a charpoy and display their wares through skimpy night gowns that conceal nothing, is spic and span. A doctor on the street below is always available. He lives above the clinic. Sometimes the girls fall sick, but Chanda has never been unwell. 'I have never fallen sick, never even had fever, I don't know how. I am so lucky. Maybe it's my prayers.'

There is order and the brothel runs without a murmur. Fights between the girls, though not uncommon, never last. There are some twenty girls in the brothel and Chanda is one of the senior ones. The others listen to her without protest. They know why they are here. Chanda helps them come to terms with the new circumstances when the old ones get frayed at the ends. The girls fight over new clothes and lovers, but it's not serious. What's a little bit of ego-bruising when they have been pulverised by life?

Chanda jokes and laughs till the tears trickle from her eyes. I simply can't fathom her and the others in the brothel. How do Chanda and the others keep laughing at life when it has always mocked them? The Buddha talked about clinging and non-clinging. This clinging response is inevitable. You become trapped in an endless web of tension and contraction. For most people, life is just this sensation.

But Chanda is like the wind song. Like the tribals of the old world, like the romantics of the thirteenth dimension. She is all of them. And even when she has been handed down all the possible venom that life has to offer, she can wipe away the tears, cover her bruises and stand up to all this and, instead of yelling back, can laugh an unadulterated, carefree laugh. There are problems: from the AIDS scare, to customers who inflict physical and mental traumas; from the land sharks who haunt the lucrative district to build swanky malls and hunt them back into the ocean, to understanding the plight of these so-called garbage bags who do not even solicit two clients per day or night, reducing them to a hand to mouth existence and an income as low as ₹20 per day. All this is there. But there is also the undying optimism of a woman I now know as Chanda.

The humid heat of Mumbai starts killing me again. I walk out of Chanda's room a different man, content in mind and spent in soul, seeking more questions than answers. My parting gift to Chanda, on her request, is a picture of me and Joan. She says that she will take the picture to the local Muslim saint's tomb and pray for our well-being. I wonder how someone so simple can harbour so much optimism. I have to tell her story to Joan. More importantly, I have to get Joan to meet her and tell her story to the world.

As I walk through the same squalid streets, the world looks different. It's as if Khan and his pervert shanty, the young girl who lifted her skirt to entice me, and the girl who had pressed herself against me have disappeared. Haunting images of the young Sameera and her much-in-demand virginity turn me into a worthless being leading a hollow existence on these never-ending streets. When out of nowhere I see Chanda's carefree smile, I instantly know that someday it will all fall into place in the grand order of things. Reaching the main bustling Grant Road, I hail a taxicab and get into it, asking him to take me to my hotel.

The radio blares with the smooth voice of the RJ who announces the next song. A slow Hindi song called 'Suno Na…' I feel it is Chanda's song. As I close my eyes, I see life dancing. I see Chanda dancing and smiling. She dances the last tango in Kamathipura as, slowly, everything fades into a distant grey background.

Hunch

KARTHIK K

'So how did you find out?'
'It was just a hunch based on a few observations.'

~⊙~

The Mumbai local train was not as crowded inside as it would be during the rest of the day. People were sitting silently in the compartment. Most of them were regular commuters. Some were travelling to open their shops early in the morning, and some didn't seem to have any destination. One of those people who didn't have a destination was Hafeez Rehman.

Having woken up early in the morning, Hafeez had chosen the Churchgate to Virar route—a slow train with twenty-six stops. He didn't have anywhere else to go, but had an important job to do today—God's job. And he felt very proud about it.

Restive as he was, he preferred to stand, even though some seats in the compartment were empty. It gave him an opportunity to observe the people around him. After all, it could be their last journey—and his too. He wanted to look them in the eye before he did his job.

'What kind of hunch? What observations?'

'Something was not right about her. Well, to begin with, what is such a young girl doing out so early in the morning?'

'She could be going to college. Didn't you see the books in her hands?'

'Going to college at that time? Are you kidding me?'

The first stop came soon enough at Marine Lines and a few more people staggered into the compartment. Hafeez still didn't take his seat. There were now some young boys, with their cricket kits slung over their shoulders. They were happily chatting about the previous day's match. They were the only ones in the compartment who didn't appear to be drowsy—their eyes were filled with dreams.

All these things didn't matter to Hafeez as he clearly knew that he was the one who held their lives in his hands now. Their dreams would come true only if he permitted them to.

'By the way, I'm buying a new bat today,' said one of the boys.

'Really? That's great. When?' asked his friend.

'In the evening,' he replied.

In the evening? You have to be alive to buy your bat today, my boy.

'Maybe she wanted to get to college early.'

'I agree. But how early? Even if she got off at Virar, the last station, it would still be just six o'clock in the morning. And no college starts before eight.'

'Hmmm. Okay. I'm with you this time. What other things led you to this conclusion?'

'I didn't come to any conclusion. I told you, it was just a hunch.'

Charni Road and Grant Road had already passed by, and the train now stopped at Mumbai Central. The compartment started filling up. Even though he was very sure of what he would do, beads of sweat started forming on his forehead. His heart palpitated. For a moment, he even thought of getting off the train at the next station and taking some other route, some other train. But something made him determined to stay where he was. He skimmed the sweat off his face and stood like a rock, waiting for the right time to carry out his mission.

The air inside the compartment started getting warmer with each passing minute. Some people were being loquacious. None of these things made Hafeez uncomfortable, for he knew everything would come to a standstill in a few minutes. All the pleasures and pains of life would go, as if they had never existed.

'All right. It was your hunch. What did you observe about her that led you to confirm it?'

'The journal and the book she was carrying.'

'The journal and the book? What about them?'

'Did you at least see what book and journal she was carrying?'

'Some medical books, I guess. I thought she was a medical student.'

'Sure she was carrying medical books. But did you happen to look at those books carefully?'

Hafeez looked out of the window and felt sick to his stomach when he saw the darkness give way to the thin rays of the sun, shining with iridescent brilliance. In a few minutes, the world would wake up, but some people on this train would be put to sleep—permanently. Including him. Wasn't your whole life meant to flash before you at a time like this?

Hafeez was born in a poor Muslim family. He had four sisters and five brothers. His childhood was spent in pain, despair, humiliation and ostracism, which embittered him greatly. His adult life was no better. But like everybody else, he too got his share of luck when he was recruited by an organization. He then learnt about suicide bombing and its effects. And now, the time had finally come for him to carry out such a mission. Two of his brothers had done it in the past, and everyone in the family and the organization was proud of them. Now, it was his chance—a chance to do Allah's work.

'I didn't really look at the titles.'

'I will tell you. One was *Surgical Modalities in Typhoid Perforation* by P. Nembang, V. Aggarwal and a few others. Another one was *Postgraduate Orthopaedics* by A.B. Paul. Now tell me, what is a seventeen-year-old girl doing with an advanced medical journal and text book? Even if she were a student, she couldn't have been a postgraduate, for she was too young.'

'Hmm... Yes, you are right.'

'Something was fishy about her right from the beginning.'

Mahalaxmi, Lower Parel, Elphinstone Road, Dadar, Matunga Road and Mahim Junction had come and gone. The train stopped at Bandra. More people poured into the compartment. Even if he wanted to sit now, he wouldn't have got a seat. Hafeez saw a sea of people around him and tried to move past them for the first time. The seats were full, of course, but there was still space to move around freely. He went and stood near the door and leaned against the cold wall. He looked outside and took a deep breath as if it were his last. He then intercepted a glance from a man who was standing at the other end of the compartment and nodded. The other man acknowledged him by nodding in return.

There were enough people in the compartment to be killed.

Just a few more minutes.

'And that's the reason you wanted to stay with her?'

'There was one more thing. She was carrying medical books, but she was not wearing an apron. She was in plain clothes—jeans and kurta. These things could have meant a lot of other things, but I didn't have any other choice except to believe in my instincts. I could have frisked her in the beginning itself, but I wanted to make sure she was alone. Had I frisked her and had she had an accomplice, I would have alerted her partner. So I decided to stay with her and observe and asked the others to keep a vigil at different places based on the tip we had got from our sources.'

Mumbai local trains form the lifeline of the city. What if one of those lifelines is snapped? Around 6.1 million passengers commute on local trains every day, from four in the morning until one the next day. What if a small part of those commuters are killed in the wee hours of the morning? What would be the impact of such a horrible occurrence? It had happened before. What if it happened again?

Hafeez was prepared to do the unthinkable. He looked at all the commuters once and made up his mind. He then saw a beautiful girl leaving her seat and standing up. She reminded him of his own daughter. She was almost her age. So many lives would be lost today. Most importantly, he wouldn't be able to get back to his family again. Nevertheless, his wife and children understood this perfectly well. But the mission had to be carried out at any cost. His forefathers and leaders would be proud of him.

Lots of other stations had passed by, and the train was about to stop at Borivali, one of the busiest stations. It was the perfect place to blow up the train and the passengers on it. Hafeez touched the area slightly below his left shoulder and felt the bulge. Would he be able to do it?

The girl who had caught his attention was now standing a few feet away, in front of him. The train was approaching its destination. The girl was walking towards the door. Her stop had come, finally. The girl looked happy and a contented smile flitted across her face. The train started to pull over and, eventually, it stopped. The station had come. People were just about to swarm the compartment. It was time.

Now.

Hafeez felt the bulge below his left shoulder once again and said, 'Yah Allah.'

And bang.

○○○

'Right. And I know the rest of the story.'

'There is still one more thing. Once I had taken my place inside the train, I noticed she was aloof all through the journey. After about an hour, I noticed an unusual thing. I saw a mark of wires against her clothing around the stomach area, which also bulged out a bit. But the thing is, she was not carrying a music player or a hearing aid. That's when my hunch grew stronger. And when Borivali came she beamed with happiness and laughed hysterically. This time I was 100% sure. You know what happened next,' said the ATS chief.

'Of course I do, sir. I was there with you, wasn't I?' said his subordinate.

○○○

Hafeez was ready for this. He blanched, but not for more than a second. The girl threw away her books, lifted her kurta a little and pulled out a small trigger from inside. But before she could blow herself up along with the train and its passengers, Hafeez took out his Glock .35 from his shoulder holster and shot her in the head.

As the girl lay motionless in a pool of blood, the compartment of the train grew noisier with each passing second. Some shouted and screamed and some kept quiet as shock held them incapacitated.

Soon, the commuters were made to vacate the compartment. The commuters waiting on the platform were blocked from getting in.

'Damn it. We should have taken her alive,' said Hafeez, evincing his disappointment.

'You couldn't have done better, sir. There were a lot of people between you and her, and I was at the other end. If you had flinched even for a second, she would have blown herself along with us,' said Hafeez's subordinate.

'Well, at least our sources turned out to be credible. Get in touch with them pronto and let me know what comes up next. I have a feeling that this is all just the beginning,' said Hafeez Rehman, the chief of Anti-Terrorism Squad (ATS), Mumbai branch.

Rajasthan Summer

AYESHA HEBLE

It was a small town on the eastern edge of the Rajasthan desert in India, the sort you might have called a one-horse town, except that the appearance of even one horse would have caused quite a sensation. The only reason I happened to be there was that I was supposed to be changing trains from one line to the other, and the Indian Railway Service had managed to ensure that I should miss the connection by a mere two and half hours, and would have to wait for the next train to pass this way at 11.15 a.m. The next day! There was nothing else for it; I would just have to spend the night in the best manner possible and catch the train the next morning.

The Station Master was most apologetic. Yes, it was too bad--the inefficiency of the Railways. What we needed was another Emergency when the trains at least ran on time. Here I was, a young man from obviously a good family, and on important business no doubt, forced to spend the night in this God-forsaken hole of a place. No, no, there was no question of my spending the night in the waiting room; it would not be suitable at all. He seemed apologetic for the lack of comforts that his small establishment could offer, but was sure I would understand, this being a small town and all.

Was there any form of hostelry, then, where I might find a room at this late hour?

'Yes, yes; we have our own little hotel in this town; it's not very grand, you understand, since we don't really have too many visitors, but it's quite clean and comfortable. Yes, yes, you're sure to find room since we don't have…Oh, you mustn't mind the old man who runs the place, he's a bit cracked, you understand.' The Station Master pointed a finger at his head and rotated it in a gesture expressive of the old man's mental condition. But who was I to mind? If I could get a decent room, it didn't matter if he was a raving lunatic as far as I was concerned.

The Station Master pointed me down the street from the station in the direction of north, and said I would find it quite easily about one kilometre away. It was set back from the road a bit but I couldn't miss it since there was no other building before it. He wished me a good night and looked forward to seeing me the next morning.

'Remember, don't worry too much about the old man…!'

I walked rather briskly along the street in the direction that he had pointed me. The town seemed absolutely deserted except for two or three pie-dogs which manage to find themselves in every street in every town in India. It was about 7.30 in the evening, the time just before dusk that has a special name in India—*godhuli*—named for the dust raised by the cows returning home at the end of the day. It is a truly magical time, when everything settles down for the evening; evening lamps are lit and evening prayers are said before the evening meal. I thought of my own family in our own home in another part of India, settling down for their evening prayers, no doubt expecting me home a little later that night. I must remember to call them and let them know about the delay.

I wondered whether the hotel I was heading for would have STD… or a telephone even?

I was jolted out of my reverie by the blaring sounds of a brass band playing their own version of *Come September*, which for some reason has been immortalized by small wedding bands in India. Anyone who has ever been to India would immediately recognize the sounds for what they heralded—the arrival of the barat, or bridegroom's party at a typical north Indian wedding ceremony. And sure enough, there they were, the bridegroom astride the traditional white mare, both looking equally uncomfortable, surrounded by various members of his family and friends, all gyrating and flinging themselves about in a mood of gay abandon. Occasionally one of the more portly women would take a hundred rupee note out of her bag and twirl it around the bridegroom's head—though this was more notional than real, since he was way out of reach—and then tuck the note into, well, wherever such notes get tucked.

The hotel itself had been brightly lit with a thousand and one fairy lights, which had been strung along its edges. A large shamiana, a temporary marquee of multi-coloured canvas, had been constructed over bamboo scaffolding in the hotel lawns, the entrance to which was a gigantic gateway constructed entirely of flower garlands. Inside one could hear the strains of shehnai music, the traditional music at Indian weddings, played on an instrument resembling a clarinet, which clashed somewhat with *Come September*. Young girls showered the guests with rose petals and scented rose water from perfume sprinklers. The bridegroom's party had brought their own set of lights, a dozen or so portable gas flares carried on the shoulders of puny-looking members of the band who had to perform this duty when not required to play.

They were just at the point of being greeted by the bride's family, traditionally a time of great tension, since this was when the groom's family could put in all sorts of extra demands, such as a new scooter for the groom's younger brother, or a honeymoon in America for the young couple, threatening to stop the proceedings if these weren't met. It was also the time when various young men of the guest party could start misbehaving with the young women of the host, but of course some of this would have to be tolerated since they were guests...and the boy's party.

But as it happened, nothing untoward transpired. I stood for a few minutes witnessing the exuberance and gaiety of the scene. The party proceeded on to the next stage of the ceremonies--the jayamala, or exchanging of garlands. I thought this might be an opportune moment for me to slip into the hotel and book my room for the night.

The receptionist, when I was able to locate him and drag him away from the far more entertaining events taking place outside, looked most bemused at my request.

'Out of question, sir. Surely you can see. The whole hotel is booked by the marriage party. Very important family, you understand, the baratis have come all the way from Jalandhar. Now, if you will please excuse me, sir.'

'But surely you can find me just a single small room somewhere? I don't mind sharing if necessary. Look, I am desperate I have to catch the train tomorrow morning'

'Sorry, out of question, sir. Everything is taken. Why don't you try the other hotel, just down the road? They are sure to have room, always empty.'

Other hotel? I didn't recall the Station Master mentioning two hotels, but there was obviously no other alternative but to try my luck there since I wasn't about to get any joy here. I picked up my bag and made my way down the road again.

The other hotel was indeed just a couple of hundred metres

further along, but I might have missed it as it was set back from the road a bit and it was absolutely pitch dark by this time. It couldn't have been more complete a contrast from the previous place. There were no lights and nothing else to advertise its charms, except for a faded sign over the door which read, *The Haveli, boarding and lodging*. Yes, this was it. Feeling slightly apprehensive I knocked as loudly as I could and nearly fell backwards as the door was opened almost immediately by one of the oldest men I have ever seen.

'Yes? Why you have come here? What you want?'

'Er...a room. Do you have a room? I want a room for the night, please.' In the distance I could hear the lonely cry of a peacock. The rains were late again this year, and the place was almost like a furnace.

'Oh, room. Yes, we have room. But no food, you understand? And no hot water. You can have room.'

The old man let me in into the darkened hotel, lit solely by a hurricane lantern, hanging from a hook on the wall. He took this same lantern off the hook and beckoned me to follow while he led me up a winding staircase. I could faintly discern paintings of old Rajput princes staring down at me from the walls. I tried to avoid their eyes as far as possible.

Pushing open a heavy wooden door at the top of the stairs, the old man showed me into my room, which was furnished with heavy, antique-looking furniture and drapes hanging from the huge four-poster bed. He flung open the window to let in some breeze and moonlight flooded into the room. I caught sight of a portrait of a much younger version of the old man, above the bed, and the old man caught me looking at it.

'My son. He died a long time ago. This was his room. Breakfast will be at 8 o'clock.'

And with that, he was gone, leaving me in the company of the moonlight, the lonely peacock's cry and his son's portrait.

I can quite honestly say that I am not a man given to superstition or unfounded fears. I sleep a sound eight hours every night. I don't have much of an imagination, a fact which causes much merriment among the younger female members of my family. But those eight or nine hours I spent in that room that night must have been the longest and most wretched of my entire life. The peacock is a beautiful bird and much deserving of its national bird status in India, except that if whoever decides these things had gone by its voice alone it would never have reached even the quarter-finals. It has one of the ugliest, most dismal cries known to man or bird. And I was to hear that cry quite a few times that night. When I tried shutting the window in desperation, the room got so stuffy that I woke drenched in sweat just as I was about to fall asleep, and after that there was no question of falling asleep again.

The old man had failed to point out a large wall clock—the old fashioned kind, with a swinging pendulum, which rang out each hour in sombre tones, regularly on the hour, every hour, and ticked out each minute in between. I tried to recall whether I could remember seeing the old man's shadow. Somewhere far away, I imagined I heard the creaking of a door. Or had I in fact imagined it? What had the Station Master meant when he had told me not to worry too much about the old man? How much was too much? In the distance the lonely peacock remembered its long-lost mate yet again. I spent the whole night walking restlessly from one end of the room to the other, followed everywhere by the eyes of the young man in the portrait. This was, after all, his room.

I must have eventually fallen asleep in the early hours of the morning, sitting in one of the old arm-chairs. I was woken by the old man, who swept into the room without knocking, carrying a tray. He greeted me cheerily. The room was flooded with strong sunlight, replacing the moonlight of the night before, and everything suddenly seemed completely normal.

"Bed tea, Sir. You sleep good? Why you not sleep in bed Sir? Much more comfortable."

I mumbled something in reply, too embarrassed to confess my condition of the night before.

"You get ready and come down Sir. I get breakfast."

Breakfast turned out to be hot aloo parathas, freshly made, with mango pickle, and a steaming tumbler of tea. The hotel seemed transformed from the previous evening. It was one of those old stately homes, or havelis, of Rajasthan that had once housed the families of the upper classes. What secrets were held behind its carved wooden panels, one could only guess at.

"Quite a place you have here. Must be very popular in the winter."

"Yes, Sir, it used to be an old Rajput haveli, but then it fell into disrepute, and my great-grandfather bought it and converted it into a hotel. It used to be a great tourist spot, but not many people come this way these days. I had big plans, but then my son died and I lost interest. Some people think I am a bit cracked." He chuckled and pointed his finger at his head, making a rotating motion, echoing the gesture of the Station Master the evening before. "But hardly anyone comes here these days. That's why I wasn't expecting you last night."

"And I suppose you must be getting quite a lot of competition from the new hotel up the road. They seemed quite packed last night. They didn't even have one room available for me."

"What new hotel, Sir? There is only one hotel in this town. We don't have any other hotel. Oh, there was one that started business about a year ago. But there was a dreadful tragedy. There was a wedding party staying that night—very important family, from Jalandhar--and there was a terrible fire. One of the gas lanterns got knocked over and the shamiana caught fire. Everything was burned down, and everyone with it. Yes, it happened exactly a year ago. Terrible tragedy."

I rushed to the window and looked out. Sure enough, the road to the station stretched out in front of me, empty and desolate. Empty, except for two or three pie-dogs that manage to find themselves in every street in every town in India.

Childish Love

REETI GADEKAR

This wasn't working. Nothing about this trip was working.

'Okay, I understand that there will be no flights and that you have a fog situation, but what about a train? I mean, there's this book, *Train to Pakistan*? So there must be a train? Can I get a ticket for the train?'

The man looked unperturbed, 'No, there is no train. Flights have been delayed or cancelled for the past two days. January weather in Delhi is always like this. Your *Travel Planet* book did not tell you?'

'No. Nobody told me that flights can get cancelled and then you don't fly. There is usually a delay and then there is a substitute flight some hours later.'

Mr Khan, or Mr J.N. Khan to be precise, smiled for the first and hopefully for the last time. It was a mean, blackened smile, a smile that took pleasure in destroying other peoples' hopes, dreams and holidays.

'Sir, flights have been cancelled for the last week. You know the backlog? By the time your substitute flight comes, you can get a new visa, not only for Pakistan but also for India!'

'So, what do I do?' There had to be a way. The connecting flight back to New York left from Karachi in a week. The airline office would probably demand five hundred dollars to change the bloody seat, to say nothing of rescheduling the itinerary.

The small mousy man next to Mr J.N. Khan muttered something that appealed to Mr J.N. Khan, who giggled, a sight even more unappealing, given that it came with audio and visual effects.

'Sir, you can go by bus.'

'Bus? I'm in Delhi and there's no train but there's a bus?'

'Yes, there is a service plying every day from Delhi to Lahore.' He pulled out an info-sheet and handed it over.

'Please read it with care, and now make way for other customers.' Considering there were no other customers, this seemed a bit rich but who's to complain?

DTC's Delhi-Lahore-Delhi Bus Service

DTC has restarted its Delhi-Lahore-Delhi Bus Service with effect from 11th July, 2003. The air-conditioned luxury bus deployed for this service has a 2x2 comfortable seating arrangement.

The service is operated from Ambedkar Stadium Bus Terminal near Delhi Gate. For the journey to Lahore, there is a DTC bus every Tuesday and Friday and a PTDC (Pakistan Tourism Development Corporation) bus every Wednesday and Saturday.

As regards the return trip to Delhi, the DTC bus leaves Lahore every Wednesday and Saturday, whereas the PTDC Bus can be had from there on every Tuesday and Friday.

1. Necessary Travel Documents…

There was going to be a catch, there always is. Ah yes…

4. Advance Booking: Up to 60 days in advance of the date of journey, after producing the original and photocopies of required documents.

※

'Today is Thursday. I need to leave...' Rapid calculation. 'I need to leave tomorrow. How do I do advance booking?'

'This is the Tourism Office. We will book the ticket from here for you. You already have all the required documents as per point number 1, that is, passport and valid visa. There will be a small extra charge. But you can pay in foreign currency, a hundred dollars.'

A hundred dollars for a bus journey?

Thought reading was a part of Mr J.N. Khan's repertoire. He read out gravely, 'The fare is inclusive of complimentary breakfast, lunch and evening tea provided at designated halts in transit.'

Right. That changes everything.

'When do I have to get there?'

'The departure time is six in the morning.'

The mousy guy got started again, this time in English.

'Khan Sahib, no tickets available. All booked out.'

Mr J.N. Khan was unperturbed. 'Foreign quota. A hundred dollars. Show me the list. Yes, this gent, why is he going? Has he left a contact number? Call and tell him he can go on Tuesday because of security reasons. We will issue duplicate ticket here. Tell him issue of duplicate ticket will be free of charge since it is an exceptional case. Sir, please come back after four-five hours. Then you can make payment. Only cash payment is acceptable in pounds, dollars or euros, if you prefer. You will not require a receipt of the same? Very well, you can make arrangements with your hotel and then come back.'

Indeed.

Well, something had worked. Hard to believe Delhi or India had ever worked.

༄

The first trip had been in 1989. Young, drugged-out couple seeks enlightenment. A one way trip to Goa was the answer—with dream hash, cheap food and even cheaper liquid refreshments. No accommodation needed. The weather was perfect and so was the sex on the beach. Maybe that's the way it should have stayed—beach, bust and dust. Nope, they'd had to grow up.

The second trip took place in 1994. Delhi had been burning because of some bloody temple crap, so it was back to the South. The plan had been Agra and Jaipur and all that jazz, but it had ended up being Ayurveda and meditation and paying for some guy to walk on you in the name of a massage. The food had been non-stop lentils, which looked like the liquid stuff coming out the other end. It had been a bad trip.

The third trip took place in 1999. Turn of the century. Agra, Jaipur, the bloody Taj and Delhi and some other monstrosities. Actually it had been fun in some silly sort of way but the point is actually to never *ever* do spiritually advanced countries with a woman, especially a woman who has no children. She always ends up adopting spirituality and avoiding sex, which is a bad combination. The relationship had gone belly-up within days. So much for enjoying the majestic North.

And that brings us to the fourth trip in 2004. Single, spiritually deprived, empty and alone, which is the best way to see the Taj and the Red bloody Fort. What a load of bollocks it had all turned out to be. Is life worth living? Depends on the liver. How was the trip? Depends on the tripper. Shop in Jaipur, for what? For whom? Photograph the Taj. For posterity. Whose? Anyway, it was ending. Pakistan would be a suitable round-up of the trip. It had never been famous for its cultural monuments, but surely a visit to a nuclear reactor and a dictatorship was a must-do, once in a lifetime thing. Hard to believe one could do it twice.

'Hi, there's been a slight change of plan. Due to the fog, most outgoing flights have been cancelled. The only way to Karachi is via Lahore by bus, which unfortunately leaves tomorrow... So tonight's actually the last...'

'Sir, that's not a problem. But sir, I am afraid we will not be able to offer full refund...'

No. Obviously you won't. No, no, no.

'How about a taxi to Ambedkar Stadium Bus Terminal near Delhi Gate? Departure is at six in the morning.'

'Sir, the problem is not with the taxi. Sir, you are saying yourself, there is fog. If you need to take bus at six in the morning, sir, then it is better to spend the night at the bus station. Fog is very dense this year.'

Much like you.

'And do I get a refund? For tonight?'

'Sir, checkout is always at noon of following day.' Perhaps it was the murderous glint; perhaps it was the milk of human kindness. 'Sir, I will ask the Senior Manager and he will be here shortly. Sir, in the meanwhile you can pack and I will arrange for the taxi to take you at ten o'clock to the bus station. ISBT, sir?'

'No, Ambedkar Stadium Bus Terminal near Delhi Gate.'

Ambedkar. Ambit? Am in bed? Am bedding? Am a bedder? Or maybe just am. Pack. Nothing to pack. Travel planet as Khan Sahib said, medical kit, never travel without it. Quinine, aspirin, ibuprofen, antacids and, failing that, Imodium—the god of small shits. Clothes, bundle, shove, bundle and shove right in. Did Pakistanis care about creases? Who cares about Pakistanis who care about creases?

And it's goodbye. Farewell to hotel and hello black-yellow, smelly taxi. Was this the famous Indo-China combine they all spoke about? It's January for fuck's sake. The windows can't be opened.

'Sir, Ambedkar Stadium Bus Terminal?'

'Yes, but first to the Tourism Office in Connaught Place. Then to the bus station. Will it take long?'

Grimace, smile. 'Depends on the fog.'

Right. The fog. Of course. Who can forget the fog? It curled around the taxi like a grey python. Closing in, closing up. Open the bloody window. Thick, damp air. Like mouldy, soft cheese.

The city is iridescent by fog. Streetlights shimmer their way through it. The entire panorama is a chiaroscuro, hiding decay and disease in the shadows.

The last few vendors pack up their wares on push carts lit with gas lamps. The bus stops are peopled with the last of the commuters. Child-waiters scuttle around the roadside restaurants carrying kettles of sweet, cooked tea and spiked omelettes. Beggars pack away their deformities. Tomorrow is another market-day. Surely the leprosy will survive the night? In the middle of town, traffic is dense again. Restaurants provide picture postcard photo-ops.

Celebrating couples, laughing children, ballooned, feted, carried. Family values shining all the way to the bank. Connaught Place. Mr Khan stands outside the office. Without the office backdrop and the greasy files, he's just an old man with thinning hair, shivering in the cold. It's been a long day and it's time to go home. 'Have a nice trip, sir.'

The traffic fades. It's another commercial centre. The shops are shut, the air desolate. Without the melee, the city is orphaned. All alone without Mummy Crowd and Daddy Noise, what should Baby Delhi do?

Beware of strangers. Why?

If a stranger beckons, do not go with him.

Does he look nice?

Don't accept candy from them.

Is it sweet?

Don't go with a stranger who wants to show you something.

What is it?

Don't go with a stranger who wants to give you money.

How much? How much? How much?

The bus terminal looms ahead. The building is in darkness, but at ground level lights blaze. The taxi driver points out the counter through the swirls of the fog as it licks its way in.

'Bus to Lahore? The departure time is six in the morning. But its departure may be delayed. Depends on…'

'The fog. Yes, I've heard. Can I stow my luggage somewhere?'

'Yes, a locker facility has been provided. Or you can even place the luggage directly in the bus. There is a waiting room just before the boarding area. Seating arrangement has also been provided.'

'Are there any restaurants?'

'Sir, it is almost midnight. Even the counter will close soon. No restaurants, but there are food vendors everywhere for the bus drivers and other passengers like yourself. Simple food but very reasonable.'

'Mineral water?'

'Of course, sir, pure like the Ganga!'

Bye-bye Mr Bus Clerk. Time for you to be going home to the

wife and the kids. If there were any left over! Indians love children. All Indians love all children. Delhi was full of children. Everywhere. In buses, trains, restaurants, museums. All full of screaming babies. Kohl-lined eyes, fat, droopy cheeks, ears pierced with gold, all clad in woolly bonnets and booties. If they cried, their mouths were stuffed with large, grubby bottles or equally large, grubby breasts.

A voice pipes up, 'Hashish, ecstasy, pills?'

Why not?

'I only need a joint. Pre-rolled?'

'Pure hashish, sir, very good quality!'

'Yes, but only one cigarette. Only one cigarette, you understand?'

'No cigarette, sir, but coke dust, cocaine?'

Why not?

'How much?'

'200 rupees.'

'Twenty rupees.'

'No, sir, 160 rupees.'

'Forty.'

'150, sir, I have to feed my children!'

Yes, of course. The children.

'Are they here?'

'No, sir. Sleeping at home. Tomorrow is school. Sir, we can go to the hut there, and there is coke and also rum.'

In for a penny, in for a rum.

The shack is strangely organized. There is no light, but the guide-dealer produces a small storm lantern which is more than adequate. Bizarre, broken pieces of furniture have been stored carefully in one corner. From the depth of this pile, a slim file bag is extracted. All the booty is carefully organized—coke, hash, grass and heroin in little screws of paper.

Unfortunately, none of the packets are labelled, so that all are carefully opened and packed away. There are multi-hued tablets, white tablets in separate plastic envelopes. Do they guarantee black-and-white or coloured dreams?

The file also yields disposable syringes for the hygienically minded. Some used syringes with traces of blood lie tastefully on the ground. The shack is a junkie paradise. Why has this shack been constructed? What was its original purpose? Is it normal to have a shack in a dark corner, so that a needy passenger can coke up before the journey? Or is this just another service along with luggage lockers and water pure as the Ganga?

A table with three legs is brought forth for the discerning coke consumer. The dealer provides the fourth leg. And we partake of the abundance. The coke dust brings power. The rum, local hooch, brings a new kind of much-needed warmth.

'Okay, sir?'

Snivelling heaven, yes, it's okay.

Outside the shack, there are two men waiting. They have observed the trip inside the shack and are awaiting the return. The streets of Delhi are full of men waiting, hanging around. If your car breaks down, if you drop a basket, if you bust a gut, if you get raped, they stand and watch. Sometimes they help you in a mauling, crude sort of way, but mostly they stand and watch, wait and watch.

'Don't they have any work?'

The other half was supposed to have the answers.

'In this country, things work differently. The rhythm of life is different.'

So different that they starve and they can afford to wait and stand and watch? Hoping some refuse will fall their way?

The two men are not moving. They seem content to stand and watch. Do they want coke? Or do they want some money? Are they thieves? Do they have weapons? One of them has his hand behind his back. They advance slowly, unwilling to give cause for retreat. But in the end, they turn to the pathetic excuse closing the door to the shack and mutter some gibberish.

'Sir, you want to eat, sir?'

Eat? Eat what? The crap you eat? Non-mineral water food?

'You have food?'

'Sir, we can go home or otherwise these are my friends. They have a restaurant here, also very good. I always eat there. Much better than the crap the bitch gives me!'

He emphasizes the crappiness of the bitch by hawking and spitting violently in the corner.

The average Indian male always emphasizes the greatness of his wife's cooking. They insist that one come home, visit the lady. This is the famed hospitality of the inscrutable orient.

So why does this one spit upon her food? Does it come so cheap? Nope, it must come at a price. The price of Indian hospitality and India—a commission.

During the time in the shack, the fog has taken over the bus station. Its soft, greying fingers mould the buses into fantastic forms. The overhead lights choke silently, their silvery brilliance dulls. Darkness comes out of the corners, chases away the light and wrestles with the fog for the spotlight.

The men close in.

'Restaurant, sir? Chicken?'

They stand on either side. Skinny sentinels bringing offerings of sustenance. The moist air carries the smell of acrid tobacco and furtive fear. Whose is it? Yours?

The restaurant, they explain as we walk into the gloom, is just behind the bus station. Here, the gas lights continue to burn gamely. Apparently, many passengers have been told to spend the night at the station. They huddle around their particular shack-restaurant. For some reason, many have brought blankets with them. They squat on the pavement and, in some instances, on the chairs, wrapped like mummies. Some are still slurping tea. Others eat what smells like an inordinate amount of raw onions.

The sentinels escort the guest to a seat of honour, which is a large ramshackle chair. It is covered with cushions of differing age and hue which, over a period of time, have been fused into one. In the fog-light it is a cushion of many colours—a seat of power, a throne.

The shack is the only one serving chicken. Scrawny birds, angry at being woken up by the knife, squawk indignantly as the foreign hand comes into the cages. Several are held over their heads for approval. They bawl their way back into the cage after the chosen one is discreetly taken into yet another back-lane. The last squawk is muted—the fog lends a helping hand.

The chicken is being plucked, the gas stove furiously pumped, onions are sliced and rice is reheated. It is an atmosphere of tremendous flurry and activity. But the SS, the skinny sentinels turned scurrying slaves, are not the only ones who are busy.

The ubiquitous children grace this stage of the bus station as well. The gas light disguises their youth. They are midget adults. The lights make their limbs thick and strong. They run with easy grace, skirt the upturned garbage and chase away the odd dog. They bear food, nourishment, sustenance. Even their voices are thickened. The shrill fluting cries are muted and gruff. The words come out thick and slow.

The SS are surprisingly efficient. One squats, a leg folded beneath him, his body light as a feather in an area a little more than a square foot. In front of him, the stove hisses and splutters but he is unperturbed by the furious oil. He is too thick-skinned, the oil does no harm. The hapless chicken is flung in with evil, unknown spices guaranteeing flatulence, and that curry smell so unique to India and Indians around the world. His colleague is now on his way to another shack, where yet another bottle of rum is unearthed.

The meal will cost ₹1,000.

'Does the price include sales tax?'

There is no answer, only raucous laughter.

Chicken, hot, spicy, scrawny. The rum, raw, bitter, potent. What a combination—a complete India packet. Will Pakistan be like this? Hot, spicy, scrawny, raw, bitter and potent?

'One thousand rupees, sir.'

'You must be crazy! I'll give you five hundred.'

'No, sir. With rum and coke also, sir.'

'The coke was extra, you bastard!'

'Sir, but police will want more, sir, if we tell, sir…'

'Tell the police what? That you sold me coke?'

'We will have to, sir—they will ask!'

The bastard policeman was probably in on the game in any case. A pie-dog comes up, avariciously sniffing the remains of the chicken. One of the SS viciously kicks it in the ribs. The dog scuttles away and stands growling some distance away. The sound is menacing and weak.

After some more snivelling, the SS agree to 800, and the original guy starts fighting with them about his commission. Time to leave the throne. It is two o'clock, but the shacks are still doing good business.

And hours to go before I sleep. Where to now?

Coke—check.

Alcohol—check.

Onion tea—rain-check.

Sex?

Children are still playing at the bus-station. Some funny kind of hopscotch. Every jump merits a cry.

Hop. *Alouette*.

Hop. *Alouette*.

Hop. *Alouette*.

The sight of a foreigner unleashes a singsong babel of languages.

Guten Tag!

Good Morning!

Namaste!

Bon jour! *Alouette*!

'You give me one dollar?'

'No.' *Alouette*!

'Okay, one pound?'

'No.' *Alouette*!

What's left of the mystic India trip? Where is India? Another India gone bad?

A figure comes out of the dark—a child. Not boy child, not girl child. It is a child person. Its eyes are shadowed, keeping its secrets hidden from me and the fog. The smiling face looks cynical. But it knows.

The song trickles between us.

Alouette!

Je te plumerai la bite,

Je te plumerai la bite,

Je te plumerai la bite,

Et la bite!

Et la bite!

I am scared. But this is food and I am sick and hungry for an old passion.

Jump, Didi

SHARATH KOMARRAJU

I count the stairs on my way up. One by one. My new shoes click harder on the granite than the old ones used to. I bought them today. They're red.

Four... Five... Six...

I know how many steps there are to the terrace. But counting has become a habit. And habits are like family, my mother used to say. Love them or hate them, you've got to keep them, she said. We were close, Aai and I.

It's sunny today. It's usually sunny in May in Bombay. Sunny and bright. Summer has always been good to me, right from the start. Baba always went away on camps in the summer—I never asked him where. I didn't care. I was just happy to be with Aai. And she was happy to be with me. We were close. Best friends.

Seven... Eight...

The staircase is dark. But my shoes still sparkle. Mehek will like them, I think. She likes high heels. She told me so yesterday. Eight year olds these days say the strangest things.

I told her heels don't suit me. I don't have long legs, you see.

'But didi,' she said. 'You have *beautiful* legs. *I* like them!' When she speaks in that adorable voice, it's hard to resist her. I haven't told her yet that I've bought them. Thought I should walk up and down the terrace to practice walking in them before I show them off to her. I haven't worn heels this high before. I wouldn't want to trip when she's watching.

I like walking up to the terrace. Baba asks me why I don't take the elevator. I suppose I could, but how would I count the steps then? And counting the steps has become a habit for me, a habit that sticks like glue. You've got to keep your habits. They're like family.

Besides, it's only a three-storey walk up to the terrace. It doesn't tire me out or anything. I walk up every day just before the kids arrive—right after breakfast. It's nice up there. I like to stand on the railing. You know, just to spread my arms out and stare down at the city.

Nine... Ten...

I took Malhar up there the other night. The little rascal's legs started hurting halfway through so I had to carry him. We just sat there watching the moon. I told him a story. Stroked his hair with my fingers. He loves it when I do that. He has such soft hair. He fell asleep on my lap, so I had to carry him back down as well. He's getting a little heavier these days. Kids do grow up fast.

Malhar likes red.

Eleven... Twelve...

Another good thing about summers is that I don't have to go to college. Not that I don't like college. It's good. Aanchal—my best friend—and I sometimes go to the movies together. Sometimes we just walk around the campus. Sometimes we go to a café. I like Aanchal. She understands me.

But Aanchal has other friends. Sometimes, when we're together, her phone beeps and she says she has to go. She never tells me where she goes, but I know it is to meet her other friends. I don't like them, but what can I do? I *want* her to spend all her time with me. I *know* I can make her much happier than any of her other friends can. But I can't tell her all that, can I? There are things that ought to be understood between friends. I don't want to sound selfish.

Besides, it's not as if I don't have a life without Aanchal. Whenever she leaves me for her other friends, I just go to the library. Or watch TV. Or paint something. Aai always said life is all about being satisfied with what you have.

Thirteen... Fourteen... Fifteen...

I am lucky in a way. When I was in school I heard stories of girls being harassed in college. Teased, molested, even raped. But none of that happened to me. Boys in the college leave me alone. Not one of them has ever given me a second look, which is good. Very good.

But Aanchal is not so lucky. She is taller, fairer and thinner than me. She wears clothes that are different from mine. Whenever we're walking down the street, the boys on the street whistle at her. She doesn't seem to mind, but it makes my blood boil.

I think Aanchal also *likes* being with boys. Most of her friends are boys. I feel as if I am eating my own vomit when I see her with a boy. All that flirting and touching and laughing—ugh! But I can't let her see it, can I? That would be selfish.

She was ragged by a group of seniors on her first day in college. All of them were boys. But within a week she had become friends with them. How can you be friends with people who have stolen your self-respect? How can you laugh with the very people who have made a laughing stock of you? How can you be so devoid of dignity? Why does Aanchal need anyone else when she has me?

But I don't ask her any of those questions. She is my best

friend. And friends should be forgiven their little foibles. Friends are like habits too—you've got to keep them.

Sixteen... Seventeen...

Books are my other best friends. Aai always said books are the only friends that will never desert you. She told me a lot of stories when I was growing up—during breakfast, during dinner, before we went to sleep. We slept on the same bed, Aai and I. Especially when Baba was away. Sometimes we slept on her bed and sometimes we slept on mine.

Aai had a very loving embrace. When I snuggled up to her, I felt that the world was a safe place, that I had no worries. She used to kiss me and tell me I was beautiful. She used to call me her treasure. She used to caress my hair. She used to hold me close to her. She used to rock me. Through the night, sometimes.

We were close, Aai and I.

Eighteen... Nineteen... Twenty...

After Aai died, we moved here. Baba said he wanted a change. The first thing I noticed about this place was the number of kids playing in the courtyard. I have always been good with kids. I know how to treat them.

A talent like that doesn't stay hidden for long in an apartment complex full of working people. Mr Khanna asked me first if I had time to babysit his son. Then it was Mrs Paranjape. Mr Nirankar soon followed. In less than a week after moving here, I was babysitting twelve kids.

Summers are good in that way too. The kids don't have school, so I get to see them every day.

Twenty-one... Twenty-two...

They call me 'didi'. They arrive at ten in the morning and leave in the evening—whenever their parents come back. I tell them stories, we act scenes from plays, we sing songs.

But lately we've moved past that.

I think it was early last month that it happened for the first time. Ruchi and I were alone in my apartment. The rest of the kids had gone home. She sidled up to me and asked, 'Didi, what does a kiss feel like?' We'd enacted *Romeo and Juliet* that afternoon.

I remembered what it was like during those long summer nights when I was a child. I told her.

She didn't understand. 'Can you show me, didi?' she asked, frowning. I showed her. She liked it.

So did I.

Twenty-three... Twenty-four... Twenty-five...

Ruchi probably spread the word to the others. Soon, all of them wanted to be shown.

I took Arpit up to the terrace that night. I was nervous because that was my first time with a boy. But I need not have been afraid. If anything, he was more willing to be shown than Ruchi was. And his nine-year-old body responded more readily than hers had. When we were done, he was a little confused.

His tired eyes looked strangely hesitant. Guilty, even.

I hugged him. 'You will be okay, my darling,' I whispered into his ear. Rocked him back and forth. He went to sleep in my arms.

Next it was Mehek's turn. Next, Malhar's. And so on.

Those twelve nights on the terrace, under the moonlight, I showed my twelve kids what it was like to be loved. To be held. To be hugged. Aai always said the love we receive from people during our lives is meant to be distributed to others. I did precisely that. Can there be any one more deserving of love—Aai's love—than my kids?

Twenty-six... Twenty-seven...

Sometimes they complain, like Mehek did last night. 'It's hurting me, didi,' she said. I told her a little bit of pain was good.

She listened. She kept quiet and swallowed the pain. She's a good, tough girl.

They always come back religiously, to sing songs, to enact plays, to hear stories, to be *shown*. They keep it to themselves too, the little dears. All they need is just a gentle reminder now and then. That their parents would be really angry with them if they ever found out. That we were doing nothing wrong. That it should all be *our* little secret.

Kids respond well to persuasion. You just need to know how to do it.

Twenty-eight...

I open the door and walk out onto the terrace.

The sun is mercilessly beating down. I wipe the sweat off the back of my neck. It has become a habit now, showing the kids. Or is 'addiction' the right term? Is there a difference?

Giving love is a million times more pleasurable than receiving it. Not all the pleasure I received from Aai over all those summer nights could hold even the smallest candle to one night with one of my kids. Up here on the terrace, with the moon as our sole witness.

I ease myself onto the top of the railing and stand on it. I look down upon the bustle of the city.

Sometimes I hear a strange beating in my heart. I can hear it only here, on the terrace. Only when I am alone. *See? There it is now!*

There it is now. It starts low, but it soon becomes an unbearable thudding underneath my chest—as though something wants to break it open.

Involuntarily, I stand up on tiptoe. A gust of wind blows. My hair flies out.

How easy it would be, I think. How easy it would be to just dive off the railing. How easy it would be to end it all, for myself and for the kids.

'Jump, didi,' Mehek's voice echoes in my ear. I close my eyes, hoping it will go away.

'A little bit of pain is good, didi,' Mehek says. *Stop!*

'Jump, didi. Jump. Jump. Jump.'

I open my eyes and stumble back on the terrace. Somehow I manage to stay on my feet. My face is awash with sweat. This is becoming more and more common of late. It's not always Mehek. Yesterday it was Ruchi, the day before it was Pradeep, and the day before...

They all said the same thing, in their sweet, cherubic voices: 'Jump, didi.'

It's just a crazy daydream. Dreams are just random signals in the brain that don't mean anything—*anything!* My kids love me. They would never want me to get hurt. They *like* what I do to them. They *tell* me so. They would never want me to jump.

No, they would never, ever want me to jump. It's just a stupid game my brain is playing with me. It must be! There's simply no other explanation.

I realize I have been gritting my teeth. My fists are closed tight. I am panting. I close my eyes and take a few deep breaths, wrenching my jaws apart. My sanity returns.

I look at my watch. It's five minutes to ten. My breathing slowly returns to normal. My body relaxes.

The kids will start arriving soon. I have to go. I will show Mehek and Malhar my new shoes. Maybe I will let them play with the shoes too... Maybe I can lure them onto the terrace tonight after the moon rises. *Together*.

I could tell them a story each, one after the other. Or I could do a play, and get all three of us involved. Or I could get them to tell each other a story while I sit back and watch. See how well they've been learning.

There is no rule, is there, that you're allowed to love only *one* person at a time?

That's what I love about kids. Isn't every day with them a whole world of new experiences? Isn't every sound they make—every word they speak, every story they tell, every song they sing—the very definition of divine music?

A couple of Dairy Milks each should help convince them to come. And of course, once we're done, one of those gentle reminders. Just in case they forget.

Kids respond well to persuasion. You just need to know how to do it.

I have always been good with kids.

It has become a habit now, all of this. And habits are like family. Love them or hate them, you've got to keep them. Treasure them. Nurture them.

I count the stairs on my way down. Like I do every day. Backwards.

Twenty-eight... Twenty-seven... Twenty-six...

Categories

ROHINI KEJRIWAL

Humans tend to categorise everything for the sake of convenience and go to sleep with a clear conscience. Everybody knows that it is a façade erected to preserve the illusion that they are good human beings. But the fact remains—it makes matters so much easier to blame someone from a category different from the one you put yourself in. For example, the relationship ended because he was a workaholic and could not spare any time for her. Or the more common one—that woman is such a whore because she has made out with many men.

The principle of 'categorise to comfort' is applied everywhere—at work, when you make yourself believe that you are not a pushover unlike that rich colleague of yours who lets people use him for his money to be popular; at home, when you wonder whether you are a bad son for trying to be cool like the other kids at school after you go to your first party where alcohol is served; or just on the roads, where you don't know the person in front of you but you ogle, judge, categorise, and place yourself in a different category from the person you have found a flaw in.

This is the story of our lives. We create façades in search of false security. And it sure works well—at least temporarily!

I was eighteen when I met him. He was only sixteen. That was the first thing that should have come to mind, but it didn't. Somehow, the fact that he was a junior did not bother me. We met in the school hospital—a small red-bricked, two-roomed structure, with one room for boys and one for girls, and a common area in the middle for patients of either gender to eat and talk in. That is where I met him. There had been a load shedding and I was sitting in the common area, clutching a hot water bottle to my stomach. He had just had his appendix removed and was prescribed rest. We sat there in the dark, talking about the most random things. I remember feeling strangely connected because someone was actually willing to listen and seemingly enjoyed my rambles and rants! When the electricity came back, we looked at each other and smiled. That night, for no reason at all, I tried to sneak into his room to give him a piece of Cadbury Crackle I had bought from the tuck shop. I didn't want to wait till the next day to give it to him because something told me that he was still awake in his bed. The nurse woke up just when I reached his room and screamed at us and took me back to the girls' room.

The next morning, I received a chit from him, commending me for my brave effort. I got discharged that day. But I kept visiting him in the evenings and having tea with him outside his window. He'd pass me a glass from the kettle he was told to finish and, since he wasn't too big on tea, I'd share it with him. He said that sharing the tea was his way of thanking me for the chocolate I'd tried to get across to him. When anyone we knew would pass by, I'd hide without even knowing why. The friendship continued for many months and we became increasingly fond of each other's company. We completely exploited the holidays and the newly discovered

Skype. I would send SMSs from Calcutta, as I ordered in from Don Giovanni's, to his mugged up mobile number in Delhi just to ask him to come online. Even if he was out pulling hookah with friends at Sheesha or Mocha, he'd apologise profusely that he couldn't come online and then, before I knew it, I'd be asked to come online. We would spend hours at night with earphones plugged in while we chatted. Music was one thing that we were both passionate about and, because of that, we never ran out of things to talk about. If there was a dry spell and neither party knew what to say, one of us would recommend a song to the other and then, after listening to it carefully, we'd discuss it. The whole world seemed to think that we liked each other more than as friends but again, that was just categorisation and nothing else.

One day, when we sat hugging in an empty class room for almost an hour, we realised that the feelings were stronger than we'd realised. But defining the feelings still felt silly and unnecessary. So we didn't. But then the day came when the insecurity seeped in and he realised that he wanted me to just be his. And in an attempt to categorise, to comfort himself, he asked me out. And I gladly became his girlfriend. The fact is that I actually liked being his, feeling wanted at a different level than I had known before.

But it didn't turn out to be as it is in the movies. I had even gotten him to see a few conventional chick flicks like *A Walk to Remember* to allow him to bring out his softer side. That side was visible while I was in school. But after I passed out, it wasn't quite the same. It was silly of me to even believe that it wouldn't change. We became the long distance couple and, unlike Justin Long in *Going the Distance*, he gave up sooner than we'd planned. I couldn't blame him completely. It was quite hard to focus on a person when you were not certain when you would see them next, even though the time you spent together was so perfect that it almost seemed unreal. We did try to make it work, we did send the occasional mix CD and the monthly card. But there was no point trying to fool ourselves. It was hard to be without him. It was hard to be with him. Other men had started to express their interest in me since they saw no tag-along boyfriend around me. But I'd tell them in my own way that I was taken, though I wasn't even sure whether I was. One of us had to be strong and put his or her foot down. I was the mature one and saw that there was no point in holding onto the nothingness that our relationship was becoming…

The narration of a love story is rarely defined by the ones who are in it. Others usually seem to have their version of it—who was the villain who brought up the idea of a break up; how romantic or unromantic the guy was, depending upon his proposal; what the boy and girl's best friend had to say about the two; and other things like that, which don't add up or make sense. It's always about the third party: the ones who categorise, have their share of fun and make a clean escape.

But that was just one story in an infinite sea of stories. Part fiction, part reality. Maybe mine. Or perhaps a story a friend told me a long time ago, which I just spiced up to please someone who might read it on a lazy Sunday afternoon and feel good about the fact that his or her not getting a fairy-tale ending in their relationship was all right. Because it always feels good to know that there is someone else who falls in the same category as you, whom you can, therefore, relate to. The characters and settings will differ, but the essence is always the same.

After all, it is only while you are on the stage of life that you need to act out the character that society assigns you. Once you're gone, only the memories of your past performances will be spoken of. The person that you were in your own skin will be left to be discovered only in the pages of your tattered journal…

Contributors

ANITA SATYAJIT
Anita Satyajit, is a journalist, writer, poet and photographer who can be found online at www.anitasatyajit.com.

ANITHA MURTHY
Anitha Murthy is a software consultant and a prize-winning writer who loves writing whenever inspiration strikes.

AYESHA HEBLE
Ayesha Heble is an Assistant Professor of English at a university in Oman; she has a home in New Zealand, which she shares with two handsome sons, a dog and a cat.

CHANDRIMA PAL
Chandrima Pal has been a journalist for fifteen years and has interviewed political bigwigs to cultural stalwarts, but she likes nothing better than disappearing in the high Himalayas with her guitar-playing husband. Her debut novel, *A Song for I*, was published in 2012

GAYATRI HINGORANI
Gayatri Hingorani, is a communications professional and closet blogger, who enjoys writing short fiction when she is not word weary.

KARTHIK K
Karthik, is an engineering graduate, blogger and a novelist in the making.
Find him on http://unalloyedwritingpleasure.blogspot.com/

MALCOLM CARVALHO
Malcolm Carvalho, is a software engineer from Pune. When not writing code or fixing the odd bug, he writes poetry and short fiction; he has also written a book and is cooking up plots for the next one.

MANISHA DHINGRA
Business writer by profession, short fiction writer by passion, Manisha Dhingra, is obsessed with cats, chocolates and blogging.
Find her on www.quickshortstory.wordpress.com

MARYANN TAYLOR
Maryann Taylor, amongst other things is primarily a teller of anecdotes, devourer of books, compulsive writer, dog lover, daydreamer and traveller, who still takes delight in reading Enid Blyton and riding bicycles.

MINI MENON
Mini Menon is a language teacher with a love for the written word. *Lesser Lives* is her debut novel.
Find her on mini1menon.wordpress.com

PARITOSH UTTAM
Paritosh Uttam, is a writer and a software engineer. He is the author of *Dreams in Prussian Blue*, and the editor of *Urban Shots and Urban Shots: Bright Lights*.

PRANAV MUKUL & AVANI RAJESH
Avani Rajesh, is a student who prefers pen and paper to a computer. Pranav Mukul, is journalist and a blogger. He is a sub-editor at *90 minutes* magazine.

REETI GADEKAR
Reeti Gadekar is the author of *Families at Home* and *Bottom of the Heap*. She lives in Berlin and can be contacted at reeti@gadekar.com

ROHAN SWAMY
Rohan Swamy is a journalist and works at *The Indian Express* in Pune.

ROHINI KEJRIWAL
Rohini Kejriwal, is the co-editor of *Down the Road*. She is also writer and an avid blogger since the last four years. She is the Editor of *TheTossedSalad.com*. Rohini enjoys exploring life and all that it has to offer, be it through different music artists, mountain trails, or film genres.

SANCHARI SUR
Sanchari Sur is a Bengali Canadian who was born in Calcutta, India. She can be found at sursanchari.wordpress.com.

SARITHA RAO
Saritha Rao Rayachoti, is a freelance journalist and writer. She lives

in Chennai and blogs at saritharao.blogspot.com

SHARATH KOMARRAJU
Sharath Komarraju is an IT Specialist based in Bangalore. He tests software by day and writes fiction by night.

SHILADITYA CHAKRABORTY
Shiladitya Chakraborty, is a freelancer in love with the written word. When not writing copy, content, game manuals, travelogues, blogs, scripts, poetry or short stories, he plods steadily away at a novel.

SHREYA MAHESHWARI
Shreya Maheshwari studies Economics at Harvard College, and writes for the *Harvard Political Review*. She loves pop-culture, travelling, reading, and red velvet cupcakes.

SIDDHARTHA BHASKER
Siddhartha Bhasker, 27, graduated from IIT Kharagpur in Industrial Chemistry, following which, he worked as an environmental consultant. Presently he teaches Social Sciences in Mumbai to make a living and writes in his free time

SRINIVASAN VENKATARAGHAVAN
S. Venkataraghavan is a tall and lanky writer from Bangalore. He enjoys solo travel, meditation and tales well-told. His writings are inspired by India, its history and geography, its people and practices, its cultures and beliefs.

VINOD GEORGE JOSEPH
Vinod Joseph, is a corporate lawyer based in Mumbai who makes up stories in his free time.

VRINDA BALIGA

Vrinda Baliga lives in Hyderabad. Her short stories have appeared in various literary journals, anthologies and magazines like *Urban Shots, Temenos, flashquake, The Shine Journal, Long Story Short, Rose & Thorn* and *Cezanne's Carrot*. She is a prize winner in the Katha Fiction Contest 2010 organized by India Currents.